ELLORA'S
CAVEMEN

SEASONS OF
Seduction
VOLUME III

ELLORA'S CAVE
ROMANTICA PUBLISHING

Ellora's Cavemen: Seasons of Seduction III

The Pirate and the Pussycat
Lacey Alexander

When Leah gets an invitation to a Halloween bash, she has mixed emotions. At last year's party, she met a man, fell for him hard and…never heard from him again. So this year she'll take a new approach. Screw emotions—she's going to find a sexy guy and do the dirty with him, no strings attached.

Arriving in her sexy cat costume, she spies a hot pirate and knows instantly that he's the man she's going to seduce. But can she succeed? Or will this naughty little kitty end up heartbroken all over again?

Panther's Pleasure
Cathryn Fox

Sash has spent her life coursing through space. She's never gotten sick before. But as they approach planet Lannar, she begins to feel very ill, and when she meets Kade, leader of Lannar, all kinds of things begin happening to her libido.

When Kade sets eyes on Sash he knows she's his mate. How it's possible that an Earth woman is the mate for a shape-shifting panther, he's not sure. All he knows is that there is only one way to help ease her pain and make her first transformation easier. Through mating. And once will never be enough.

On Her Back
Renee Luke

Simone Harris is experienced when it comes to loss—most recently, that of her brother Jerold. But when his best friend Elijah, wounded in the same fray that killed Jerold, returns home, Simone tries to put her pain aside and offer him her support. She wants to give him anything and everything he needs.

Elijah Russell survived every night he spent in the desert—and, later, in the hospital—by invoking fantasies of Simone. On her back. Beneath him. Now, just being near her again is enough to make him forget his pain for a moment. But his heated emotions seem to be mutual, and soon those fantasies might become a reality.

Simone and Elijah both need time to heal, but it's a lot easier to wait together.

I Was an Alien's Love Slave
Charlene Teglia

Micki Sloane needs a hero and she needs him now. She's got a deadline, writer's block and no inspiration. What to do? Wish on a star.

Keelan Os'tana has been seeking his bondmate, the one woman who is on his wavelength—literally. He answers Micki's mental call by beaming her up into erotic adventure beyond her wildest imaginings. Her options? Form the permanent telepathic bond with Keelan or go home and write for the tabloids. "I Was an Alien's Love Slave" is a sure seller, but Keelan tempts her to live the fantasy instead.

Sunshine for a Vampire
N. J. Walters

Sunshine DeMarco is a blonde-haired, blue-eyed vampire who just doesn't fit in with her own people. She doesn't really like the whole vampire lifestyle—the opulent surroundings and overindulgence in everything from food to drink to blood. But even she has family and social obligations.

While attending a party for a special European dignitary, she finds herself captivated by a tall, dark stranger. One sensual dance between them leads to a passionate tryst in the host's garden.

Reality intrudes and Sunshine flees, but she hasn't seen the last of her mystery lover.

A Man of Vision
Kate Willoughby

For Cristoforo, sculpting marble is his life, but the price of creation is a libido that rides him like a demon. When he discovers his sculpting days are numbered, he hires a mistress to satisfy him night and day.

Modern-day courtesan Delphine arrives at Cristoforo's villa prepared for the rigors of being on call 24/7. What she isn't prepared for, however, is the intensity of her body's response to Cristoforo. When she learns what is driving him so ruthlessly, she wonders if she can protect her heart…or if it's already too late.

An Ellora's Cave Romantica Publication

www.ellorascave.com

ELLORA'S CAVEMEN:
SEASONS OF SEDUCTION III

ଅଚ

THE PIRATE AND THE PUSSYCAT

By Lacey Alexander

Trademarks Acknowledgement

ℰↃ

The author acknowledges the trademarked status and trademark owners of the following wordmarks mentioned in this work of fiction:

Captain Morgan's Rum: Diageo North America Inc.

Superman: DC Comics

Chapter One

ഇ

"So what are you wearing to my Halloween bash this year?"

Sipping on her latte, Leah cringed at her best friend's question. "Oh God, I totally forgot. It's October already." She gave her head a sad tilt, designed to garner sympathy. "Would you hate me if I skipped out this year?"

Across the table from her in the busy coffee shop, Tracy's eyes narrowed in controlled irritation. "*Yes.*" Then she shook her head as if in disbelief. "What are you even *thinking*? How could you want to miss my big party? You know people far and wide look forward to this all year long."

Leah just sighed, thinking the answer was obvious. "Need I remind you that I always have terrible luck with men at your Halloween party? Three years ago there was that freaky guy in the priest costume who kept trying to get me to sit on his lap. Then the year after that was the cowboy who I *thought* I liked until he kept lassoing me and practically forcing me to kiss him. And last year was the worst."

"Patrick the Fireman," Tracy said somberly. Then *both* girls sighed, remembering. While decked out as a hula dancer, Leah had met a totally handsome, confident, funny guy costumed as a firefighter. They'd hit it off and spent the whole evening together, sharing a few long, slow kisses before finally saying goodnight at two a.m. He'd taken her number and promised to call. No, more than promised really. They'd already talked about dates they were going to go on—movies they'd see, places they'd eat, and even the picnics they'd have as soon as it turned warm. That's how right it had felt.

And despite loving what a perfect gentleman he'd been, waiting until the end of the night to even kiss her — after they'd parted ways, she'd been dying to get in his pants. She'd fallen asleep night after night remembering the way she'd felt him growing hard against the apex of her thighs as they'd made out on Tracy's front porch, and thinking she couldn't wait to get more of that lovely sensation — until she'd finally figured out that he wasn't going to call.

And though she'd known it was stupid to be so hung up on a guy she'd spent one lone evening with, it had hurt. She'd *really* thought he liked her, and she'd let herself get *way* too wrapped up in him *way* too fast. And as it had turned out, the party had been so busy that Tracy didn't even *know* Patrick or who he had come with.

"Surely you remember what high hopes I had for him," she reminded Tracy. "And frankly, I'm just not up for another heartbreak — or more of those goofballs Mike works with." Mike was Tracy's husband, and the cowboy and priest had come from his side of the "friend pool".

"You know what you need?" Tracy asked, a conniving glint in her eye.

Leah *hated* Tracy's conniving glint — it always ended up getting one or both of them into trouble. "What?" She let her gaze narrow suspiciously.

"A night of no-strings-attached sex."

Leah simply let out a tired breath. "And why do I need *that*?"

"Because you haven't gotten any in a while?"

Hmm. Good point. She hadn't dated anyone in nearly six months, in fact. So as much as she hated to play into Tracy's scheme, whatever it may be, she asked, "Exactly what are you suggesting?"

"Nothing too heinous — I promise. I just say you wear something ultra-sexy this year, and then you find some hot guy and do the dirty with him. You know, be a seductress.

Call the shots. Have your way with him. That way, you get some good, nasty sex and you have no worries when it's over."

Leah's heart beat harder at the notion, even if she had some concerns. "I've never been good at casual sex."

Tracy waved a dismissive hand. "That's because you've never really tried it. You're all hearts and romance. But I say, for once, you just sex it up—be a tart and find some guy to make you feel good. I guarantee you'll go home glad you did it."

Leah rolled her eyes. "Says the happily married woman of five years. How would *you* know?"

"If you'll recall, I was pretty good at casual sex before Mike. It got me through many a lonely dating period. And besides, I intend to have this party every year forever, and I expect you to be there, so you need to find a way to make it work for you."

Taking another sip of her latte, Leah turned the idea over in her head. Could she do it? Be a sexy, seductive vixen for one night? To her surprise, she was actually tempted.

"The more I think about this," Tracy added, eyes blazing with mischief, "the more I like it. Just think—sex with costumes on, not even being able to see each other's faces. That's kinda kinky hot, don't you think?"

The truth was, Leah's pussy fluttered at the naughty vision Tracy had just planted in her head. And maybe, just maybe, if she fucked a guy she couldn't even see, she wouldn't get emotionally attached and it would be only about sex.

"Okay," she said. "I'll do it."

Tracy nearly choked on her coffee, sputtering and spewing before she managed to speak again. "You will?"

"I will." And seeing Tracy's surprise increased Leah's resolve even more. "In fact, I'm going to shock us both. I'm going to be the hottest, sluttiest little seductress you've ever seen. Prepare to be amazed."

Chapter Two

ഇ

Well, she'd really done it. She'd dressed herself up as a total sexpot—in the form of a cat. Black, of course, complete with whiskers drawn with eyeliner and a sparkly little black mask that covered her eyes. Below, she wore a stretchy, skintight black top with long sleeves and a sinfully short—also skintight—black miniskirt with a long, stuffed tail pinned to the back. The hem was *so* short that it revealed the lace tops of her black stockings and the attached garter belt. On her feet she wore strappy fuck-me heels and on her head black velvet ears with pink satin centers. The final touch—a thick faux diamond choker that doubled as a collar. She'd decided she was a *rich* kitty-cat.

And if all that wasn't enough, she'd left off panties. Because if she was really going to do this—really going to go into Tracy's party and pull some masked guy into a closet and have her way with him—panties would only get in the way.

It was easily the most daring outfit she'd ever worn, and it was definitely the first time she'd left home knowing she looked dressed for sex.

So she was feeling proud...but nervous.

Thus she remained sitting in her car in front of Tracy's house a full ten minutes after arriving. Watching costumed people through the brightly lit windows, listening to "Monster Mash" pouring from an open door. And now she had to make herself go inside. Being brave enough to dress like this had been one thing, but gathering the courage to go *into* the party, where there were *people*, was another.

But hadn't she told herself she was going to do this thing and do it right? "You can't do it if you don't get out and go inside," she told herself, stuffing her keys in the tiny black clutch she'd brought and checking her mask in the rearview mirror. "And you can't do it if you don't go in with *attitude*, either. You have to want it."

And she *did* want it. The truth was, her pussy had been damp and tingly all week just anticipating being a dirty little sex kitten tonight. She'd decided it was something every single girl should do just once, for the thrill, for the sense of power and excitement, and at twenty-nine, there was no time like the present.

So she tried her damnedest to put on that new attitude now. Glancing back in the mirror, she ran her tongue over lush lips painted pink, then hefted her breasts upward in her tight demi-bra until they curved provocatively from her low-cut top. She even delicately pinched her nipples, just enough to stimulate them, to—hopefully—make them slightly visible through her top and bra.

Her cunt spasmed slightly as she told herself, "You can do this. You can walk into this party looking for sex, and you can get it, *take* it, just the way you want it."

With that, she got out of the car, slammed the door and felt the whoosh of cool October-in-the-Midwest air rush up under her tiny skirt and sweep across her freshly shaven cunt.

And as she strode boldly up the sidewalk, her high heels clicking confidently with each step, she *did* want this. More than she'd even known up to now. She wanted it bad.

Chapter Three

∽

"Oh my God, you look fabulous. Like, like...some kind of Halloween centerfold or something!" Tracy said, greeting her at the door in a naughty nurse costume.

"Doctor" Mike, complete with stethoscope and one of those little silver discs strapped onto his head, stepped up behind his wife—then blinked. "Holy shit, Leah, is that you?"

Leah struggled to keep feeling sexy even as a bit of sheepishness snuck in. Mike knew her only as the normal, conservatively dressed, not-especially-wild woman that she was. "Yes, it's me—and you can blame your wife for this. She dared me to wear something sexy tonight and bet me I couldn't do it, so I win. Pay up," she said, holding her palm out to Tracy. It hadn't exactly been a dare *or* a bet, of course, but it seemed like a good enough explanation to give Mike.

"What is it that you win again?" Tracy asked, smiling at Leah's slightly exaggerated rationalization.

"I think I win a cosmo for now. And you can buy me a latte the next time we go shopping. But at the moment, I definitely need a cosmo."

To Leah's surprise, stepping into the party dressed as she was turned out not to be as overwhelming as she'd feared. Sure, she'd taken the sex nymph thing farther than most girls at the party, but she wasn't the only woman showing some cleavage and leg. Just following Tracy across the room to the drink counter, she passed a sexy devil, a tawdry saloon girl and a witch wearing only a tiny black slip dress in addition to her tall hat and boots. Still, maybe it was the lack of panties that made her feel...less dressed than everyone else.

"So you're really going for it, huh?" Tracy asked, pouring her a glass of premixed cosmo from a pitcher. Cosmopolitans had been their drink of choice since college.

"Wasn't I supposed to?"

"Yes, yes. I'm just...surprised. I didn't think you'd really go through with it."

"Well, I am. Now, have you scouted out any hot guys for me yet?"

Tracy tilted her head, her little nurse's cap leaning to one side. "Well, there's a hunk-a-licious Superman playing pool in the basement."

Hunk-a-licious sounded fine, but Leah shook her head. "Guys in tights don't do it for me. And besides, they'd probably be hell to get him out of."

Tracy held up one finger. "Oh, I know. Mike's friend, Dell, is here. He's a really nice guy and just broke up with a longtime girlfriend."

"What's he dressed as?"

Tracy pursed her lips and looked a little worried. "Well, he came as...a clown."

Leah rolled her eyes. "Damn it, Tracy, I am not having sex with a clown, and I think that goes without saying. In fact, don't even think about fixing me up on a date with him, either, because I am not having sex with any man who even *thinks* it's a good idea to dress like a clown under any circumstance."

"Okay, okay," Tracy said. "Point taken. Clowns aren't sexy. Let me think." She took a sip of the pink concoction in her own martini glass. "Okay, I've got it. I just saw a guy dressed as a cop. Cops are sexy, right?"

Hmm, cops *were* sexy. Or they definitely *could* be. "Is he hot?"

Tracy's eyes flashed a hint of dismay. "Eh...so-so." Then she tried to be more enthusiastic. "But he has handcuffs. Handcuffs are hot."

Yet Leah only scowled. "Look, this is simple. I need a hot guy in a hot costume — nothing else will do."

"Why is the costume such a big deal?"

"You said it yourself — costumes make it kind of kinky. And I've embraced that. And if some guy gets to do *me* dressed like *this*," she said, using her free hand to motion down at her curves, "I get to do some guy who is equally as appealing."

Tracy nodded, sighing. "Okay, you're right, I totally get your position on this. But the bad news is…"

"Yes?" Leah braced herself.

"I'm not sure there's anyone here who fits the bill."

Oh hell. Where was Patrick the Fireman when you needed him?

Chapter Four

ରୀ

Twenty minutes later, Leah sat on the sofa chatting with one of Tracy's neighbors—currently masquerading as a mermaid, right down to her iridescent green tail—when she felt someone's palm move smoothly down the back of her head over her shoulder-length brown hair, making her scalp tingle.

She looked up to see the most handsome pirate she could have imagined. Yet despite the long raven tresses, tricorn hat and a full-length red captain's coat, what she noticed most about him were his dark, arresting eyes. They seemed to possess her on contact. Or at least undress her. Or maybe he just made her *want* to be undressed. Whatever the case, she felt an instant chemistry with him, even before he said, "Nice kitty," and boldly petted her again.

Her first response? She purred, peering up at him and feeling the slight swell of her pussy—that fast.

"Mmm, that feels good, now does it?" he asked, sporting a classic pirate accent.

"Um...meow," she said in a softer, sexier voice than she'd ever heard leave her lips before.

He cast a wicked grin, clearly liking her cat games, but kept his pirate voice on. "What's yer name, pussycat?"

Glancing over to see that, thankfully, the mermaid had already tuned in to someone else's conversation, Leah bit her lip, then let out her own naughty little grin. "Kitty," she said. She hadn't planned to be so coy with whoever she met, but it had just dawned on her that if she was going to play out the whole costumed stranger fantasy, keeping her name to herself would make it that much easier.

"Aye, you're a cute one, me beauty."

"And *you* are?"

"Morgan," he said. *"Cap'n* Morgan. But you can call me Cap'n fer short."

She laughed lightly. "I *thought* you looked familiar." Indeed, now she knew where she'd seen him—he was dressed like the pirate in the logo for Captain Morgan's Rum, right down to the sexy little goatee. And she'd never really had a pirate fantasy before, but she was having one *now*. About being plundered. He wasn't Johnny-Depp-pretty—instead he was strong and commanding, clearly the captain of any ship he wished to take. "So," she said, *still* practically purring as she spoke, "what are you doing so far inland?"

"Arrrr—I be lookin' fer wenches." Then his gaze narrowed on her seductively. "But a pretty little kitten might do. I bet you could keep ole Cap'n Morgan right warm at night, snuggled up against him in the bunk." Then he leaned closer, spoke softer, deeper. "Interested in the job, pussycat?"

Leah's cunt practically hummed. This was exactly the kind of guy she'd come here looking for tonight—hot, sexy and into casual, naughty fun. Moreover, he was exactly what she needed to help her pull this off. Of course, her second cosmo was helping, too. "What's in it for *me*?" she whispered up to him, arching her chest, hoping he could see her nipples through her top.

"What would ye like, me beauty? Name it and 'tis yers."

Boldly meeting his gaze, Leah ran her tongue across her upper lip. "Will you…let me play with your sword?"

His eyes blazed with heat, buffered with a hint of amusement. "'Tis called a cutlass amongst we pirates, pussycat, but yes—ye may play with it 'til yer heart's content."

"That sounds fun," she said, barely able to speak now beneath the weight of her lust.

"Would ye care to join me for a walk on the beach then?"

She raised her eyebrows. "The beach?"

He winked. "Ye seem to think we're inland, beauty, but the beach lies just outside, and my sloop waits in the distance." His voice deepened. "Come outside, pussycat, and you can play with my cutlass in private."

Chapter Five

ഇ

This was it. The invitation to sin. To fuck a stranger.

The truth was that, even as Leah had dressed tonight, even as she'd entered the party, even as she'd started exchanging flirtatious banter with this tall, broad, sexy as hell pirate, she'd been unsure if she could take that last step. But now, she was ready. And taking it.

She answered merely by pushing to her feet on her do-me heels and sashaying slowly around the couch to where he stood. His gaze dropped to the lace tops of her stockings before rising back to her eyes, and her pussy creamed once more.

"Arrrr — you're a *naughty* kitty, aren't you?" he said, voice low and hungry.

She didn't hold back — she said exactly what she was thinking. "I want to rub up against you. But fortunately, I'm taller than most cats, so I'll reach better parts than just your ankles."

"My cutlass," he murmured, and she could almost sense the hardening of that particular metaphorical tool just from the tone of his voice.

"Meow," she said, soft, suggestive.

Taking her hand, he led her through the house toward the back door. Leah barely even noticed the various superheroes and celebrities and monsters they passed along the way. Her heartbeat pulsed through her whole body and her cunt felt like the largest part of her — warm, sensitive, needy. She didn't give a thought to where they were going because she instantly trusted him to take charge. When they reached their destination, then *she'd* take charge.

Her pirate drew her through a pair of open French doors and onto the sun porch. Tracy had opened it for the party, but only candles lit the space, so no one had ventured back here yet. Releasing her hand, he smoothly closed the doors behind them, shutting out the sounds of laughter and chatter and muting the music — currently an old song by the Hooters, "All You Zombies".

Then he turned to face her, a glint in his eye. "Arrr, my beauty — alone at last."

She didn't answer — merely bit her lip, felt her breasts swell within the cups of her bra and took a step toward him. Again, logically, she thought she should be shying away by now, reverting to her usual self — but she wasn't. Despite all the suggestive talk and the fact that she'd just agreed to "play with his cutlass" less than five minutes after meeting him, she felt strangely safe with "Captain Morgan", as if such hedonism was A-okay.

He stepped toward her, too. Slid one palm to her hip, then lifted his other hand to touch her face. He drew the tip of his index finger around the edge of her mask, under one eye, and the sensation made her shiver.

"Can I take this off, pussycat?" he whispered. Not quite so pirate-ish this time. Warmer. More seductive.

"No," she answered gently. "You can take off anything *else* you want — but not that."

He gave a succinct, acceptant nod. "Understood."

Then he kissed her.

His lush mouth molded hot and moist over hers, turning her whole body molten in mere seconds. When his tongue pressed between her lips, she met it with her own, lost that quickly to passion. One kiss became two, and more, as she curled her fingernails into the ruffled pirate shirt covering his chest, clamoring for more of this hot, hunky man — the answer to her Halloween fantasy.

When his hand eased up onto her breast, she sucked in her breath and murmured, "Oh God," against his mouth. It had been awhile since she'd been touched there and the sensation ricocheted through her body like a pinball.

Her response clearly encouraged him. He stopped kissing and pulled back just enough to meet her gaze—close, so very close—and molded her breast full and hard in his hand. The intense, raw contact sent a jolt of lightning through her cunt, made her cry out softly. To look at him while he...while he...took such solid *possession* of her transported her to a more feral place than she'd ever been. She'd never let a guy touch her anyplace intimate this quickly after meeting him, and she'd certainly never experienced such a hot, fierce connection with a man she didn't know. His eyes shone glassy with lusty intent, and she could only *imagine* what he saw in hers, even with the sparkly black mask surrounding them.

Soon both his hands massaged her breasts—his thumbs raked across taut, pointed nipples and she arched forward involuntarily, offering herself to him.

"Does my dirty kitty like that?" he asked, back in pirate voice again but still sexy as hell.

The only other thing she could hear was her labored breath and she suspected that was answer enough, but still she managed to reply, "Mmm, meow, yes." She also liked being called dirty. Not usually. But tonight it sounded positively delicious coming from her big, strong pirate man.

"I want more," he growled then.

"Take it," she demanded.

And he didn't hesitate. Lowering his palms from her breasts, he found the bottom of her stretchy black pullover and pushed it up, up, over the top of her bra. She knew her breasts looked plump, practically spilling from the tight cups, and as he studied her curves, she found herself licking her upper lip, peering at him through half-shut eyes, loving the feel of his gaze on her.

Cupping the undersides of her breasts, he pushed them even higher and began to rain hot, tiny kisses across the swelling ridges above the stiffened lace. Her breath came faster as she reveled in the ministrations, his long, dark hair brushing over her sensitive flesh as he worked. At some point, she lifted her arms above her head, jutting her chest out even farther, offering herself to him completely. Behind her, her cat's tail pressed provocatively into the crack of her ass now that she leaned against the wall.

Of course, delivering such chaste affections didn't occupy her lusty pirate for long. The next thing Leah knew, he'd curled his fingers into the black cups holding her and was slowly pulling them down—so slowly that the slide of the lace abraded her nipples, so slowly that they both watched the bra's descent, and when the beaded pink peaks finally popped free, they both sighed.

When their gazes met as he gently licked her, she knew without doubt that it was the most erotic experience she'd ever had. "Yes," she whispered, drawing out the "s", letting him see the pleasure in her eyes. He tongued her elongated nipple, then drew back to blow on it, making her shiver in delight.

He grinned darkly. "'Tis breezy at sea, me beauty," he rasped at her breast.

"Then I like being at sea, Captain," she replied on another catlike purr.

After that, he feasted on her nipples some more, licking, kissing, suckling, even once gently biting as she held his head in her hands, running her fingers through that dark mane of hair and being careful not to knock his tricorn askew because she was enjoying the fantasy so much—the fantasy of being some pirate's wench, ravished at sea, and also the lurid fantasy she was actually *living out*, fucking a stranger while both of them wore costumes.

She could only imagine how she looked to him, still dressed, her top and bra framing her breasts above and below, and the friction from both garments only added to the sensations taking her over.

Leah feared she would die of pleasure. Even though they were standing up, just steps away from a rollicking party — and right next to a set of windowed doors, no less — she wasn't sure any man had ever treated her breasts so nicely, brought her such extreme joy just by using his mouth and hands on that part of her body. It was the only moment in her life when she'd ever wondered if it was possible to climax just from breast stimulation — until his arms twined around her, his hands sinking to her ass, and he pressed his erection into her crotch.

"Ohhh," she moaned. God, why would she even *want* to come from mere breast play when her pussy could be involved?

And his cock felt...large. *Huge.* And it made her hungry — so, so hungry.

Then, for the first time since exiting onto the sun porch, she remembered — she'd intended to take control here.

And play with his cutlass.

Chapter Six

ၼ

She had to have his cock, needed to feel it beneath her palm. So after letting her body move against his, pelvis to pelvis, just for a few blissful seconds, she reached boldly down between them and pressed her open hand to the bulge in his navy blue captain's pants.

"Jesus God," he moaned.

"Does my nasty pirate man like *that?*" she asked, playful and hot.

"Aye..." he managed, a hint of role-playing amusement leaking from his expression just before his head dropped back in pleasure.

She'd been right—his cock was big. The rock-hard column of flesh arced upward over his belly beneath her touch, and even through fabric, she knew he possessed the largest penis to ever to cross her path. If she'd thought she was hungry for it before, that measured nothing compared to now. She caressed him firmly, letting her fingers mold around him, squeezing, massaging his length.

"Ah God, pussycat, yeah," he murmured, quickly lost in a haze of passion, and she liked him that way, liked the sense of power it gave her. Wasn't that what she'd wanted here? Oh sure, at first the whole notion had just been about getting laid and making sure she had a better time at the party than in years past. But she'd felt that to reap the most from it, she'd need to take control, be a true seductress—and now, suddenly, she was. She was wrenching moan after moan from him and wanted, very soon, to wrench more than just mere sounds from the sexy man before her.

29

A thought that drove her to undo his pants. Glancing down between them, she worked at his belt buckle, then found herself unbuttoning and unzipping the "breeches" above his black boots. Underneath, standard white briefs, his erection jutting up from the elastic band. Quickly she yanked that down, hooking the underwear beneath his balls—and stood amazed.

Dear God, he had to be at least nine full inches long. "Oh, *Captain!*" she heard herself squeal in delight as she wrapped her hand around his naked shaft.

His voice sounded only slightly strained—and fully pirate-like—as he said, "So ye like me trusty cutlass, eh?"

She was getting into the play aspect of this even more now. "Mmm, very much." She squeezed him, then ran her fist up and down. "It's so big. I hope I can...handle it properly."

His response was a bit more labored this time, but still confident and full of heat. "I've tremendous faith in ye, pussycat. Give it a go."

And give it a go she would. She dropped to her knees, felt the hard, cool porch tiles through her stockings, gripped his cock still more possessively and went down on him. Smoothly licking away the pre-come at the tip of his cock, she eased her lips over his width and took him into her mouth.

Oh God. Even without him moving, it felt like being fucked by him. The entry into her body had been that direct, deliberate, impactful. The sensation of having him fill her mouth made her ravenous, made her slide her lips farther down, sucking intently, wanting him to feel it deep, wanting to give him the best blowjob he'd ever had.

And how strange such desire felt as it overtook her. She'd always done this in a bed or, back in college, a car—she'd never actually dropped to her knees before a man until now. Strange how putting herself in such a submissive position made her feel so distinctly powerful.

He gently kneaded her scalp with his fingertips, heightening her pleasure, driving her onward as she took him deeper, deeper, all the way to her throat, wanting to swallow as much of him as she could. And there was so much to swallow—somehow it presented an inherent challenge and she wanted to prove she was up to the task. When only a few inches of the hard phallus remained outside her mouth, she felt amazed, accomplished, and looked up at him.

His eyes said she was incredible. And his mouth said, "Ah, damn, pussycat, that's so fucking good. You're taking me so fucking deep."

And then she began to move, to slide her wet lips up and down his majestic shaft while she gripped the root of his cock in one hand. She let her eyes fall shut now, let herself become fully absorbed, lost in the pleasure she delivered. Sometimes it *was* better to give than to receive, even in sex. More of that lovely power flowed from him into her, pumping through her veins, fueling her to continue, no matter how swollen or tired her mouth became.

"That's right, pussycat, suck my cock. You suck it so good."

His dirty talk pushed her onward, too, until finally her hot pirate began to gently fuck her mouth, thrusting lightly— and even as it threatened to steal a little of her power, making her *take* it, forcing it into the recesses of her mouth, even *that* somehow ultimately delivered still more control. Because she *wanted* to take it. She wanted to take as much as he wanted to give.

After a while, though, she backed off. Not completely, but because she found herself wanting to...play with his cutlass. Really *play* with it.

Curving both hands around his length, she found herself licking teasingly at the rounded head, flicking the tip of her tongue across the tiny slit there. Then she ran her tongue in a circle around it, almost as if French-kissing it. She let just the end of his cock back between her lips, focusing on how smooth he was there, how soft that part of him felt despite the impossibly hard shaft just below it.

Every move she made caused a fresh reaction in him—a moan or a sigh or a whispered obscenity. And soon she couldn't help herself—she went back down on him with pure vigor, wanting to take his stiff length back inside her again, wanting to make him crazy with pleasure.

After which she looked up, met his eyes. And this time she *kept* her gaze on him, never looking away. She sucked him, moved up and down his tremendous cock while he watched her. His breath came labored and heavy and his eyes looked wild, his fingers clenched tight at her scalp—until he pushed her back. "God, stop," he breathed.

She peered up at him, still on her knees, her lips feeling more delightfully stretched and well-used than ever in her life.

"I don't want to come," he told her. "And if you don't stop, I will. Hard."

With her heartbeat in her throat, her mouth hungered for more of him. But *she* didn't want him to come either.

Somewhere Michael Jackson sang "Thriller". So she gently grasped her pirate's shaft again and said with a soft smile, "I think he's singing about *this*."

A small grin stole over her handsome brigand's face.

But just as quickly, it disappeared.

"Stand up, pussycat," he said, hot possession filling his eyes.

So he was ready to take control again. She didn't mind trading it back and forth.

Thus, with a gentle kiss to the tip of his cock and a move designed to let his length slide between her bare breasts as she rose, she pushed to her feet and stood before him, ready for whatever came next.

She loved the way his eyes raked over her, but she was so hungry for more, dying to kiss him, dying to fuck him, that she wanted him to hurry. When his gaze stopped, as it had once before, on the sexy lace tops of her stockings, he resumed a hint of the pirate voice. "Now what kind of panties does a naughty little kitty-cat wear under such a short skirt?"

She couldn't help flashing a seductive smile. "The *best* kind—for what *we're* doing."

He didn't hesitate to grab onto the skirt's hem and ease it upward to her hips. Which revealed, of course, that the best panties were...none.

A low moan left him, and apparently the sight drove *him* to *his* knees—from weakness or for a better view, she wasn't sure and didn't care. Since the moment she'd met him, she'd enjoyed his eyes on her, relishing his bold, unabashed study.

He glanced up at her. "No fur here, pussycat."

"Maybe I'm a rare breed."

"No maybe about it," he said, then skimmed his fingertips over the smooth flesh between her legs. She didn't always keep the area shaved, but she'd figured if she was going to be a bad girl tonight, she might as well go all the way. When, still staring at her denuded cunt, he said, "Damn, that's fucking hot," she was glad she'd followed her instincts. So she followed another and parted her legs.

"God," he said. "You look so wet."

"Drenched," she assured him.

And then his tongue sliced into her.

She cried out at the shock of pleasure, then covered her mouth, fearing they'd be heard. But Captain Morgan didn't seem concerned—no, he was far too busy licking her, dragging his tongue full up her parted slit, making her legs weak as her breath grew wild and thready.

She found herself clutching at the wall behind her, trying to find something—anything—to hold onto to keep her from collapsing, but nothing was there. She felt herself pumping her pussy at his hot mouth, needing the blessed attention, drinking it in with every thrust against his face. And in back, her kitty tail still rubbed softly at her center, only adding to the sensations.

"Lick me," she begged. "Lick me hard."

She never did that—never pleaded or begged. But tonight, her body was propelling her far beyond her normal sexual boundaries, and the words left her without thought or care. She loved the way he looked between her legs, servicing her, giving her back that sense of control so very quickly, making her bold enough to work her hungry cunt so eagerly against his tongue.

She wanted to see herself, wanted to see how she looked, and even in the midst of her hard lust, she found herself scanning the room until she caught sight of their reflection in one of the many large windows. It was dim, dark, difficult to see, but enough that she witnessed her own utter abandon— and took obscene delight in it.

His tongue raked over her clit again, again, as she bucked at him, and she even found herself molding her breasts in her own hands, pinching her nipples between her fingertips.

"Oh God, oh God," she heard herself mutter.

And then the orgasm washed over her, wave after intense wave of pleasure expanding from her cunt outward through her arms and legs, making her grip his head, curl her fingers into his hair, just to hold on to something, just to keep her upright.

And as the waves eased, passing, she sensed one kind of need inside her almost...crumpling, dissolving, to give way to another.

"You've got the prettiest little pussy, honey," he murmured, his breath warm on the tender flesh there.

Her voice came ragged. "I want you in it."

She'd climaxed, assuaged that urgent, gnawing lust—and now she needed something simpler, baser. She needed his cock inside her. She needed to be fucked.

She watched as he rushed to his feet, then began to reach inside his captain's coat, likely going for a condom.

"I've got it," she said, halting his search. Her tiny little skirt had a tiny little pocket, and she'd come prepared.

Chapter Seven

🔊

Dipping her fingers into the pocket, she plucked out a square foil packet and tore it open, then began to put it on. He hissed in his breath as they both watched her fingertips rolling it tightly over his much larger than average appendage.

Then she lifted her gaze to his—again, he stood so close and his eyes remained so dark and possessive—and she began to tremble. She wasn't sure why.

"You okay, pussycat?"

She nodded. She was. The trembling was about lust. "Just want you," she told him. "Inside me."

He answered by twining both arms around her, firmly gripping her ass. She gasped as he pulled her tight, his enormous cock stretching up the front of her slit.

"I've never…" She hadn't meant to start talking, but the words had just come out. "I've never been with a guy as big as you."

He kissed her, short but sizzling, then leaned his forehead against hers. "No worries. I won't hurt you."

Somehow she believed him, trusted him just as she had from the start to make this good, *keep* this good.

The next thing she knew, he was lifting her slightly, positioning her, and his sheathed cock nudged at her opening. Then eased inside. Slow. Deep. As easy as that. They both groaned. And then he was in her. Her pirate was in her.

Again, their faces were so close—they were eye to eye as he began to move, to thrust slow but deep up into her pussy. And this didn't feel like sex with a stranger anymore. This felt like sex with a masterful man who let her take control from time to time, whenever she wanted it, but now he'd taken it back. Having his big cock in her made her whimper—he was now the giver, she the taker.

"Your sweet pussy's so tight," he murmured deeply.

She heard herself whisper a reply. "Because you're so huge."

"I'm not hurting you, am I?"

She shook her head. He wasn't. "No, you're just...filling me. So deep. So good."

"Your cunt is so warm, pussycat. So warm and snug." He still moved slowly in her but used his hands on her ass to maneuver her body the way he wanted—and just then, he plunged deeper. She moaned and wrapped her legs around him tight, letting him support her completely.

"Oh God," he said, "your heels are digging into my ass."

"Does it hurt?"

"No, I like it."

He'd long since left the pirate accent behind. And part of her missed that, because the fantasy was such lusty fun. But part of her liked hearing the *real* him, the warmth of his voice, the depth of his passion.

She *shouldn't* like that, because this was a one-night thing, and when it was over, she was going to push down her skirt and leave—leave the fantasy perfect and untarnished and just walk away, mask intact.

But she couldn't help it. They were experiencing profound physical intimacy. She couldn't help wanting to know him just a little.

Shit. Looking into his eyes, having him hold her, feeling his length drive to her very core, was drawing her in too deep. Into emotion. She had to take control again. And she'd do well to keep it this time.

So she lowered her shoes to the tile floor and planted her hands at his waist, pushing him back. She immediately missed the fullness of having his penis inside her, but she was going to take him over to the little wicker couch a few steps away. She was going to mount him, going to ride him. Going to re-seize control.

Only that didn't happen.

Instead, his hands gripped her hips—hard, almost forceful, his fingers digging into her flesh. And a strange desire shot through her, unbidden. It must have blazed in her eyes because the commanding pirate captain was suddenly back. "Aye, do you like it rough, pussycat?"

God. She didn't even know. She'd never wanted anything "rough" with a guy before, but maybe she did. With him. Now. Tonight. "Make me find out," she heard herself say.

With that, the slow, rhythmic tempo of their sex changed—he turned her around to face away from him and pressed her hands flat to the wall. The wallpaper—displaying, ironically, a beachy, windblown seascape on which a woman might well fuck a pirate—possessed textures she'd not noticed up to now. Wavy portions were lined in the lightest velveteen, and now she felt the softness beneath her fingertips just as he plunged his huge cock deep into her.

She cried out but no longer cared if anyone heard. She'd never felt so...taken. *God*, he was big, and now she experienced his size in a way she hadn't before. Because he no longer went slow—now he fucked her harder, faster, delivering punishing thrusts that reverberated out through her fingers and toes. She tried to be quiet, but she kept sobbing her pleasure, amazed at how something that bordered on pain could also bring her such hot, dirty joy.

His hands gripped her hips tight as he drove into her again, again, but occasionally he slapped her ass, and good Lord, even *that* felt good—echoing through her, heightening other pleasures, simply making her feel. Feel. Feel. Everywhere.

"Do you, pussycat?" he asked near her ear, sounding as if his teeth were clenched. "Do you like it rough?"

She responded between brutally hot plunges that made her legs threaten to fold beneath her. "God... Yes... Fuck me!"

As for control, she'd forgotten it. She just wanted to be fucked. She just wanted to feel everything he had to give. She wanted her body, her whole *being*, to soak it in, to revel in it.

Soon she found herself pressed further against the wall. She still arched her ass, welcoming his forceful strokes, but now her breasts rubbed at the wallpaper, the plush ridges teasing her nipples, delivering the softest sort of pleasure even as he dealt out the hardest. She found herself sobbing louder. "Oh *God*. Oh *God*. Oh *God*." She felt consumed by him.

And it was delicious and dirty and more pleasure than she'd ever known—yet also *dangerous*. This was supposed to be good, hot sex, but...but not like *this*. She'd imagined something quicker—a frantic coupling. This was...stunning. Life-changing. She was feeling things she'd never felt before. Maybe it was a G-spot thing currently making her feel so crazed, so possessed, so wild, but it was...too much. Just too much to experience with a man she was never going to see again, a man who, in a few short minutes, would be nothing more than a memory.

And finally, finally, she was going to take back the control. *Now*. "Let me ride you," she demanded as harshly as she could.

Behind her, he gripped her hips tighter and went still. "What?" He sounded frustrated and she couldn't blame him, but she persisted.

She looked over her shoulder. "I want on top. I want to feel your cock stretching up inside me. I want to put my weight on it so that I have to take every inch, all the way."

Apparently her reasoning swayed him since he pulled out of her, leaving her to suffer that emptiness again as she turned to face him. Yet his eyes, framed by that long, dark pirate hair, still looked forceful, almost angry.

Well, she didn't care. She was angry, too. Angry at *herself* for letting this get so out of hand. She was taking it *back* in hand.

They moved together to the couch — him half dragging her, her half pushing him. They were a tangle of limbs as he landed on his ass and she moved to straddle him. Neither bothered mentioning that this part of the room was much more visible through the French doors if anyone looked.

She peered down at how grandly his shaft rose between them — and sighed. "Oh God," she heard herself utter once more. It seemed they were the only words that described all the things he made her feel.

And suddenly, for some insane reason, she wanted to be more tender with him again, move slower. She'd intended to bring him over here and fuck his brains out to end this crazy liaison, but to her surprise, now she wanted to go slow again. She even found herself leaning forward to kiss him.

He seemed resistant to that at first, kissing her too hard, but then he softened toward her and she felt it once more, the power of seduction.

Their mouths met, slow and languid, kisses that melted through Leah like warm syrup — until she kissed her way over his jaw and down onto his neck. He groaned as she explored the tender flesh spanning his throat, so soft beneath her lips — until finally stopping to raise back up. Meeting his gaze, she purred deeply, letting a gentle smile unfurl.

He returned it and she knew they were friends again, the weird, frantic sexual animosity gone now. "Arrr — ye be a hell of a lover, pussycat," he said, but just as quickly, the pirate voice dissipated once more. "This is the best sex I've ever had."

The words sifted through her, perilous and sweet. *Me too,* she wanted to say. But couldn't. Couldn't let herself feel any closer to him than she already did. So instead she said a soft, sexy, slightly raspy, "Meow."

"Ride me," he said deeply.

And she rose up onto her knees and slowly, surely, sheathed him with her welcoming cunt. They both sighed with the pleasure of being connected again, joined together. And when she did as she'd promised, sank down with her full weight, taking every long, hard inch of his majestic shaft—oh God, it was nearly overwhelming.

She'd thought this position would bring back that power she'd wanted so badly, but it didn't. Instead, it took them to a place where *neither* had the power. And where they *both* had the power. Adjusting to his size, she rode him in tight but leisurely circles that delivered perfect friction to her clit even as he stretched to impossible lengths inside her. He slowly massaged her ass as he thrust gently deeper, deeper.

Working on pure impulse now, she looped her arms around his neck and rubbed her nipples against his chest, simply needing to connect with him in yet another way.

Which was ridiculous. She didn't even know him. She didn't even really know what he looked like without the dark hair—which she suspected was a wig but wasn't sure—and all his other pirate trappings.

This was why casual sex never worked for her. She could never keep it casual. Never. And she'd always known that about herself. She might've thought she was old enough now, mature enough, not to succumb to that odd feeling of *emotional* attachment that always grew out of *physical* attachment for her, but she'd been wrong. She felt crazily close to this hot man. And how could she not? She'd tasted his lips, felt his warm breath on her neck, his mouth at her breasts. She'd sucked his cock, for God's sake. And now their bodies were interlocked, tight as puzzle pieces. *Of course* she felt close to him.

So she refused to think ahead even five minutes, focusing only on now—and on pleasure. Because, *oh God*, did the man deliver pleasure! She'd never known the joys of such a large male specimen, and mmm, size *did* matter, she realized for the first time. Not that she'd kick a guy with a lesser penis out of bed, but she certainly liked this nice, big one. She liked the way it filled her so full, so full that she suffered nearly devastating pleasure and each stroke echoed all the way out through her arms and legs to her fingers and toes.

As minutes passed, their breathing grew shallow, ragged in tandem. She lifted her hands to his face to kiss him, liking the way his soft, thin mustache and goatee tickled her skin. He slid his hands to her breasts, molding, caressing, then whispered, "Let me suck them, pussycat." She didn't refuse, leaning inward, rising slightly, feeling the delight dart straight down to her cunt when he pulled one beaded nipple into his mouth.

It was exactly what she needed, combined with the sensations below, to push her over the edge. And she'd never had multiple orgasms in her life—until now.

"Oh God," she moaned. "*Yes. Yes. Yes.*" This one came on faster than the first, with less warning, but the pleasure itself was softer, somehow deeper, wafting through her slowly to leave her feeling ready to curl into his arms and fall asleep.

She did curl into his arms, just for a moment. But then he pushed down on her hips, hard, thrust deep, making her cry out as he said, "Me too, pussycat—I'm coming in you. I'm coming in your perfect little pussy."

His cock nearly lifted her from the couch in four powerful upward drives, but she absorbed them, relishing how amazingly deep he was inside her body.

And then he went still below, but continued kissing her mouth and whispering in her ear, "Damn, pussycat, you were amazing." With no pirate voice at all. In fact, now, coming out of the haze of orgasmic sex, his voice suddenly sounded so warm, comforting, that it almost made her feel a little...empty to have played so coy, not giving him her name. It made her feel like she'd taken immeasurably great sex and turned it into nothing but a game. And it made her feel like...her usual self, and like she'd just come crashing down to earth.

"Oh God," she said, knowing she sounded pained. But she couldn't help it, couldn't hide it.

He sounded worried. "Pussycat, what's wrong? Are you okay?"

She shook her head. "No." God, they were still joined, his cock still arcing magnificently up inside her cunt, still filling her so astonishingly full.

His fingertips brushed her cheek. "What's wrong?"

She found herself shaking her head some more. "This isn't me."

Of course, he was confused. "What?"

She tried to be honest, thinking through it aloud. "Well, it's *me*—of course it's me. And I'd be lying if I said I haven't loved every dirty minute of this. But..." She dropped her gaze, focusing on the white ruffles at his throat. "I've just never done anything like this before. I'm not usually this forward. I don't usually fuck guys I don't know."

"Oh."

And since that was all he said, and she was afraid she was freaking him out, she started talking more, just spilling it all—she couldn't stop it. "I only dressed like this because last year at this same party, I met a guy and really liked him, but he never called, and I was really hurt, you know? I know that sounds crazy after just spending a few hours with him, but that's what happened. And I suppose I was just trying to get Patrick out of my system by doing this." *And now I guess I'll spend the next who-knows-how-long trying to get you out of my system. Captain Morgan.*

But then he said, "Wait, *who?*"

"Huh?"

"*Who* are you trying to get out of your system? The name?"

43

"Patrick. Why?"

"Jesus." His head dropped slightly, his expression dumbfounded. "*I'm* Patrick. Are you… God, I can't believe this…are you Leah?"

Chapter Eight

ഔ

Leah blinked, amazed. How could this be? How was it possible? "Oh God. Yes. Are you really him? Really Patrick? You..." She sighed. "You don't look the same."

"I'm dressed as a freaking pirate," he reminded her with just a hint of dryness, then lifted the mask from her eyes. "I didn't recognize you, either. You had long black hair when we met."

"My hula girl wig," she said. "Kinda like this one." She lifted a lock of the hair near his face. It was *great* hair, but now she knew it was fake. The Patrick she'd met last year had possessed dark brown hair cut in a classic, professional style. Suddenly she suspected his goatee must be artificial, as well.

"It's not just the way you look, though," he said, reminding her. "Tonight you were so...so different."

She exhaled, expelling all the air from her lungs. And remembering. The things she'd done with him tonight. The things she'd said. Total hedonistic abandon. "Oh God," she murmured, letting her eyes fall shut in mortification and regret.

But then he cupped her cheek in his palm. "No, tonight you were different *good*, pussycat, I promise. *Very* good. You were...fucking incredible."

Which is when it hit her. "I guess you were pretty different, too."

"Funny what a costume can do for you, huh? I mean, last year I didn't feel as...disguised as I do this year. And for some reason, well..." He grinned. "I guess I really let go of my inhibitions."

"I hear ya on that," she said, giggling, even if a bit nervously. Thank God he didn't hold tonight against her, but it was still hard to believe…any of this.

"And I'm so sorry about last year," he went on—and suddenly, beneath the wig, behind the new bits of facial hair, she could see him, see the guy she'd spent those lovely hours with last Halloween. She now recognized his eyes, his smile, his voice. "I lost your number—couldn't find it anywhere. I hadn't gotten your last name, and like tonight, I was kind of tagging along to the party with a friend of a friend, so I didn't even know who to ask about you. Then my company unexpectedly sent me to New York for six months and my social life kind of fell off my radar screen for a while. I really am sorry."

Lord. Why hadn't something like that occurred to her? She'd never even considered the fact that maybe he'd simply lost her number. Or that big life issues had gotten in the way. On one hand, she felt like a dunce to have been so brokenhearted and hurt over it, but on the other, guys were so historically famous for taking girls' numbers and then not calling that it had just seemed like a typical guy/girl slap in the face when she hadn't heard from him.

"I'm kind of embarrassed," she admitted.

"About the stuff we did?" His grin turned surprisingly boyish. "Don't be, pussycat. I loved it. And I love knowing that the sweet girl I met last year also has a naughty side. I mean, in guy world, that makes you the perfect girl."

She couldn't help laughing, but said, "Well, yeah, I'm embarrassed about all *that*, too, but I meant I was embarrassed about what I just told you. About getting so attached to you last year." In fact, she felt a warm blush staining her cheeks at reminding him.

But Patrick simply shook his head, looking far kinder now than she'd known a pirate could. "Don't be. I…felt pretty strongly about you, too, and I was in the process of trying to track you down when the New York thing came up. So...just know you weren't the only one who was disappointed."

She bit her lip, her heart filling with joy. This was magical. But then again, it *was* Halloween, a night for magic.

Tracy was *so* not going to believe this. And Leah couldn't believe her luck—that the guy she'd so effectively seduced for a night of hot sex was also the guy she held in her heart. She could only conclude that, somehow, maybe the two of them really were meant to be.

And everything felt so good and right between them suddenly, so wholesome and pure, as she recalled last Halloween, as they exchanged such caring words—but things *also* felt really *dirty* when she remembered... "Um, do you realize you're still inside me?"

He glanced down between them, his eyes turning heated again and his voice going all pirate. "Aye, me beauty—and 'tis a fine place for a man's cannon."

Despite herself, she laughed. "A cannon? No longer a cutlass?"

He shrugged. "Arrr, pussycat, Cap'n Morgan likes to mix up his pirate metaphors a bit."

God, he was adorable. Hot but funny. Drop-dead sexy but playful. And even as she smiled at him, her humor began to fade and she started moving against him in a slow, sensual rhythm she knew they both felt in all the right places. "I want to make that cannon of yours hard as steel again, Captain."

"Mmm," he growled, low, "'twill be an easy enough thing, lass. Just grind your hot little pussy on it. Aye, like that."

Oh my. That fast, Leah could feel his not-yet-wilted cock beginning to grow more rock-hard again, expanding inside her. "Oooh," she said, then did her best cat's purr.

"Aye, ya like that, do ya, me beauty? And I'm only yet at half mast."

Then, feeling unexpectedly bold once again, swept up in the heat of the evening, she leaned back slightly, lifted her hands and twirled her nipples between her fingertips while her pirate lover watched. Then sighed. Then got bigger and bigger inside her.

Soon he filled her cunt, as large and commanding as he'd been before, leaving her astounded anew at the length of his cock. "So *big*, Captain," she said.

"Just fer you, pussycat."

She rode him again, and he pumped up into her, making her feel every stroke. And this time when they looked into each other's eyes, the intimacy grew even deeper because she knew it wouldn't end with the night.

"Oh God," she said, her clit connecting with his body just above where his cock sprang upward into her. "Oh God, Captain Morgan, you have the most powerful cannon I've ever felt."

"'Twill explode in ye soon, naughty girl."

Rubbing against him even harder now, she smiled into his dark eyes and admitted, "I'm kinda digging the whole pirate fantasy thing. You make a *very* hot pirate."

"Well, then, me beauty, maybe tomorrow night we'll get you a costume, too. We'll dress you up as the lusty wench you are—even if you *do* make a sexy little kitty."

Just then, she came, hard and fast, dumbfounded that she could achieve orgasm three times in such a short period. This one was almost violent, rocking her body, making her buck and jolt on her pirate's big cock until he said, "Ah, pussycat, watching you come just took me there, too," and he drove deep into her, just like last time, nearly lifting her with his powerful shaft as he groaned his pleasure.

When finally they both went still, his arms fell around her and they leaned close, letting their foreheads touch. "Was that good?" he asked.

Mere words could not describe Leah's joy, so she simply said on a hot sigh, "Me-*ow*, baby. Me-*ow*." Then she whispered. "One thing, though. Just promise me you won't lose track of me this time."

"Not a chance," he said low, near her ear. "Because you're coming home with me tonight. We're going to see exactly how warm a naughty kitty can keep Cap'n Morgan in bed."

Also by Lacey Alexander

❧

Behind the Mask (*anthology*)
Brides of Caralon: Seductress of Caralon
Brides of Caralon 1: Rituals of Passion
Brides of Caralon 2: Master of Desire
Brides of Caralon 3: Carnal Sacrifice
City Heat: Carter's Cuffs
City Heat: Lynda's Lace
Hot In the City: French Quarter
Hot In the City: Key West
Hot In the City: Sin City
Hot For Santa!
Unwrapped

About the Author

ॐ

Lacey Alexander's books have been called deliciously decadent, unbelievably erotic, exceptionally arousing, blazingly sexual, and downright sinful. In each book, Lacey strives to take her readers on the ultimate erotic adventure and hopes her stories will encourage women to embrace their sexual fantasies.

Lacey resides in the Midwest with her husband, and when not penning romantic erotica, she enjoys history and traveling, often incorporating favorite travel destinations into her work.

Lacey welcomes comments from readers. You can find her website and email address on her author bio page at www.ellorascave.com.

Tell Us What You Think

We appreciate hearing reader opinions about our books. You can email us at Comments@EllorasCave.com.

PANTHER'S PLEASURE

By Cathryn Fox

Chapter One
Year 3040

ഔ

Sash stepped from the shower and balked at the ghostly reflection staring back at her. She grabbed her steamy oval mirror, propped it up over her steel sink and angled it for a better viewing. Surely to God that wasn't her. Her skin looked alabaster, her tongue pale. She swallowed down the scratchy feeling clogging her throat, and cursed under her breath. When she looked and felt this bad, she at least wanted a good reason for it and maybe even a few satisfying memories. But she couldn't even blame the peaked, wide-eyed apparition on a wild night of partying or a wild night of sex. Nope. She'd spent all of last evening in her quarters, traveling through the Taconian Galaxy on starship *Anthon*.

What the hell was wrong with her? She never got sick. Ever. Not once in her twenty-five years could she ever remember being ill. Sickness was for the weak of mind and the weak of spirit. She was anything but.

Her vision went a little fuzzy around the edges as she glanced around her cramped quarters. The lights embedded overhead stung her eyes. She pinched them shut and tried to ward off an impending headache. Her itchy skin felt ultra-sensitive, even the tiny hairs on her arms hurt. Moisture pebbled her feverish flesh as her gaze skirted over her unmade bunk with longing. Christ, she needed to pull herself together and haul her ass to the bridge where the rest of the crew awaited her arrival. They'd be landing on Lannar in less than twelve Earth hours, and as the ship's chief mechanic, she didn't have time for such inconveniences.

She pinched her cheek, hoping to add a tinge of color to her ashen skin. Nothing. She eyed her tray of makeup and considered her dilemma. Sash only bothered with makeup at the docking stations, never while on a mission. Which meant that ninety-nine percent of the time, she'd gone without. Because ninety-nine percent of the time, since the day her mother had given birth to her onboard the ship, she'd been coursing through space. And she didn't see that changing anytime soon.

After Sash had lost her mother in her early teens, Captain Mike Cavanaugh, her mother's dear friend and confidant, had taken her under his wing. The captain tried to be the father she'd never had. He'd tried to do right by her, buying her pretty dresses and barrettes, grooming her for ship's liaison, a position held by only the finest of women, but damned if she wanted anything to do with that. Not her. The captain assumed she'd prefer to work as a liaison, like her mother Aasia had, but she was a tomboy through and through, preferring to hang out with the guys in the engine room. Sash had spent years working under the chief mechanic, learning the trade, paying her dues, and when the chief retired, she rightfully stepped into his position.

Even though Mike had treated her like his own child, she insisted on paying her own way in life. It was simply in her nature, her genetic makeup perhaps, to rely only on herself after her mother had died. Those who knew her well often called her regimented, a control seeker. It was a label that suited her just fine. What was so wrong with having a fierce determination to maintain control over every aspect of her life, her work and wanting to earn her own keep? Not a damn thing.

Although she'd spent her entire life on the ship and the crew treated her like one of the family, she'd never truly felt a sense of belonging. They were her friends, yes, her family, no. And even though she'd never found a man strong enough to tame her, a man she wanted to spend the rest of her nights with, that didn't mean she went without the finer things in life. And by finer, she meant sex. She had a sexual appetite that could rival any man.

On any planet.

Every couple of new moons they'd schedule an overnight stop on the infamous Pleasure Planet in the Clarion Galaxy, a place where the drinks were free and the locals were freer. Sash would smack on some makeup, bang around the nightclubs for the evening and, if she was lucky, do a little banging of her own.

She stole another glance at herself. Shit. If the ship's doctor got a whiff of her sickness, she'd find herself confined to her quarters. Like a caged panther, she paced and considered her dilemma. It had taken three full weeks to reach Lannar and she wasn't about to find herself locked inside the ship while the rest of the crew were granted shore leave. She too was anxious to step foot on the planet that Earth had recently reopened trade with. No doubt a night intermingling with another species at the docking station was just the thing she needed to make her feel as right as rain.

Sash grabbed her tray and hastily applied a thick layer of pink blush to her cheeks. After coating her short, spiky black strands with hair tamer—the only part of her being ever to be tamed—she gave herself a once-over. Lovely. Now she looked like a ghost suffering from anaphylactic shock.

Giving up her efforts, she pulled on her one-piece skintight suit and began her long trek to the bridge. In a bid to maintain her balance, she trailed her fingers along the smooth polymer bulkhead. The lights embedded in the metal grates below her feet seemed brighter than usual, enhancing the rather drab gray steel of the passageway. Fellow crew members milled about. The scent of their coffee reached her nostrils and turned her stomach. The simple gesture of nodding a good morning greeting nearly made her lose her cookies.

Link, Chief of Security, hurried his steps to catch up with her, just like he did on most mornings. "Hey," he said.

"Hey yourself."

His scrutinizing eyes swept over her features, assessing her. A wide smirk curled his too plump, too girlish lips.

"What the hell are you looking at?" If she'd had the strength, she'd have twisted sideways and smacked that grin off his face, but in her quest to make it to the bridge without collapsing, she needed to conserve her energy.

"I guess it's that time again."

She didn't want to ask. She really didn't, but her inquisitive nature got the better of her. "Guess it's what time again?"

His eyes traced the pattern of her curves. "Since you're wearing makeup, I figured it was time for the old grease job and oil change."

One little smack. Surely just one little smack wouldn't completely drain her of her energy. She settled for a halfhearted jab to his rib. Anything less would have raised his suspicions.

"Real romantic, Link." She rolled her eyes. "And you wonder why you can't get laid." Nodding her head toward his hands, she said, "Haven't I told you that when you spout shit like that, it only ends up getting you a date with the palm twins?" The sound of their heavy boots pinging off the bulkhead ceased as they both stopped outside the bridge.

He grunted, pressed the lock and the hatch whirred open, granting them entrance. Humor laced his voice. "You're such a bitch, Sash," he replied, grinning from ear to ear, obviously entertained by their good-natured jibes and witty banter.

Sash stepped through the portal. "I might be a bitch, but I'm a bitch who can get laid," she shot back over her shoulder, even though the movement took effort.

Plastering on an air of professionalism while hiding the sick feeling in her stomach, Sash met with the captain and the rest of the crew.

Once it was clear that things were running smoothly and her crew was manning their stations, she made herself scarce and proceeded to count down the hours until they reached Lannar.

Unfortunately, the closer they came to the planet, the worse she felt. As she trekked back through the passageway, making her way to the living quarters, she glanced up in time to see the ship's doctor round the corner just ahead. In an attempt to avoid an encounter, Sash darted out of sight and then made her way to her chambers. She secured her door behind her, welcoming the peace and quiet of her room. Her body fell with a clunk as she dropped onto her bunk.

"Jesus, what the hell is wrong with me?"

Maybe she should go get checked out. It really would be the right thing to do. After all, she didn't want to infect the species on Lannar with whatever bug had found its way into her gastrointestinal track.

She rolled her eyes and scoffed. Talk about making a great impression. Earth could kiss their trading goodbye if she brought a foreign bacterium to Lannar.

After a quick consultation with herself, she backtracked. Perhaps she just needed air, she surmised, not wanting to risk having her shore leave denied. Not to mention not wanting the ship's medic to doctor her. She could damn well take care of herself.

Once they docked at their destination, she'd disembark for the evening and avoid mingling with the locals. Yeah, she mused, stretching her legs at the docking station and pounding back a few drinks was all she needed. Seconds later, her heavy lids slipped shut and the room around her faded from her vision as she drifted off to sleep.

The sound of her intercom woke her. Blurry-eyed, she pressed her comlink to communicate with Radner, her lead mechanic.

She cleared her throat, hoping her voice didn't come out as rough as she felt. "Report," Sash barked out, wincing at how horrible she sounded.

"We've reached Lannar," Radner responded.

Jesus, it felt like she'd just faced an all-out assault from the deadly rebels on Dortan. Except she replaced gunfights, air attacks and hand-to-hand combat with drooling, tossing fitfully and snoring.

Sash scratched her itchy skin and then gathered herself. "System check," she blurted, running her checklist through her mind.

"All systems are running smoothly," Radner responded.

"I'll be there in five."

"Copy that."

After a thorough check of her systems, Sash dismissed the bulk of her crew, granting them shore leave. A few members remained on board for any emergencies, not that any were expected, but when venturing onto any planet—trade invitation or not—emergency measures were always set in place.

Needing to escape herself, Sash reported to her captain and gave him her briefing. When in uniform, he treated her like every other member of his crew. Except today, he seemed to be taking an extra interest in her. Sash shifted her stance, worried that he could read her too easily.

After the captain dismissed his crew and before she could make her exit, his commanding voice stopped her mid-stride. "Is everything okay, Sash?"

Damn, he used her name, not her rank, which meant this conversation was about to turn personal. She twisted back around to face him and schooled her features, attempting to keep things professional. "Yes, Captain."

He stepped closer, scrutinizing her. "You look pale." The concerned look in his eyes touched her deeply. She really did care a great deal for him.

"Just in need of shore leave, Captain. It's been a long three weeks."

"Very well, then. You are dismissed."

She turned to leave.

"One more thing."

"Yes, Captain."

He got quiet, thoughtful for a moment, then he said, "Be safe on Lannar, Sash, and remember, you don't always have to be in control of everything. It's okay to let others take care of you."

Shit, he must have guessed she was sick and refused to go to the doctor for medical attention. Appreciating that he hadn't pushed the issue, she gave a curt nod of acknowledgement and twisted around to leave. After Sash cleared her shore leave, she made her way to the exit and considered the captain's cryptic words a moment longer, wondering if they held some deeper meaning. Maybe they did, then again, maybe they didn't.

Either way, she needed a drink.

Sash stepped onto the tarmac. Chilly air rushed over her flesh and helped cool her feverish skin. She drew the fresh air into her lungs and made her way into the docking station, which proved to be no different than any other docking station on any other planet. Broken down into quadrants, it housed sleeping quarters for visitors, a lounge area where business was conducted and dining areas where they could sample the local cuisine. At this particular moment she didn't care about food or sleep, she needed a drink and hoped they were serving something that would help her forget how crappy she felt.

As she moved through the bustling building and into the lounge area, she spotted the beautiful Dahara, the ship's liaison, sharing a drink with a man. Dahara, with her long blonde hair and hourglass figure, was the antithesis of Sash, who sported a short, spiked cut and a lithe body that could easily pass for a preteen boy. Only the finest of women, like her mother, assumed the role of liaison. Where her mother had been fair and curvaceous, Sash was dark and thin, making her believe she took after her father's side. Not that she knew who he was. In the past, whenever she had brought up the subject, her mother had always redirected the conversation, but Sash never missed the look of longing in her eyes.

On closer inspection, Sash acknowledged that the man sitting with Dahara didn't look like an extraterrestrial being at all, something she had grown accustomed to seeing during her planetary endeavors. In fact, Mr. Gorgeous resembled a human male from Earth. Except he looked wild and unkempt, with piercing green eyes that were panty-soaking gorgeous.

It was unexpected, really.

But interesting, definitely.

Why the hell did she have to be too goddamned sick to do anything about it? Because Link was right, it was well past time for the old grease job and oil change.

Out of her peripheral vision, Sash eyed the man as she made her way to the bar. She assumed the ship's liaison was conducting intergalactic business, not that she knew for certain what kind of trade deals they were making. It didn't really concern her. All she cared about during each mission was keeping her ship and her crew running smoothly.

But damned if *she* was the one who wasn't running smoothly during this particular mission.

With little finesse, she plunked her small mass onto a barstool and summoned the barkeep. He moved toward her. At least the appealing sight of his long legs and muscular body helped keep her mind off her itchy flesh. If only momentarily. Restless, she shuffled in her chair and clawed at her arm. She glanced down at the long red marks left by her scratching.

Damn, when had her nails gotten that long? And the hairs on her arms seemed much longer as well, and darker. How peculiar.

Shifting her attention, she caught the barkeep's glance and noticed that he too had those same mesmerizing green eyes. They reminded her of cat eyes, actually. A wild cat. Dangerous. Unpredictable. Fierce.

She found her thoughts drifting, wondering for an instant if the men from Lannar were as wild in the bedroom as they looked. Her pulse raced with excitement, anxious to find out as her gaze raked over him once again. It was always pleasant when a species appealed to her sensibilities.

Slut that she was.

When he stepped up to the counter opposite her, his eyes widened, as though startled. He inhaled, his jaw muscles twitched. "You're a..." Before he finished the sentence, Mr. Barkeep slanted his head sideways and caught the attention of Mr. Gorgeous. Sash watched the action in mute fascination. They exchanged a look and Mr. Gorgeous gave a slow side-to-side shake of his head. It was slight, but it hadn't gone unnoticed.

Never one to be subtle, she arched one brow and twisted on her stool to get a better look at Mr. Gorgeous. Her glance panned the man, registering every detail. Talk about dark, dangerous and sexy. Her gaze flitted across his handsome face, taking in his firm, square jaw, his dark unshaven skin and his sensuous mouth, a mouth that Sash would love to feel on her neck, her breasts, between her legs.

As though he sensed her watching him, examining him, green eyes shifted and met hers. When their eyes connected and locked, awareness flared through her, catching her off guard.

Holy shit!

The smoldering look he shot her fired her blood. Her stomach clenched like she'd just taken a blow. Her entire body reacted with heated urgency. Liquid fire prowled through her as lust clawed its way to the surface, clamoring for attention. Jesus, she'd felt sexual desire before, but never this potent. She felt like a wild animal in heat.

Sensuous lips turned up over perfect white teeth as he, in turn, devoured her. The hunger she saw in his gorgeous green eyes brought on a shiver. He watched her for several more moments and then let his attention drift back to the ship's liaison.

Feeling slightly lightheaded from the whole encounter, Sash turned her focus to the barkeep and worked to keep her mind off Mr. Gorgeous. Her efforts proved futile.

The barkeep continued to stare at her. Glaring back, she cut her hand through the air, giving him an opening to continue with their earlier conversation. "You were saying?" she asked, even though speaking took effort.

He cleared his throat. "You're a...human."

She grunted and ran her fingers through her hair, feeling anything but. "Today, that's debatable."

He narrowed his eyes, assessing her. "Do you feel...feral?"

What kind of stupid question was that? She looked at him, perplexed, then decided the men from Lannar really were no different from Earth men, nice package on the outside, a little hollow upstairs. She shrugged. "I feel just fine," she lied and propped her elbows on the counter.

Mr. Barkeep continued to look at her like she was some goddamn intergalactic mating experiment gone wrong. It made her feel uncomfortable, awkward and annoyed. "I'll have a Passion Peach. And make it strong," she said, hoping he'd take the hint and leave her in peace.

After her drink arrived, she twirled on her stool and watched the crew mingle with the locals. She nursed the sour elixir, but the fuzzy peach concoction did little to keep her headache at bay.

The sound of a chair scraping across the floor gained her attention. She turned in time to see Mr. Gorgeous stand. He crossed the room and moved hastily past her, stepping outdoors.

She caught a whiff of his natural scent. It called out to her and aroused new feelings deep inside. Her skin prickled, her heart raced and everything inside her urged her to answer that call. Inhaling deeply, she pulled it into her lungs, letting it rush through her bloodstream, letting it awaken all her senses, letting it awaken all her...*memories*. Memories? Why would his scent be familiar to her? Myriad sensations and emotions rushed through her. She shivered, almost violently.

Sash stood and stretched. A fierce need to step outside, to follow the animalistic scent emanating from that intoxicating man overcame her. Even though there were planetary laws prohibiting them from stepping outside the docking station, she made her way across the wide expanse of floor. A strange sense of déjà vu washed over her. How odd. As far as she knew, she'd never stepped foot on Lannar before, but something deep in her mind stirred to life. Some weird sense that she'd been here before. Had her mother taken her here as a child? She didn't think so. She searched her memories, but they were too far back, too out of reach to grasp.

Savvy that she was, she slipped past a few security guards, and pushed through the steel doors, needing, in some unfathomable way, to touch the soil, to become one with the land, the environment and the wildlife. Sash was never inclined to take risks with her career or balk the system, but the strange pull, the strange connection and sense of belonging she felt with this foreign planet had her going against her own best interests.

Perhaps it was just her fever playing havoc with her mind.

She scanned the area. The first thing she noticed was that the docking station was surrounded by tall trees and mountains. Tall trees and mountains that beckoned her.

Eyes alert, she took a quick glance over her shoulder and, despite her best interests, moved farther from the docking compound. The closer she came to the natural habitat, the worse she felt. But despite that she continued forward.

* * * * *

From the minute she stepped foot into the docking compound, Kade's instincts went on high alert, and as soon as he looked into the little Earth woman's hazel eyes and got a whiff of her natural scent, he knew it beyond a shadow of a doubt. She was his mate. And she needed him.

How it was possible, he wasn't sure. But he knew underneath that human exterior existed a wildcat itching to get out.

And there was only one way to help make her first transition easier.

Through mating.

And only one way to mark her as his mate.

Through submission.

For that was the way of the panther.

Barely able to keep his focus on the beautiful Dahara and their important trade negotiations, Kade had left the compound, instinctively knowing the Earth woman would follow, knowing her panther would feel the strong pull of the environment and the need to seek out her mate. As Kade waited for her, his skin itched to return to its natural form, to lay his mark on his life partner, to claim what was rightfully his.

Kade had no real answer as to why or how a woman from Earth was his mate, he just knew it deep in his soul. All others like him on Lannar had found their mate by the time they reached maturity, but not him. He'd spent most of his youth waiting, watching and wondering. As those around him paired with their partners, he worked to fight down the pang of envy that ate at his very being. In the face of all that, he remained calm and affectionate, as was their kind, learning to harness his pent-up energy, his restlessness and use it to become the powerful leader he was today.

He'd been physical with others, of course, but alpha that he was, Kade knew he'd never settle for anything less than his *true* mate. Nor would he settle for anything less than her submission. He'd almost given up hope of finding her. Almost.

Heart beating with exhilaration and the rush of excitement hitting him hard, he ripped off his clothes, shape-shifted into his panther form and followed her. His natural state allowed him to negotiate the jungle with ease and keep his presence undetected until he desired otherwise.

Inhaling, he caught the scent of another panther close by. He turned to find his brother Macon walking up behind him.

"Kade, what is she doing outside the compound?" Macon asked, alarm in his voice.

"I lured her here."

"Why?"

Kade angled his head, his nostrils flared, the animal in him roaring to life, demanding he claim the Earth woman immediately and mark her as his. Forever. Passion and possession raced through him. For the panthers on Lannar were unlike any other panther. Not only were they able to shape-shift, they mated for life. "She is my mate."

"How is this possible?"

With no easy answer, Kade shook his head and peered at her through the trees. Everything inside him tightened as he took in the paleness of her face, the tension in her body. "I have no idea." They watched her a moment longer. She looked lost, confused. A rush of tenderness overcame him, his deep-rooted compassion prompting him into action. He moved closer, knowing his mere presence would lessen her pain.

"She doesn't know," Macon said, stating the obvious.

"No, but her body must be in terrible discomfort as her first transformation begins." It pained him to think that his mate felt such distress. Everything in him reached out to her, his entire body longing to ease her discomfort, to own it himself and, for the first time, he understood what it truly meant to have a mate. The unbreakable connection, a connection he knew she felt too.

Sure, he was surrounded by family that he loved, but this felt different—it empowered him in a way he'd never felt before. As he filled his lungs with her scent, his heart pounded harder in his chest as a barrage of emotions swamped him. His entire body shook with need as a low growl sounded in his throat.

Nails extended on his thick paws as he negotiated the jungle floor, anxious to aid her. He could not, would not, see his mate in such a state. "I need to help her."

"Yes, you do. But I've never seen anything like this, Kade. Our first transformation is always reversed, panther to human. How is this possible?"

"I'm not sure."

When the little Earth woman clutched her stomach, Macon said, "You better go to her."

Kade nodded, knowing his presence alone would help ease her pain and that the only way to ease her first transformation was through lovemaking, since their seed had natural medicinal properties.

As he mulled over his approach, he got a whiff of Tallia's scent. He was pleased to know his brother's mate was close by. This tiny little Earth woman might need her during her transformation as well. "Where is Tallia?"

"Up there," Macon nodded to the tree line. Kade glanced up to see her watching from above. Kade's gaze went from Tallia to Macon. Their presence warmed his heart. Kade knew both Macon and Tallia were loyal to him and would provide support should he need it.

"Stay close, brother. I've never heard of an Earth woman shifting to a panther either. She may need us both."

As much as he wanted to go to her, to tell her what she was, he knew he couldn't be so candid. Although he wanted to make love to her immediately, splash his seed up inside her and make her shift easier, he resisted. He sensed he had to let her accept it slowly, for fear that the human part of her would rebel, fight off the change, and that could prove to be dangerous to her health. He'd never dealt with such a dilemma before, but deep down instinct told him to suppress the alpha in him and go easy with her. When she was up to full strength, then he'd have her submit to him and claim her completely. With her health and safety paramount, Kade, fighting the natural inclination to dominate her, transformed back into his human form, gathered and pulled on his clothes, and stepped onto the path.

Chapter Two

&

Twigs crunched and snapped beneath Sash's booted feet. Ever determined to reach whatever it was beckoning her, she moved deeper into the jungle. With stealth and precision, she ventured farther into the rough terrain, dodging the low-slung branches and carefully stepping over fallen trees.

With each step, the pain in her body amplified, making her trek that much more difficult. Her head felt heavy, her eyes stung. An incessant ache began at the back of her neck and traveled all the way down her spine.

She glanced up. The thick canopy of leaves blocked the moon, darkening her path. Despite the pain biting at her body, her other senses came to life. Not only could she hear the wildlife as though they were up close and personal, she could feel their presence and somehow see the unlit path before her.

Once again, the strong animalistic scent emanating from the man in the docking station curled around her. The wildlife suddenly went silent. She knew he was here, watching her, even before she saw him. Holding her stomach, she spun around, searching. She knew she should be afraid, but when she saw him standing in the shadows, she sensed she'd stumbled upon the very thing that had been beckoning her. Her mouth opened, but before she could get any words out, he spoke.

He stepped toward her, his voice low, soothing. "Don't be afraid, little one." When she remained quiet, he went on to ask, "Are you okay?"

She caught his glance and swallowed. Hard. Of course she wasn't okay. How could he possibly expect her to be okay when those gorgeous green eyes were undressing her and devouring her and she was too damn ill to lay herself out like a buffet? She lifted her chin. "Yes," she replied firmly, suspecting he'd followed her on purpose after that heated exchange they had back at the docking station. Either that or she was in big trouble for breaching the boundaries.

Long determined steps closed the distance between them. He leaned forward, crowding her. He cocked his head, his green eyes fairly glowing, an aura of ferociousness about him.

One large hand touched her elbow and tugged gently until her body collided with his. He brought his mouth close to hers. As her flesh absorbed his heat, her libido roared to life in a way it never had before. Christ, she knew she had a healthy sexual appetite, but the sudden craving for this man both frightened and excited her. He slipped his arms around her waist and rested his large hands on the small of her back.

What kind of strange, primal power did he have over her?

"What's your name, little one?" he breathed the words into her mouth.

His warm breath fanned out over her flesh, making her feel wild with need. Ensconced in the circle of his arms, the sudden need to touch him in return overwhelmed her. When he dipped his head and brought one hand around to touch her cheek, she had to lock her knees to avoid collapsing. The look in his eyes made her forget every sane thought. His fingers brushed against her flesh as he tucked a wayward lock behind her ear, the intimate contact easing her pain in some mysterious way. Her legs began to quiver and she became hyper-aware of the moistness in her panties.

She cocked her head. "What's yours?" she countered.

His eyes narrowed and she sensed that he was trying to control himself. Everything about his stance, posture and body language told her he wasn't a man who liked to be toyed with.

"Tell me your name," he repeated again, firmly. Lord, she could have sworn she heard him growl, deep in his throat. When she still didn't answer, he offered her a smile that stirred all her senses and had her resolve melting like sugar in water, which really caught her off guard. Her reactions were unexpected really, because no one had ever accomplished such an impossible feat before.

"It's Sash."

"Sash," he said as though tasting her name. His dark tone sent shivers skittering down her spine. "Sash," he said again, letting that one syllable roll off his tongue.

She furrowed her brow, studying his intoxicating green eyes, his pitch-black hair and his unshaven face. "Do I know you?"

He hesitated and pulled back slightly. His voice dropped an octave. "No, you don't know me."

She searched her memory. "I think we've met."

He touched her cheek and a weird tingling began in her bloodstream. "My name is Kade," he said softly. "I am here to help you."

She balked and furrowed her brow. "Help me? How? Who said I needed help?" Had Link sent him after her, knowing how desperately she needed the old grease job and oil change? "Was it Link?"

He blew an exasperated breath and angled his head. "You know, you ask an awful lot of questions for a woman who is in pain." He ran his tongue over his bottom lip, making saliva pool in her own mouth. He crushed her against his chest and joined them, pelvis to pelvis. She quaked under his touch and became aware of the passion rising in him.

She straightened. "Who says I'm in pain?"

"I do."

"How the hell—" She stepped back, assessing him. But the farther she moved away from him, the worse she felt.

He cupped her elbow and drew her back. He brought his mouth to hers and pitched his voice low. "Kiss me, Sash, and let me make love to you. It will help take care of the pain."

If her head didn't hurt so damn bad, she would have thrown it back and hooted. She settled for a halfhearted snort instead. "What the hell kind of lame-ass line is that?"

"It's not a line, it's our way."

She cocked her head, studying him. "Are you for real?"

He waved his hand around the jungle. "Things are different here on Lannar."

She snorted and decided to indulge him for a minute. "So you're telling me that if I have sex with you, it will make me feel better?" Man, the guys on the ship are going to love this angle, she mused.

"That's exactly what I'm telling you."

As her gaze panned him, it generated need and longing. She considered things further as she took in his magnificent body and the intensity in his smoldering gaze. If this hot delusional alien thought sex would cure her illness, who was she to tell him different? "Are you talking full-blown—"

Clearly flabbergasted, he cut her off and said, "Enough questions." Taking charge, he smashed his lips to hers, silencing her with a kiss. The minute they touched down, all thoughts fragmented. Warmth washed over her as his rough tongue moved in to mate with hers. He kissed her with such passion, it left her breathless. She'd never felt anything so divine. Blood rushed through her veins, pushing back the pain, clearing a path for the lust.

As pain segued into desire, her whole body went up in flames, this time not from the fever. She had no idea what kind of spell he had on her, but when he made her feel this good, she didn't care.

She touched him, suddenly unable to get enough. She tore at his shirt, ripping the buttons. Controlling the pace, he grabbed her trembling arms and pinned them to her side.

"Soon, little one, soon. We must go slower. Let me undress you and taste you first."

Kade reached for her zipper at the back of her neck and tugged, bringing them to a deeper lever of intimacy. Her skin came alive at the unhurried sound of the hiss. His seduction was far too slow, she needed him to take her fast. She'd never felt so frenzied, so wild or out of control before. "I need you inside me, now," she rushed out.

When she met his glance, she knew his need and desire matched her own. "I know what you need, little one, and I know how to give it to you. Now I want you to hand yourself over to me and trust that I can take care of you and your pleasures." He tugged her suit and panties to her feet and she kicked them away. She stood before him, naked and wanting. She heard his sharp intake of breath as his gaze panned her body. "You are the most beautiful female I've ever set eyes on."

His mouth connected with hers, kissing her long and deep, his hands tracing the pattern of her curves. She quaked and drew in air. Kade dropped to his knees, wrapped his arms around her body and pulled her to him. He held her to him for a long moment, just holding her, seducing her senses as well as her heart. He pressed his mouth to her stomach, his nose taking in her scent.

She touched his hair, aware of the emotions he brought out in her, emotions she'd never felt with any man, ever. Large hands came around to touch her small breasts. His voice sounded broken, labored. "You are so perfect, Sash, so damn perfect. I am the luckiest animal in the world."

Animal?

She didn't have time to consider that one word further, not when he was palming her breasts and circling her nipple with his warm, wet tongue. All she could think about was the desire, the need welling up inside her, threatening to burn her up from the inside out.

He drew one nipple into his warm mouth and savored her. She nearly lost all control of her legs right then and there. And her losing control was completely unheard of, completely unacceptable, but the way this man aroused her made her temporarily forget she was a control seeker. He pulled back to glance up at her. A cool breeze rushed across her breasts, cooling her hot flesh. She shivered.

"How do you feel?"

Pain momentarily forgotten, she ran her fingers through his hair and guided his mouth back. It felt too good to stop. "More," she demanded, answering his question. Jesus, she needed him more than she needed her next breath. She'd never felt such a powerful connection before.

He chuckled and then nipped at her swollen buds until they puckered in heavenly bliss. After a thorough taste of her breasts, he trailed his tongue lower, over her stomach, stopping to dip into her navel and then even lower still, until he was just a hairbreadth away from her cunt.

She spread her legs in silent invitation, but instead of answering the demands of her body, Kade eased himself out from between her thighs and stood.

He had to be kidding. She grabbed his head, ready to guide him back down, but a sudden burst of pain ripped through her. She glanced at her arm, noting the fine hairs appeared darker, longer. "What the fu—"

"Shhhh," he soothed. Without answering her question, Kade scooped her into his arms and laid her out on a soft bed of leaves.

"Let me make it better. I need to be inside you, Sash. I need to make love to you."

Once again, she spread her legs. Wide. "Then please, get on with it."

He stroked her cunt. "Let me get you ready."

She put her fingers between her legs, touched her drenched pussy and then brought her finger to his mouth. "I am ready," she pressed, not wanting to wait another second. Kade drew her finger into her mouth and groaned as he tasted her creamy essence.

He stood, and tore off his clothes. She took in his long torso, his bronzed muscles, and his magnificent, rock-hard cock. Ah, now she understood what he meant. He needed to prepare her for his length and thickness.

Now for that, she'd wait.

Kade dropped to his knees and insinuated himself between her legs. He stroked her skin, softly, gently, his finger coming perilously close to her clit, but never quite touching where she needed it the most. She bucked forward, encouraging him.

Answering the demands of her body, Kade pulled open her folds until he exposed her delicate pink flesh. His eyes filled with lust and longing. He swallowed and she sensed he was fighting for control, she could feel it in every fiber of her being. Kade was so feral, so strong, so animalistic, yet he was taking his time with her. But she wanted him to lose that control and take her, hard and fast.

His chest rose and fell in an erratic pattern. "I've waited far too long for you, little one," he whispered, his words choppy, his breathing rough.

He pressed his mouth to her pussy. She cried out and raked her hands through his hair, holding him between her legs. "That feels so good," she murmured, writhing beneath him. "Don't stop."

He licked her all the way from the back to the front and then inched back ever so slightly. "I won't ever stop loving you or making love to you, Sash. Ever. I promise, and a panther's promise can never be broken." With that, his mouth closed over her clit, licking and sucking and nibbling until her body shook uncontrollably. One thick finger slipped inside her. He pressed deep and then began the erotic motion of in and out, in and out, driving her passion to never before known heights of excitement.

Barely able to comprehend anything he was saying, she thrust her hips forward and moaned. He growled in response.

His low sensual rumble rushed through her blood, driving her into a wild frenzy.

He pushed another finger inside her, filling her with his thickness. She arched into the touch. He increased the pressure, driving his fingers in and out faster, his tongue circling her clit until her pussy clenched and convulsed in bliss.

"Yesss..." she hissed. Bright lights danced before her eyes as she gave herself over to her climax. Panting, she gripped for something to hold on to. A low moan crawled out of her throat as a powerful orgasm ripped through her. But it wasn't enough, not nearly enough. She needed to feel him inside her. Now.

As though sensing what she needed, Kade didn't wait for her to catch her breath. Instead, he climbed over her and, in one quick thrust, pushed his cock into her.

He drove himself inside her hot cunt, plunging deeper and deeper, unable to get enough of her. When her tight pussy gripped his shaft and squeezed, Kade knew he was going to lose all control and empty himself into her. And he couldn't lose it just yet, not until her transformation began, because it was then that she'd need his seed the most.

He calmed himself and gazed at the strong alpha woman beneath him. Sucking in air, he struggled to tamp down the animal clawing its way out. His panther struggled for dominance, wild with the need to claim her, mark her and make her submit to him. It was the way of their species.

With softer strokes, he continued to pump, angling her body to provide deeper penetration. He brought his mouth to hers and drew her in for a soul-stirring kiss. He could feel her heat and her love reach out to him. Like himself, he suspected she'd never dealt with these powerful, all-consuming emotions before either. He inched back and looked at her. She was close to shifting now, so very, very close. Her joints were swelling, her skin, hair and eyes darkening.

With gentle hands, he brushed her hair from her forehead and swiped at the perspiration dotting her forehead. Whispering into her ear, he asked, "How do you feel?"

She bucked against him and he felt her urgency, her panther fighting for dominance. "More."

She was close enough now that he needed to prepare her. "You are changing now, Sash, and I don't want you to fight it. Just let it happen naturally. I can help ease the pain with my seed."

"What do you mean, changing?" she asked breathlessly.

"You belong here now, with me. You are changing, becoming one of us." For a brief moment, he allowed his face to morph into panther form. He knew once he exposed his panther to hers, it would hasten her shift.

Her eyes sprang open, her mouth formed a perfect circle. He pressed his lips to hers, smothering her questions, and continued to drive his cock into her, thrusting harder and harder, encouraging her panther to find its way out.

She clawed at his back, but he continued to pound into her. When he felt her sex muscles clench around his cock, he let his own orgasm take hold. His seed splashed up inside her just as her body began to shift.

As her transformation began, he pulled his cock out of her, stepped back and morphed into his natural form.

A moment later, the most gorgeous, graceful panther stood before him. Long, lean muscles, shiny black fur and wide hazel eyes.

"Sash," he stepped closer. "Don't be afraid."

Her glance went from him, to herself and then back to him. He could almost hear her heart race and her blood rush frantically through her veins. "What the hell is going on?" she asked.

She spoke in panther, easily communicating in their tongue as though it was ingrained into her DNA, the same way it was ingrained into their DNA.

He kept his voice low and softened his words. "You are a panther. Like me."

"How can this be?" His heart went out to her when he heard the panic in her voice. He called for Macon and Tallia to join them. In their panther forms, they leapt from the trees and landed on the ground beside Sash, one on either side of her, giving her their protection, their comfort.

Kade waved his paw toward them. "We are all panthers."

She backed up slightly. Stumbling with the use of her four paws. She lifted one, examining it carefully.

Her eyes widened. "But how? How come I was never told of this before?"

"I'm not sure, little one." Kade moved toward her, needing the physical contact, needing to comfort her. She was being brave, he knew, but he could smell her confusion, her fear. He circled her, brushing up against her, nuzzling her.

He nudged her head with his own and watched her sort through things. He saw the first glimmer of understanding when she glanced at him. "The closer I got to the planet, the worse I felt." She looked at Macon and Tallia, and then around at the jungle. "It makes sense now. It must have been my panther trying to get out." She began to calm, much faster than Kade ever would have suspected.

His heart filled with love, proud of his mate for her strength of character. "I think you're right," Kade replied.

She examined her paws again. "I've seen lots of strange things in my travels, but never anything like this." She brought her paw to her face and studied her claws. "But why now? Why has this never happened to me before?"

He struggled to understand it himself. "Perhaps your panther needed to connect with its natural habitat first." He got quiet for a moment and then continued. "And then when you got closer to the planet, closer to me, your mate, your panther stirred to life." But why she had panther in her, he still didn't know.

He could almost hear her mind race, sifting through the information. Her head lifted. "And the lovemaking, it helps ease the pain?"

"Yes, our seed has properties that can help lessen the pain for our females."

Her eyes lit, hopeful. "So we have to do that every time I shift?"

He chuckled. "No, only for the first shift. Each one will be easier from here on out." Kade circled her again, his panther stirring, itching to claim her. Waiting for her to be ready. He wasn't sure how long he could suppress the alpha in him. He knew she was a strong Earth woman as well, but would she be submissive enough to submit to him?

When Sash glanced into his green eyes, her breath caught. They shimmered with lust and dark sensuality. She could sense his rising passion, his need to lay claim to his mate, to mark her. She turned to look at Macon and Tallia. They had begun to walk circles around her, their paws creating a path, as though preparing for some ritualistic mating dance.

Tallia glanced at her. "It is the way of our family, Sash. You are a strong female, but you must submit to your alpha mate. It is our way."

Submit? "I don't submit to anyone." She was strong, independent and self-reliant. She prided herself on those traits. She shot Kade a glance and watched him stalk back and forth like a caged animal, thick claws wearing a path in the bed of leaves beneath them. His nostrils flared, his eyes glowed green, his silky black coat bristled in the evening breeze and it surprised her that she wanted him again, badly.

"It is our way," Tallia repeated. "Give yourself freely, let your mate mark you and then you will understand how much he truly loves you. Once you've given yourself to him, he will cherish you and protect you with his life."

"Give myself freely? Forever?" Not f...ing likely.

He circled her and she could sense he was fighting down his wild animal, fighting to maintain control. "Sash, I've spent my life waiting for you." His voice was rough, his breath deep, labored. "I value your strength, I really do, but I am the leader here, the alpha, and I *need* your submission. I won't settle for anything less."

He couldn't be serious. When she caught the intent look his eyes, she gave a humorless laugh and then swallowed, her mind going a million miles an hour. Shit, he *was* serious.

She glanced around. Three to one. She was outnumbered on this strange planet, but the strange thing was, she didn't feel threatened, she felt...*loved*. And for the first time in her life, she felt like she belonged. Like she'd found her place.

Suddenly, as though he could no longer suppress the animal in him, Kade stalked up behind her and went up on his back paws, his front paws landing on her back, driving her front shoulders to the ground. Her blood began to burn hotter when she felt the weight of his body on hers. A deep low growl filled the air as he mounted her from behind.

God, he was so strong, so alpha. So amazing. And for the first time in her life, she suspected she'd met her match. His paws scraped along her back, his thick cock probed her opening a second time, alerting her to his raging arousal.

His claws bit into her flesh. "Sash, you are mine," he growled loud enough for the entire jungle to hear. In that instant, as his claws branded her, something powerful and intimate passed between, and she knew it beyond a shadow of a doubt. She was his and only his.

She glanced at Macon and Tallia and felt the intimate connection to her people too. Her heart swelled and pounded harder in her chest. She now understood why she'd never felt a sense of belonging on the ship or a family connection with the crew. This was her family, here in the jungle, and this is where she truly belonged.

Instinctively, her body began reacting to Kade's arousing animal scent and his lean powerful body. Everything in her reached out to him, wanting to give herself to him in a way like she'd never given herself to another. Giving him her body, her heart and her control. Sash had never relied on anyone, always taking care of herself, but it was not the way in this panther family. A family she wanted to belong to with all her heart. And in order to belong to that family, she had to let go of old ways and open herself up to this new primal way of life. She drew a rejuvenating breath, rattled by the emotions they all brought out in her.

Wanting — no, needing — him in a way she'd never needed another, Sash extended her front paws and lowered her head, keeping her backside in the air, offering herself up to him. Gifting him with the dominance he needed to claim her.

Kade spread her open with his erect tip and sank his cock deep inside her. As he plunged into her, her shoulders pressed on the ground, her claws scraping the dirt ground beneath her. A deep primal growl rumbled from the depths of Kade's throat. With the mating process underway, Macon and Tallia walked away, granting them their privacy.

Sash pulled in air as the powerful panther behind her marked her as his mate. His thick cock pushed open the tight walls of her cunt, bringing her closer and closer to her peak for the third time.

"Give yourself over to me, Sash."

There was nothing she'd like better. With a deep sense of belonging rushing through her veins, she wanted him to feel her love for him. She bucked against him and squeezed her sex around his cock.

Kade's voice came out strangled. "Tell me you are mine and mine only."

"I am yours, Kade." Her voice wobbled with emotion. As soon as she said the words, a powerful orgasm ripped through her.

Kade threw his head back when her cream drenched his cock. A moment later, he joined her in release. She could feel his hot seed splash up inside her, warming her body from the inside out, filling her with love and happiness and a sense of belonging.

Her chest ached from the joy welling up inside her. She was his. And he was hers. They now truly belonged to one another. Forever. No one would ever come between them. It was the way of this panther family. Her family.

Kade eased his cock out of her and crawled up beside her on the ground. He nudged her with his mouth. She took in the animal before her. He was so lean, so muscular and so beautiful.

"Are you okay?" he asked, his soft tone evoking myriad emotions inside her.

"I'm better than okay." She reached out with her paw and touched his fur. Wanting to be completely honest with him, she said, "This is just going to take some getting used to,"

A frown line furrowed his brow. "Do I appeal to you in this form, Sash?"

She nodded and addressed his worries. "Oh, yeah." Her pussy lubricated as she gazed at him in rapture. Desire reverberated through her blood. Honestly, she couldn't resist him in any form. She was about to bend over again to show him how much he appealed to her, but stopped when she noticed a puzzled look in his eyes.

She nudged him with her jaw, not wanting him to keep any secrets from her. From this moment on, she wanted them to share everything. "What is it?"

"I just don't understand all this. I know you are my mate. But how? You are an Earth woman."

Sash shook her head. "My mother was an Earth woman, but I never knew who my father was."

Kade rose to all fours. "Come on. There is one panther that should have the answers we seek."

Chapter Three

✆

Kade's heart filled with love and admiration for his new mate. Knowing they had to search out answers, he suppressed his need to lose himself in her again, over and over until they were both drained and sated. To think he'd almost given up hope that there was another feline strong enough to mate with the feral alpha cat inside him, yet submissive enough to allow him to claim her.

He watched her move with such grace as she negotiated the jungle floor in her panther form. He was amazed at how stealthy she'd become in such a short time. Continually touching, both needing the intimate physical contact at all times, they climbed the mountain together until they came to an opening in the rock.

"In here," he said, gesturing with a sway of his head.

"Who is in there?"

"Baback, one of our elders. He might have the answers to the questions we seek."

With Sash at his side, Kade stepped into his den and spotted Baback napping. Cautiously, not wanting to startle his elder, Kade stepped up to him. "Baback, we seek your assistance."

Baback opened his eyes. His glance went from Kade to Sash, back to Kade again. "Who have you brought to see me." Kade didn't answer, knowing it was a statement, not a question. Baback stretched and climbed to his four feet slowly. Without speaking, he circled Sash, inhaling her scent, his eyes focusing, assessing.

Then he stepped back. Kade didn't miss the conflicting emotions passing over his eyes. "This is Sash," Kade explained. "She is my mate, but she is also an Earth woman, an Earth woman who can shape-shift into a panther."

There was a long drawn-out silence and then Baback whispered, "It is you." He touched her as though to confirm she was real. "Aasia's daughter." He lowered his voice and added, "My daughter."

Kade watched Sash falter backward, water filling her eyes. He stepped closer to her, their bodies touching as he whispered soothing words. He rubbed against her, offering his comfort and his support, knowing they both had so much to understand.

Sash felt her throat constrict. "How can I be your daughter?"

Baback circled her slowly, his voice sounded tired, aged. "Because I loved your mother, my young child."

Sash's voice choked at the mention of her mother. She swallowed. "How did you know her?" she whispered.

"Years ago, our planet used to trade commodities with Earth. I met your mother and fell in love with her." He cut his paw through the air. "I wanted to keep her here with me forever. Our leaders back then forbade it. You see, species intermingling with other species was unheard of and one species transporting to another planet was prohibited. Our leaders worried that if we secretly allowed one human to reside here, others would follow."

Sash glanced around before moving in next to Kade, taking her rightful place at his side. "And that would be so terrible, why?"

"People fear the unknown. And the ability to shape-shift is unknown to others. We didn't want our kind to be hunted out of fear or simply for sport. It is a secret we must protect."

Sash nodded, encouraging him to continue. Kade touched her back and she felt his love reach out to her. Her heart swelled. Actions ruled by emotions, she eased in closer. She knew the bond between them was strong, unbreakable.

"A little over twenty-five years ago, after my indiscretion with your mother, our leaders shut down our docking station, prohibiting trade with other species for fear of it happening again. Your mother was taken from me, forced to leave. I fought the system and I fought hard. But I was forbidden to go with her by my people here and by your people on Earth. Intergalactic rules were set in place and such things were just not allowed." He gave a heavy, resigned sigh. "It is only recently, after your captain fought so valiantly to reopen trade, that our newest leader, Kade, and his brother, Macon, second-in-command, had welcomed a few select species back to our planet."

"My captain?" Why would he do that? Once again his words came back to her. "Be safe on Lannar, Sash, and remember, you don't always have to be in control of everything. It's okay to let others take care of you." The captain was her mother's dearest friend. Had Aasia told him of her love for Baback? Had he known all along what she was and that, when she met her mate, she would have to give up her control and submit?

Baback's voice pulled her back. "And now you stand before me. How did you find your way home?"

She didn't answer his question. Instead, she asked a question of her own. "Did you know my mother was pregnant?"

He lowered his head. "Not until now." Green eyes met with hers. "But now that you're here, will you let me make up for the lost time?"

Sash nodded, her heart going out to him, sad for the love both he and her mother had lost. She put her paw over his. Emotion thickened her voice. "She passed away many years ago, but I want you to know that she always loved you."

"And I've always loved her." Then he said, "You must stay with us now."

"How can I stay? Won't it be prohibited?"

"Times have changed." He nodded toward Kade. "Leaders have changed. That's not to say you won't meet with some resistance, you will. Some may be threatened by you; you are an Earth woman, and some will be fearful that you will reveal our secret. We must always be prepared for that." He brushed his face against hers. "The question is, do you want to stay?"

She lifted her chin. "Yes. I want to stay with Kade. I feel as if I'm finally where I'm meant to be, where I belong." At the mention of his name, Kade spoke up.

"What will you tell your captain?" Kade asked.

"I believe he already knows."

Both Kade and Baback looked startled.

She addressed their worries. "Since he's kept our secret this long, I'm certain he has no intentions of revealing it now. Besides, I am a daughter to him and he will do whatever is necessary to protect me."

"I'm your protector now, Sash," Kade said, his deep voice firm, unwavering. She smiled at him, knowing she could take care of herself, but granting him the right to do it.

"Come on, let's go talk to your captain." Kade turned to Baback. "When we return, we'll gather the family and apprise them of the situation." He turned back to Sash and guided her outside the cave.

As they made their way down the mountain, she stopped, confused. "How do I shift back to human? We certainly can't face my captain this way."

Kade nuzzled her neck. "You do it at will, little one. Close your eyes, Sash, and visualize your human form."

A brief second later both Sash and Kade stood before one another, both in their human form, both naked. She had to admit, she really liked seeing his gorgeous bronzed body in such a state. Her salacious mind wandered, thinking about all the delicious things she'd like to do to him.

As though he read her mind and even had the same indecent thoughts himself, he grinned and circled his arms around her. "Soon, Sash, after we've talked to your captain."

Damn. She returned his grin. "I guess we'll need clothes for that."

After walking back to find their clothes, Sash and Kade dressed and made their way to the docking station. Sash found her captain sitting in the lounge, nursing a drink. She glanced at Kade. "I need to do this alone." He seemed hesitant at first but she insisted. When he frowned, she planted her hands on her hips. "Kade, you can stay close, but I need to take care of these matters myself."

He scowled, clearly not in agreement. When she continued to glare at him, he gave a resigned sigh. "I guess I'm going to have to get used to an alpha female."

She kissed his cheek with all the love inside her. "Thank you." Then she winked at him. "You will be rewarded for your cooperation later."

"I like the sound of that." Kade took a seat not too far away.

Sash stepped up to her captain. "Mind if I join you?"

"It'd be my pleasure." His gaze panned her. "I see you're feeling better."

Never one to mince words, she got right to the point. "You know, don't you?"

He nodded. "Yes."

Her heart went out to him, knowing he was the man responsible for connecting her with her kind. "And this is the reason you wanted to come to Lannar. To reconnect me with my people."

Again, he nodded.

"Why now?"

He shifted in his chair and took her hand. "As you grew into a beautiful young woman, you also grew increasingly restless on the ship. I knew I had to take you here, to see if it was where you truly belonged. I wasn't sure whether you had the ability to shape-shift or not, since you never exhibited any signs, but I suspected we wouldn't know for certain until you came to Lannar."

"Why didn't you ever tell me?"

"I promised your mother I wouldn't. It was for your own safety, Sash. But I could no longer keep it from you. I had to know for certain. And now I do."

She squeezed his hand and offered him a genuine smile. "Thank you."

He swallowed and she heard his voice crack. "You're welcome. Now go, be with your other family. I promise to come and visit often."

They both stood and hugged. It pained her to leave like this, but they both knew it was the right thing. She had to be with her mate, the man—the panther—she loved like no other. "I'll miss you." Before she left, she asked, "What about the crew? What will you tell them? We can't have others thinking they can reside here. We must protect my family."

"I'll tell them only what they need to know. That you hopped on a ship headed to Pleasure Planet in the Clarion Galaxy and plan on taking an early retirement. They'll all believe that," he added, smirking. "Now go, be with your family." He glanced at Kade. "Your mate is getting restless."

Kade stood when she turned to face him. He closed the distance between them and nodded at Captain Cavanaugh. "Thank you," he said, his eyes sincere, his voice heartfelt. The captain nodded, then made his way back to his ship.

Kade grabbed her hand. "Let's get out of here." Without preamble, he led her out into the night. Once deep into the jungle, Kade became restless.

When she caught his glance, everything in her reached out to him. God, she loved him so much. She could tell he was about to shift again, to make their trek though the jungle easier.

"Not just yet." Sash slipped her hands under his shirt.

His gorgeous green eyes lit up, intrigued. "No?"

A burst of heat arced between them. "You showed me how alpha you were in panther form, now it's my turn to show you how alpha I am in human form."

He furrowed his brow. "Yeah?" The pleasure she heard in his voice excited her.

She trailed her hand higher until she touched his nipples. "You marked me, now it's my turn to mark you and claim you as mine." Sash didn't give him time to answer. Instead, she dropped to her knees, drew his pants to his ankles and insinuated herself between his thighs. She inhaled the scent of his magnificent cock and sheathed him in her hands.

"So good," he murmured.

She brushed her fingers over his long, hard shaft. "You are so gorgeous." Gently, she massaged his balls and drew him into her mouth. Moaning, she licked and stroked his length with her tongue until a low growl welled up from his throat.

"Sash, that feels—" His words fell off as she caressed his balls and scraped her teeth over his bulbous head.

He raked his fingers through her hair. "That feels damn good, Sash, but if you keep it up, I won't be able to control myself."

"I want you to let go. Come in my mouth," she whispered from between his thighs.

She sucked harder, swirling her tongue around his engorged head, loving the way he swelled and pulsed in her mouth. His hips jerked forward and she knew he was close. She licked his slit and could taste his tangy juice. She'd never tasted anything finer. Despite knowing he was on the brink, she spent a long time between his legs, savoring the taste of him, never wanting the moment to end, yet never allowing him to tumble over.

As she drew him in deeper, fire licked over her thighs, her blood pressure soared from simmer to inferno. Lust and desire for her mate raced through her. She worked her hands over his cock, milking his erection. Dark veins filled with blood and she felt his approaching orgasm. Poising his tip over her lips, she continued stroking. She could feel his body tremble. A moment later, his warm liquid spilled into her mouth.

After she licked every last drop, Sash stood and tore off her clothes. "Lie down," she commanded, her whole body quaking.

He did as she requested. Driven by need, Sash parted her lips and climbed onto his still rock-hard cock. It thickened and throbbed deep inside her. He felt so damn good. Rotating her hips, she gripped her breasts, thumbed her nipples and rode him with wild abandon. She writhed and moaned and thrust her pelvis forward, pressure building inside her, consuming her. As her own orgasm peaked, she leaned forward and raked her nails over his chest, branding him, claiming him as hers.

Still, she couldn't seem to get enough of him. Fever gripped her and the need to have him take her, all of her, consumed her. She wanted—no, needed—him inside her, everywhere. Trembling and panting, she hungered for so much more.

She lifted herself from his cock, dipped her fingers into her feminine cream and lubricated her back puckered passage. She bent forward and presented him with her ass.

"Sash, what are you doing?" His voice sounded strangled.

"I want you to take me like this, Kade."

He came up behind her and spread her cheeks. Lust exploded through her as his cock probed her opening.

"Who knew Earth women were such sexual beings."

She fought to find her voice in her haze of passion. "Combine that with the insatiable panther in me and you're not going to get a moment's rest."

He gave her another inch and groaned deep in his throat. "You are amazing," he whispered. "I am the luckiest male alive." A fierce possessiveness raced through her when she heard the emotion and love in his voice.

His velvet thickness pushed deeper inside her, spreading her wide open. A whimper escaped her lips as he sank his girth between her puckered cheeks.

As slow pumps became more frenzied, more demanding, it fueled her hunger for him. Her whole body went up in flames. She reached between her legs and stroked her clit. Her sex muscles clenched and tightened.

"You are so tight, Sash. I won't last."

Her voice came out rough, impatient. "I want to feel your seed inside me, Kade."

Kade groaned and released his liquid heat deep inside her. His warmth rushed through her, the erotic pulse of his cock bringing on her own orgasm.

"You are incredible," Kade whispered.

"You're not so bad yourself," she teased.

"Come here, little one." Kade gathered her into his arms and drew her to him.

They lay on the grassy bed for a long time, stroking, caressing and just holding one another. She'd never felt such a sense of belonging before. As though he read her mind, he asked, "Would you like to go meet the rest of your family?"

It sounded like a great idea and she couldn't wait to meet them, but at this particular moment, Sash had other ideas in mind. With ease, she morphed into her panther and then lowered her upper body to the ground. With casual aplomb, she said, "I'm sorry, did you somehow think I was finished with you?"

Kade followed suit and morphed into panther form. He stalked up behind her and let out a low chuckle. "And here I thought the day I met my match would never come."

"I believe I was worth the wait."

Kade laughed out loud. "I had no idea an alpha Earth woman could be so aggressive, so..." he paused as though searching for the right word. Then he added, "So feral."

Grinning, she said, "You have so much to learn, my wild alpha panther. So much to learn."

His mouth curved enticingly. "How lucky for me." He put his paws on her back, his panther roaring to life. "Come here, you little vixen."

Also by Cathryn Fox

Liquid Dreams
Unleashed
Web of Desire

About the Author

If you're looking for Cathryn Fox you'd never find her living in Eastern Canada with a husband, two young children and a chocolate Labrador retriever. Nor would you ever find her in a small corner office, writing all day in her pajamas.

Oh no, if you're looking for Cathryn you might find her gracing the Hollywood elite with her presence, sunbathing naked on an exotic beach in Southern France, or mingling with the rich and famous as she sips champagne on a luxury yacht in the Caribbean. Perhaps you can catch her before she slips between the sheets with a man who is as handsome as he is wealthy, a man who promises her the world.

Cathryn Fox is no ordinary woman. Men love her. Women want to be her.

Cathryn is bold, sensuous and sophisticated. And she is my alter ego.

Cathryn welcomes comments from readers. You can find her website and email address on her author bio page at www.ellorascave.com.

Tell Us What You Think

We appreciate hearing reader opinions about our books. You can email us at Comments@EllorasCave.com.

ON HER BACK

By Renee Luke

Chapter One
His Return

Simone Harris closed her eyes, willing away the burn of tears, swallowing past the tightness in her throat. She shouldn't be the one to do this, shouldn't have to do it alone. But there was no one else. Jerold, her brother, was gone, his body tucked beneath six feet of soil at Arlington National Cemetery.

And now his best friend, Elijah Russell, was coming home injured, two months too late to see his grandma before she succumbed to cancer.

Sucking in a shaky breath, she opened her eyes and lifted her gaze to the top of the escalator where a man in camouflage stepped into view. He looked breathtaking in his service uniform—proud to wear it, powerful, determined.

With her heart pumping like mad, she took in the sight of him—broad shoulders, coffee-and-cream skin and pale hazel eyes.

Intoxicating eyes.

Eyes she knew and loved.

Eyes that made her insides knot up and her pussy go wet.

Even with their distance, he met her gaze and held it as the metal stairs slowly carried him closer. Her hands were shaking. Hell, so were her knees, but this wasn't a time for weakness. She wiped her sweaty palms across her skirt and took a few calming breaths.

He needed her strength, and she just needed him. Needed him so badly. In her life. In her bed. Needed him like crazy to ease the ache between her legs. To fill the void in her heart reserved for him.

Thinking back, she couldn't recall when hanging around Jerold and Elijah to be a pest had changed to wanting to be around them because she was crushing hard on her brother's friend. Or when the innocence of her crush had turned into love and womanly desire.

But it had. And she did desire him.

As she stared into his eyes all the longing from those solitary nights of masturbation resurfaced, mixed with the heavy, unforgettable sorrow of the last few months, and she felt torn — emotionally battered. It wasn't until the escalator delivered him to the airport's lower level and he stepped off that Simone noticed the cane he gripped in his right hand and the way his once-upon-a-time swagger had turned into a limp. Her chest tightened up. This man — this beautiful man — who'd gone away to war with a touch of arrogance had returned with his body damaged and a look of defeat in his eyes.

She ached to help him. To ease his pain. To see the gleam of confidence in his amazing eyes return to replace the dull emptiness.

"Hi, Elijah," she whispered when he'd closed the remaining distance between them. His heat seeped across her skin, the scent of him clean and sexy. Her mouth watered, her nipples beading beneath her silk bra.

"Hey, Shortie." His voice was rich and thick, and it cracked a little on her nickname. He lifted his left hand, touching his fingertips softly to her chin, slowly sliding them back over her cheek, down the slope of her neck, then around her back as he tugged her forward into his warm embrace.

His chest was a wall of muscle, and it felt so right to be there. She closed her eyes, knowing there was no way to hold back the lonely tears as they dripped past her lashes and slipped from her chin. They were silent tears, but he knew. His strong arms tightened and he held her, rocking slowly back and forth, one hand smoothing circles down her spine. Setting her body ablaze.

They stood in silence in each other's arms as people flowed around them like water. But Simone didn't care about their public location, not when the hard ridges of his body were pressed so closely to her. His heart thumped steadily beneath her cheek.

Turning slightly, she pressed a kiss to his chest as she clutched at his clothing. A low mumbled sound escaped him, followed by the swelling of his cock against her belly. She could feel the solid length of him, feel the rhythm of his pulse throbbing against her. And the ache, the ever-insatiable ache of lust, intensified in her clit.

She kissed him again, wishing it was his naked flesh beneath her lips rather than fabric, and tried to rationalize the meaning of his hard-on. He'd been away at war, then hospitalized—surely it'd been a long time since he'd fucked, since he'd busted a nut. As much as she longed for his physical response to be solely about her, doubt interfered and she feared his arousal was about her gender. Nothing personal.

But that didn't mean she couldn't enjoy how good it felt to have his rocked-up dick pressed against her stomach, couldn't long for it to be pushed up in her wet pussy. She'd take what she could get and she hugged him tighter, enjoying everything about the embrace.

After a few moments, Simone sucked in a breath, trembling as she regained control, remembering her need to show him strength. Nothing but strength. She put desire on a back burner. There'd be time for that. She hoped.

"You have a lot of bags?" she asked, straightening away from him and swiping her palm across her damp cheeks, ignoring the slickness between her thighs. "I'll take you to Mami's. Home."

His hands flexed, his fingers curling into a fist, and she watched as his throat worked, undoubtedly struggling to put arousal and emotion in check. "Nah, just one duffel." He reached for her, twining their fingers, and leaned heavily on his cane. "Come on, Shortie, let's get out of here."

* * * * *

The house still smelled like Mami, Elijah realized as he slowly walked into the home he'd grown up in, leaning too damned much on the cane. Inhaling, he caught the sweet fragrance of lemon bars and the subtle scent of oil from years of frying chicken.

"I shoulda been here," he mumbled, anger and regret burning a hole in his gut. He should have been home caring for his grandma while cancer ravished her body. Instead he'd been deployed and had returned half a man, unable to even walk unassisted.

A warm hand touched his forearm, her fingers soft and gentle against his skin, but no matter how light her caress his arousal was nonetheless intense and immediate. Blood rushed to his cock. Lust caught in his throat.

"She passed in her sleep," she whispered. "She's free from pain."

Nodding, he looked at Simone's face, saw the faint lines of dried salt against her smooth brown skin, the evidence of her tears. God, he should have been home to kiss every single one away.

She shouldn't have had to deal with the death of her brother—the only family she had—alone. She shouldn't have had to care for Mami all alone.

He stepped away from her, feeling an immediate loss as her hand dropped away. He had to put distance between them, or he risked turning on her and claiming the lips he'd spent the last year dreaming about. Risked backing her against the door and sinking his dick into her tight flesh, fucking her hard and relentlessly.

He swallowed past the clawing need, past the rush of blood swelling his cock into a hard-on. Hell, it wasn't just her lips he'd dreamt of, but also doing exactly what he wanted now. Sex, and making this honey his.

Back in his tent, as bombs blasted loud and angry in the distance, his body had matched the heat of the desert. It wasn't until he was injured that he realized just how deeply he loved her, that it wasn't just lust. And nothing close to brotherly. When he had thought he was dying, he'd fought to live so he could go back for her. To keep his promises.

But then guilt had set in. Guilt because what he wanted from Simone—to have her on her back—wasn't the kind of care he'd promised Jerold he'd provide for her. Jesus, he could still remember so sharply the day Jerold wrung the pledge from him to care for her if anything ever happened to him.

There, as their convoy slowly crept across the desert, the sand swirling so thickly around them they were blind to the road and their surroundings, they'd talked of their shared childhoods, struggles of today and what to expect from all of the unknown tomorrows.

It had been like hell with that heat and wind. Swallowing, Elijah remembered Jerold's words, remembered his fears, remembered Jerold's predictions that he'd never be going home, and his crushing worry for his sister's future.

And so he'd promised, without doubt or hesitation, to care for Simone, because as much as he desired her, he also loved her. Had always loved her.

Leaning heavily on his damned cane, he swallowed against the tightness in his throat and took a few more steps from her, shaking off the memories of half a world away. Clearing his throat, he said, "Thanks for taking care of her."

"I loved her, too." Her voice was low, but she'd followed him across the room.

"I know you did." He turned to look at her.

"She was like family, Elijah. She took care of Jerold and me when," she glanced away, her body trembling, "when...when no one else would. I was glad I was there when she needed me."

There were tears again. Fuck, he hated to see her pain. It affected him so strongly he felt it like a vise tightening around his chest. He took a deep breath, exhaustion seeping through him.

It'd been a long flight, a long recovery and too damned long since he'd slept in his own bed.

"And who was there for you when you dealt with Jerold's death? Mami's?" He didn't want to hurt her more, but he had to know—dammit, he had to know—who she'd turned to when she needed comfort. If she had a man.

Her dark eyes shimmered, liquid brimming and threatening to run over. She slanted her chin, brought her shoulders back and lifted her gaze to his. "I dealt with it the same way I've always done. On my own."

He nodded, a smile tugging slightly at his lips as relief that she wasn't hooked up with someone flooded through him. A smile hindered by remorse.

Leaning on his cane, he moved toward his bedroom. He needed sleep. And after he slept he planned on telling Simone how much he loved her.

Simone watched him limp away, his wide shoulders slumped slightly. Lawdy, after all this time with him on the other side of the globe, his bedroom seemed too far away. With Elijah in the room with her, she'd felt a spark of life, felt the loneliness ease slightly. But as he moved inside his room, the distance between them grew and she couldn't take it. Her heart thumped hard beneath her breasts. Her throat was dry and tight.

Closing her eyes, she tried to calm down, to rein in her desire to be near him. He was tired, she knew that. He needed sleep, and she'd let him. She just wanted to be in the same space.

Opening her eyes, she followed him through the door,

which he'd only slightly closed. By the time she arrived he'd stripped down to only a white T-shirt and his pants, having released the button of his fly.

He paused, his hands not leaving his pants as he lifted his amazing hazel gaze to hers.

She closed the distance, halting when a mere foot remained between them. "I don't want to…"

Silence descended around them for a lingering moment. "Don't want to what, Shortie?"

She inched closer, licking her lips as she allowed her gaze to drift over his handsome face. "Be alone."

A growl escaped his perfect full lips and his large hands came up to frame her face. "You don't have to, boo. You don't have to."

And then his mouth was there, slanting over hers. He nipped at her lips, then soothed them with the glide of his tongue. He held her in place as he pushed deeper, pressing past her teeth. He tasted like mint and male. Warm and strong. Perfect and exactly what she needed.

She touched his tongue with hers, absorbed the heat, learned his texture. He stroked into her mouth, changing the angle and moving into her in a rhythm she wanted his cock thrusting into her body.

The tingle of desire built, swelled her clit, soaked her panties. Moaning, she leaned into him, her hands settling on his chest as he deepened the kiss, his tongue relentless and exploring. Trailing her fingertips down the slope of his body, she caressed the warm skin of his chiseled abdomen beneath the hem of his shirt.

His muscles quivered beneath her fingertips. She kept her hands under the fabric. Moving in small circles, she swirled around his bellybutton, scraped her nail through the line of hair that plunged downward, a trail she longed to follow.

He moaned into her mouth.

She pressed upward, skimming his chest and feeling the

puckered flesh of new scars, wounds from the shrapnel he'd had removed. "Oh, Elijah," she whispered against his lips, then kissed him deeply while wishing she'd been by his side when he'd come out of surgery.

He groaned, his body trembling under her touch. Against her wrist she could feel the rise of his erection, solid and thick and still growing. A whimper lodged in her chest, the need to touch him, stroke him, fuck him overwhelming.

Without his cane, pain shot up his leg, but Elijah ignored it. Screw the pain, he thought, for it couldn't hurt worse than how bad his hard cock needed to be buried within her.

Her lips were soft and yielding, and her kiss tasted sweetly feminine. Everything he'd imagined. More. Drinking in her breathy moans, he slanted over her, allowing his hands to drift from her face down her body. He settled a palm over one ripe breast, feeling the arousal of her hardened nipple. He stroked his thumb over the beaded flesh, causing her to whimper and arch her back into him.

Her hands were roaming over him, dropping low on his belly, toying with his unbuttoned fly, fully releasing the zipper. Her touch, light and alluring, dipped beneath his boxers. Delicate yet insistent fingers curled around him.

His body shook, her hand coaxing the throb from his dick, sending him to the brink of coming. He fought for control.

She moaned, a hungry little sound that drove him damn near crazy. Across the head she swiped her thumb, then swirled it in the bead of moisture, and his balls pulled up tight again, climax threatening.

He moved from her mouth, kissing her jaw, her cheek, her neck, the silken skin below her ear. He nipped at her fleshy lobe, inhaling the floral scent of her skin, acutely aware of the sweet scent of her arousal perfuming the air.

"You going to stop me?" he asked, knowing there was no way in hell he could stop himself.

"No." Her free hand grabbed onto his shirt and clung to him, a sob escaping before she spoke. "Please, Elijah, please don't stop."

Fuck—his control fled. He turned their bodies, angling for the bed, and used his size to ease her back onto his mattress, sliding a hand up her thigh as he followed her down. The short pink skirt she wore slid upward, bunching around her waist, her legs spreading to welcome him.

Lifting her smooth leg over his hip, he was frantic now, shoving at his pants and boxers, shrugging them over his ass and easing one foot out of the material. The other pant leg caught and bunched around his splint and bandages, but he didn't give a shit. The only thing that mattered now was Simone—and loving her the way she deserved.

She was moving with him, rolling her hips against his, her hands and mouth eager on his skin. The scent of her arousal, the hungry mewing of desire and trust tore at his heart. She wanted him as fiercely as he desired her.

He didn't bother removing her panties—just shoved the thin line of silk to the side, felt her slickness on his hand and plunged his forefinger inside. His thumb went to her clit and circled.

She was wet. So wet and hot and tight. Clenching his jaw, he strove to slow down, to keep from just moving his hand and getting his cock pushed up into her. But he wanted her ready, wanted her as close to the brink of climax as he was. Wanted her begging.

"Please, baby," she whispered, shoving his T-shirt upward, her mouth touching his bare chest. She kissed him, then smoothed her tongue across a scar. "I'm sorry for these. So sorry." And she lavished his flesh tenderly, like her sugared mouth could erase the pain. Erase the memories. And it was working. He couldn't think of the injuries. Only sexing her.

In and out he thrust his finger into her welcoming cunt. Each time, her hips rose to meet his hand, to grind against his hand, her muscles clamping and sucking at him. The shudders of her building orgasm shredded his control.

Removing his hand, he grabbed his dick and changed the angle of their bodies. He touched his head to the slickness between her creamy thighs, rubbed against her clit then drove inside. Hard.

"Elijah," she cried, her hands gripping his shoulders beneath his shirt.

She was so tight and so hot and wet around him. She held him in her grip, and when he thought to go slow, to make it last longer than a few quick strokes, she curled her other leg around his back and lifted her hips.

He thrust in again, pressing against her womb. Out, then in again as a steady rhythm pumped through his system. Her nails scraped against his skin, her head arched back, mouth open with breathless whimpers on a long, slow moan. Leaning forward, he kissed the slender column of her neck, licked her pulse point, ran his tongue over her delicate collarbone.

She worked with him, matching his movements. Thrust her hips upward as he slid his cock inside her over and over again. She accepted him within her, whimpered on his retreats, cried out as he came into her again. As he ground against her clit. Ground their bodies into the plush mattress.

Her arms banded around his neck and she pulled his mouth back to hers, kissing him with so much tenderness he had to do a reality check to be sure he hadn't actually died and gone to heaven.

Her body arched off the bed, trembling. A tiny fluttering of contractions tightened around him, then intensified and she cried out as she climaxed.

"Aw, shit." That was all he could handle. He'd held off longer than he thought possible, and with her body soaking him with orgasm, he let himself go with one final thrust and came powerfully inside her.

She caressed his back through his spasms. Hugged him,

kissed his neck, licked his earlobe, pressed her moist lips to his closed eyelids.

Elijah struggled to breathe. Here he was, still half hard inside the woman he loved, and he had yet to even confess his feelings for her. Here he was, secure in her gentle embrace, enjoying her warmth and touch with the lingering pain from war throbbing up his leg. With his best friend killed in battle. And in his grandma's house, with her gone.

He tightened his arms around her, put his face to her heart and let his emotions go.

Simone felt Elijah's body shake, so much differently than he had when he came. And then she felt the moisture. The fat salty tears of exhaustion. Of heartache. Tears she'd shed so many lonely nights.

Oh, God, she loved him. This man, this strong muscular man who'd survived war, seen death and loved her thoroughly, was weeping. Heart-twisting, body-shuddering sobs.

Her heart ached for him. Her throat closed, thick with emotion. All she could do was hold him and hope he felt her love.

It wasn't long before the tension left his body and the weight of him increased above her. She shifted, rolling them on his mattress as sleep overtook him.

And then she lay there beside him, in his arms, and watched his chest rise and fall. Watched the movement behind his eyelids. Filled her soul with his nearness and beauty. She closed her eyes and inhaled his musky masculine scent. Elijah was home and she'd made love to him.

* * * * *

It was just after dawn, the pale yellow sunshine just beginning to creep through the windows when Simone was roused from sleep by the ridge of hard dick pressed against her ass. Smiling, she kept her eyes closed and listened to the sound of Elijah's breathing, still steady and even with sleep.

Shifting slightly, she pressed backward, enjoying the feel of his morning erection pulsing against her bare flesh. Sometime during the night they'd kicked off their clothes and found their way beneath the feather comforter, and cocooned in each other's body heat and bliss.

She was thankful now to be naked, to have Elijah bare behind her. Suppressing a yawn with the back of her hand, she turned toward him, backing up slightly so she could gaze at him. He absently reached for her, but his strong fingers fell to the off-white bedding in the spot she'd just vacated.

Opening her eyes, Simone looked at him. His brown skin looked rich and yummy in contrast to the light-colored sheets. In the pale light of early morning, the angry gashes of his healing wounds looked silvery and puckered. But they didn't tarnish the perfection of his chiseled body. There were badges of honor.

Swallowing the emotion tightening her throat, she licked her lips and suppressed a soft moan. She'd lost so much over the last few months, but Elijah was here now — home — and she wanted to cherish him. To taste him, kiss him, lick him.

Lifting the blankets from his body, she pushed them back, causing him to grunt in sleepy disapproval of the cool air washing across his flesh. He rolled slightly from his side to nearly on his back.

All ten inches of his hard cock rose toward the ceiling from the dark curls around his base and balls. Wide and long, with skin shimmering as smooth as taut satin. A vein pulsed, disappearing at the ridge of his swollen head. A dewy pearl glistened on the slit.

Her nipples beaded, her breasts felt heavy with need, her pussy wet with desire. Clamping her bottom lip between her teeth, she tucked her knees beneath her and drew up over him. Her thighs ached, partially in protest from being unused for so long, partially from fucking so hard last night. And partially from her yearning to fuck him again, now. To climb on top of him and ride that cock until the emptiness inside was filled, until her lust for him was appeased.

Releasing her lip, she soothed the tooth marks with her tongue, then bent forward and touched her puffy lips to the tip of his rocked-up cock. His flesh leapt, pressing more firmly against her mouth.

Scooting closer, she wrapped her hand around the thick length of him, holding his erection steady as she licked away the moisture. He moaned, moving his head on the pillow. Glancing toward his face, she watched his lashes flutter but his eyelids remained closed. His chest rose and fell steadily.

Smiling, she licked the satiny plum-shaped head all the way around the ridge, then closed her lips around him, taking him deep inside her mouth. He throbbed against her tongue and tasted of their sex, of cum and climax. The saltiness of his sweat mingled with the flavor of her pussy.

Closing her eyes, she whimpered against her rising need. She tightened her fingers. The saliva slid down his shaft, lubricating her hand as she began to stroke, rubbing her thumb up and down the engorged veins.

With her other hand, she cupped his balls, massaging them gently. Air hissed between his teeth, but his eyes remained closed and she wondered how deeply he was sleeping—if he was faking rest or dreaming.

Drawing in her cheeks, she added suction as she moved over him, taking him deeply into her mouth, stroking with her hand the inches she couldn't manage down her throat. He was solid. Delicious. Intoxicating.

His sac drew up. His breathing changed, but all the while the shadows of his eyelashes remained on his cheeks. Simone picked up her rhythm. Down. Caressed his length with her tongue. Up. Faster, until the salty bitterness of pre-cum filled her mouth.

Oh lawdy, arousal was heavy at her clit, and she longed

for a third hand so she could ease the ache a bit. Squeezing her legs together, she increased her pace over Elijah's rocked-up flesh, twisting her palm as she worked him.

His hips bucked off the mattress. His hands fisted in the sheets, the corded muscles bunched on his forearms and shoulders, a sheen of sweat covering his smooth brown skin. And his breathing had changed, rapid and shallow. His response to her blowjob was making her creamy, making her nipples pebble and elongate.

With her lips around him, she moaned against her own need and increased the suction, feeling the cum increasing its pressure at his base. His body trembled. A deep groan rumbled from his chest.

She could tell that he was fighting against climax now, his body shifting on the bed. But she wasn't letting up. His hand touched her head, strong fingers curling into her hair, gripping it firmly.

"Damn, Shortie, I want you on your back."

He moved to sit up, to turn them so he could fuck, but she wasn't having it. She was eager now for the flavor of his cock, wanted his orgasm damn near desperately.

With a growl between clenched teeth, he struggled, climax building. Using her thumb, she worked the sensitive vein as she stroked and sucked. One more time. Down. And he was gone. His body roared off the bed and his cum, hot and sticky, filled her cheeks, pulsed down her throat.

His body was shaking when he collapsed against the pillows, his cock still throbbing in her hand and mouth as she licked up every last drop.

Sitting up, Simone couldn't help the satisfied smile as she slid her tongue across her lips and turned toward Elijah. His eyes were open, expressive pools of green and brown, intent upon her. A shiver danced down her spine.

"That's the best damn way I've ever been woken up."

"I couldn't help myself." Heat infused her face and

scurried down her neck. Glancing away, she felt her heart pick up speed and she wondered what he thought of her now — that maybe he'd intended last night to be a one-night stand that wouldn't be happening again.

"Let me take care of you," he said.

Quickly turning her head, she caught his gaze. Her breath snagged in her lungs. Tempting, so damned tempting. Juices dampened her inner thighs and the tingle of repressed passion increased. Slowly he allowed his eyes to roam over her, across breasts that begged for his mouth. She felt her nipples tighten further under his appraisal.

Eventually his gaze dropped to the triangular patch of curls between her legs, his pointed look conveying his intent. Then his amazing hazel eyes were looking into hers again, his stare intense and pondering. And it felt as if her heart and soul were stripped bare.

She cleared her throat, swallowing several times against the dryness. "No, baby, that was just for you." Scurrying backward off the bed, she had to put some distance between them, had to get to the bathroom before the tears that burned behind her eyes dropped shamefully from her lashes.

"Go back to sleep," she said as she walked away. "Your body needs it to heal." Closing the bathroom door behind her, she dropped her face into her hands.

For a second there after he'd said *Let me take care of you* she'd thought he'd meant something other than sex. Dared to dream that he could have meant her heart, her life, her future. Struggling to breathe, struggling to keep the sobs muffled in her palms, she realized just how badly she longed for that from him. Just how desperately she yearned to be cared for, because all her life no man ever had.

Chapter Two
Sexual Healing

෯

Simone sat down on the stone wall, looking out over the Feather River. The California sun was high, a soft breeze swaying off the slow-moving water. Letting out a breath, she rolled her shoulders, trying to ease the tension, trying to forget how she'd escaped Mami's earlier that morning.

Work she'd told him, but really she'd taken the rest of the week off so she'd have time to be with him. To help him if he needed it.

So she'd washed her face, dressed quickly and gone home to shower. And to hide. Though she'd loved Elijah and wanted him, she hadn't set out to seduce him last night. Or this morning. She hadn't intended to welcome him home with open legs. But she had, and now she feared where it left them. Their bond. Their friendship.

She knew one thing for damned sure, she would never survive this fling if he washed up and moved on. Could never deal with seeing him with another woman and pretending she didn't care. She'd have to walk way, to distance herself from him, no matter how bad it hurt.

It was at times like this Simone longed for her momma—or an ideal of what a momma should be. As a foster child who'd never been adopted, she didn't have one. And because trust hadn't come easy when she'd been bustled from one home to the next, she'd never really developed any deep relationships.

Beside her brother, the only exception had been Mami. Lawdy, she missed that woman. And Elijah.

The pain and resentment of childhood had solidly formed

who she was today. Maybe it was the reason she'd become a social worker, so she could help children because no one had helped her and Jerold.

Squeezing her eyes closed against the brilliance of the day, she exhaled slowly. No more tears. There were no more left anyway.

After a moment, she pulled out her cell phone and scrolled through her digital phone book. She may have had the day off work, but that didn't mean she couldn't check up on a case she was particularly concerned about. A seven-year-old girl who'd recently been returned to her mother because the mother had met the court-ordered requirement of rehab.

Her job was heart-wrenching at times, but rewarding at others. Her work helped ease some of her own pain, and today, it'd help relieve her mind from thoughts of Elijah and the incredible way he fucked.

* * * * *

Propping his bandaged leg up on some pillows he'd placed on the coffee table, Elijah settled the photo album on his lap and flipped it open to the first page, to Mami and his granddad. He'd never met the man, because he'd passed before Elijah was born.

Mami looked so young and happy, a hand curled protectively around her pregnant belly. *His mother.*

Leaning his head back on the couch cushions, he stared at the ceiling. Everything was different now, and he had to find a way to be cool with that. To find acceptance of what his life would be now, without his best friend Jerold, without his grandma. With the physical expression of his love that he'd shared with Simone last night, and how it'd affect their relationship.

Groaning, his mind shifted back to the morning. Blood filled his cock, swelling just from him thinking of how it had felt to have her mouth on him. Her tongue lavishing him. Her hand working and stroking.

He set the album aside, gritting his teeth as he shoved his erection to the right to make room, glad he'd worn boxers under his sweats and not briefs. Curling his fingers around his dick, he closed his eyes and willed away the throb of lust.

Hell, he couldn't be getting hard every time he thought of Simone. He'd end up blue, his mind always drifting back to her, back to the way she sucked his dick, back to the way it'd felt to be buried deep inside her tight pussy. Arousal poured through his body, making his pulse thump at his temples. "Damn…" This shit was going to drive him crazy, wanting her every second. Wanting her now.

"Waiting for me?"

Elijah opened his eyes, lifting his head off the couch as he dropped his hand away from his cock. *Damn.* Changing positions, he made sure the photo album covered the evidence of his rocked-up flesh and willed the blood to let up a bit.

Simone stood a few yards away, looking fresh and clean and completely beautiful. Her eyes shimmered with humor and a pink blush crept across her cheeks, but he didn't miss the way her nipples had puckered beneath her sundress.

"Yeah," he replied, patting the sofa beside him. "Come sit down."

She grinned, her dark eyes sparkling. She walked in his direction, lifting a white bag as she closed the distance between them. "You hungry? I brought Chinese." She put the bag on the table before them, then tucked her feet beneath her as she settled next to him, the hem of her dress barely reaching mid-thigh.

Hungry? Hell yeah, he was hungry, but despite how his stomach grumbled at the smell of the food, his body was responding to something else he wanted.

His mouth watered as his gaze drifted to the shadows cast beneath her skirt. "You smell good."

"That's orange chicken, not me."

116

"Nah, it's you. Like peaches and honey."

The rose blush on her skin deepened, but a smile turned the corners of her lush, damp lips. "My lotion. So, you're hungry, yeah?"

He wanted to lean her back, push away the cloth and sink into her like he had last night. But first he needed to find out what was happening between them. Where their relationship stood.

"Starved. Thanks, Shortie," he said, reaching for the bag and pulling out a white carton and a plastic fork, then shoving a couple big bites into his mouth. Screw chopsticks. He hadn't eaten all day.

Elijah watched as Simone leaned forward and took out a box and a pair of sticks, but she didn't take a bite right away, just sat quietly so near he could feel her soft feathery breaths. "How was work?" he asked, the words muffled as he chewed.

She didn't answer right away, but looked down at her food and shrugged her delicate shoulders. When she looked back at him, her big eyes were rimmed with liquid—unshed tears that left him feeling sucker-punched.

"Elijah, can I ask you something?" Her voice was just a whisper, hushed but full of pain.

He longed to reach for her, to give her the comfort she clearly needed, despite the raging of his pulse, the fear of the inevitable talk and possible disappointment over what had happened between them.

He took a deep breath, then dropped his fork into the food carton and grabbed Simone's hand. "Sure, boo, ask me anything."

"About Jerold." Her hand trembled beneath his, but she disguised it by turning her hand and twining their fingers. "Did he die peacefully?" Her voice cracked, her plump lips quivered.

Elijah took a moment, wondering what she'd been told about her brother's death, trying to keep the sorrow from

117

overshadowing the truth. He cleared his throat. "He never saw it coming, Shortie, and was gone instantly."

"He didn't know what was happening? He didn't lie there in pain wondering when help would come? Die knowing it never did?" She pulled back a strangled sob, but tears slid silently down her smooth brown cheeks. "I can't stand the thought of him...of him being scared." Another sob escaped. "And alone."

Leaning forward, he caught a fat tear on his fingertips, then brushed the silvery liquid trails from her cheeks. "Nah, boo, it didn't go down like that." He slid his thumb over lush, trembling lips.

She blinked, then whispered against the pad of his fingers, "Tell me how."

Letting out a sigh, he put the box of orange chicken on the table, then pulled Simone into his lap, his hand settling on the small of her slender back. "We were just riding along, going from our base to set up a checkpoint." His throat felt as if it was filled with shards of glass. His voice was low and raspy.

He'd told this story many times—to his commanding officers, to doctors, nurses and the media. He'd grown to telling it fact by fact, putting aside the depth of his emotion. But he'd never told Jerold's sister, though he'd imagined this conversation a thousand times while he lay in his hospital bed.

Pulling her closer, he shifted her so she faced him more fully, then started making small soothing circles up and down her spine, hoping like hell the tremors in her body would let up some. Her pain did something physical to him. Something he didn't like, that churned his gut and made it hard to think.

"Just driving. And then a blast." He clamped his eyes closed, inhaled. After a second he exhaled and looked back at Simone's shimmering eyes. "I didn't know what happened at first. I just remember...I remember looking up and seeing him across the sand."

He embraced her, drawing her forward, and nuzzled his

face into the hollow of her throat, infusing his senses with the sweetness of her scent. "He was gone already, Shortie. Didn't feel a thing."

"Are you telling me straight?"

"For sure, Shortie. I wouldn't lie to you." The whispered words felt stuck in his dry throat.

"Not just what I wanna hear?"

He felt her tremble, suck in a breath and hold it as she waited for his reply. "Nah, I'm tellin' you, he didn't suffer." The damned truth, too—Jerold hadn't suffered, but that didn't ease the guilt over living while watching his friend die.

She was silent, but he could hear her uneven breathing, feel the warmth of it across his skin. She held on to him, and he could feel her tension in the way her fingers tightly grasped his shirt, in the way her inner thighs pressed against his legs.

Taking a breath, she shifted, moving more squarely toward him, her ass brushing against his hardened dick. A whistle of air escaped his lips. She moved again, landing on his leg in a way that caused a sharp pain to shoot up from his damaged foot, which he'd propped up on the coffee table.

"Hmph," he mumbled, trying to ward off the ache.

She sat up and glanced back at his foot, her eyes wide and glistening when she turned to face him again. Her lips were damp and formed a silent O. She looked at him, her dark stare so assessing, so vivid he'd have sworn she was seeing right into his soul.

"But you did, didn't you?" Her delicate fingers smoothed down his cheek. Slid down his neck and around his back.

He could feel her swallow, could feel the movement of her shallow breaths. Could hear the sympathy and pain in her sweet, sweet voice.

She kissed his temple. Whispered against his skin. "You remember. Every second. You remember, and it haunts you." She kissed him again, his temple, his closed eye, the corner of his lips. "And you suffer from the scars." In her low voice, her emotion-filled words, he could have sworn that she wasn't just talking about his memory and pain, but hers.

And he didn't want her to hurt anymore. To hell with the pain he'd suffered. To hell with the scars and the memory. The scars on his flesh would eventually fade to almost nothing. The memories... He'd make new ones.

Starting now.

Shifting, he cupped her face in his hand, angling so her lips were slanted over his. "The suffering's over, Simone." He kissed her. Lightly at first, just a feathering of lips, a brushing of emotions. Just a mingling of breaths, the sharing of the same warmed air. Then he pressed closer, sliding his tongue along the plump seam of her mouth. "We don't have to linger in it, boo. We can move on."

And then he pushed further, touching his tongue to the sugary sweetness of hers, stroking and swirling and thrusting. The tender movements shifted into the kind of hungry kiss done when making love. Urgent and fiery.

His hands slid from her cheeks, down her slender throat, across delicate shoulders. He circled and caressed gently down her bare arms, rubbed his thumbs across the swells of her breasts as he moved downward across her ribs to her narrow waist.

Her arms circled his shoulders, her mouth just as demanding in her answering kiss. She tasted of honey, sweet and alluring, but there was the unshakable hint of the saltiness of her tears.

Screw the tears. He wanted to taste the saltiness of sweat.

He curled his fingers over the slope of her ass, down and forward over her thighs to where the hem of her sundress rested against her satiny smooth skin. Teasing the material against her leg, he moved lower, creeping his fingers beneath the thin material, the damp heat of her pussy pulling at his need. Urging his fingers farther.

Her inner thighs quivered against his palm and she

shifted on his lap, opening for him. His fingers pressed upward, caressing the tender flesh.

Hell, the girl wore no panties.

Elijah groaned into her mouth, his body pulling in the needy rhythm throbbing in his rocked-up dick. Rolling his hips up, he swallowed the desire to shove away his sweats and boxers and get between her slick thighs. With his thumb and forefinger, he parted her lips and sank two digits into her wet, tight pussy.

"El—Elijah," she whispered, tearing her mouth from his. Her lips were swollen and glistening, opened slightly as she whimpered and ground her body onto his hand. Her dark eyes caught his, a plea for release silently exchanged. Then her long lashes fluttered, the shadows falling to her creamy cheeks. Her head lolled back, her body moving on his, taking his fingers into the juiciness and her heat. Riding him. Hard.

Cum curled at the base of his cock, his balls pulled up tight to his body. About to lose it and he hadn't even fucked her yet. Tightening his jaw, he pushed away his orgasm, held his body in check. Moving his thumb against her slickness, he found her clit, pressed against it then circled.

With his other hand, he slid up her spine, holding her as she moved her pussy up and down his fingers and ground her center against his thumb. Pulling her forward, he found her nipple, extended and firm, and closed his lips around it through the thin sundress.

She smelled of sunshine, floral and feminine, mingled with the pleasing fragrance of desire. So heady and enthralling. He scraped his teeth over her nipple, then swirled around the elongated flesh with his tongue. The beaded tip was like candy in his mouth, even when barred by her clothing.

Simone shook hard, tension winding through her blood, but no matter how good Elijah's fingers felt inside, no matter how good his thumb felt working against her clit, it wasn't enough. Part of her still felt so empty, and she knew what she needed. Knew what she had to have.

The thick erection pressed against her ass—hell, yeah, baby, she needed it naked and inside her. Needed his solid cock pounding into her.

Loosening her grip on his T-shirt, she thrust her hands between them, rising on her knees, reluctantly leaving the pleasure of his hand for the promised temptation of having something bigger, thicker and hotter filling her pussy.

Frantic now, her body on fire, cold need prickling along her back, she shoved at his pants, pushing them down, breathing a sigh of relief when his engorged deep purple cock head was stripped of clothing. With one hand, she curled her fingers around his length, and used the other to push the material down his legs and out of the way.

"I need you, Elijah," she said, smoothing her thumb across the teardrop opening, wetting her fingertips in his pre-cum. "I need to feel you." His flesh throbbed, blood-filled veins pressed against her palm.

"Aw, dayum, girl..." The low rumbled moan poured from his lips and every muscle in his body was tightly coiled beneath his skin. "Feel me, boo. Anything you need."

Stroking downward, she found the ridge below his head and rubbed against it until his body shot up from the couch, pushing fully into her hand, lifting them both. Then, trembling, he attempted to relax back against the cushions.

Giggling, Simone ignored her own need, her own desperate desire to fuck, and took pure pleasure from watching his responses, from commanding his body with her caresses. Keeping her fingers tight, she slid down him, rotating her wrist over the rock-solid shaft, cupped his sac and massaged lightly before stroking back toward the head.

"Do that more often," he said, his words broken by pants.

"Rub you?"

He shook his head. "Laugh."

She smiled at him, knowing he knew damned well she hadn't had much of a reason. Until he'd come back. Glancing at his face, she saw his amazing hazel eyes half covered with heavy lids. Beads of sweat shimmered on his brow and upper lip. His jaw was held tight, and at the base of his neck, his pulse raged the same drumming beat his cock was dancing to in her hand.

Stroking down, then slowly up again, she drew out her movements, let her thumb slide along the sensitive underside as she watched how her actions made his breathing change.

More glistening lubricant beaded on his swollen head. Her mouth watered, the remembered flavor of his cock lingering on her tongue. Licking her lips, she had the urge to scoot back so she could make room to take him into her mouth, but unlike this morning, her body needed sex too badly to give him a nut without getting one of her own.

Elijah must have figured out the look in her eyes, the hungry motions of her mouth. He chuckled, then closed strong fingers over hers as she worked his dick with her hand. "Whatcha gunna do with this, boo?"

She smiled, sucked her bottom lip into her mouth then bit down while she decided if she was going to suck or fuck. Her heart raced beneath her breasts. Heat swirled at the apex of her thighs, her pussy nearly weeping for him now.

Laughing again, she lifted herself up on her knees. "This is crazy, Elijah. Crazy." She rubbed his head against her clit, felt him pulse, fought the urge to just drop down on him, taking all those inches in. "Crazy," she shook her head, somehow trying to make sense of when their friendship had turned into raw sex, "I've got to fuck. I need you."

"Then let's fuck." He shifted his hips, pressing an inch inside her. "I need you, too, Shortie."

I need you, too... Simone closed her eyes against the rush of emotion, and relaxed her legs so all those rocked-up inches of his erection thrust into her. Deep, so deep she could swear she felt him press against her heart, her soul. When he was all the way in, she ground her clit into him, shaking as her body stretched around him, as heat poured to her toes, as arousal elongated her nipples beneath the damp material where his mouth had been.

Gulping for air, she remained still for a moment, allowing the connection between them to flow through her. Remained still so the tingle of climax would subside just long enough for her to ride him right.

But after a second of sitting on his lap, her pussy stuffed with his stiff cock wasn't enough anymore. She needed to move, to ease him out of her body and then take him in again. Deeper, harder.

Her hands fisted the cotton of his shirt, her nails scraping at his pecs. She lifted, rolling her hips, then moaned long and low as she dropped, fucking that dick again. And the frenzy of need returned. Deeper now. Harder. She slammed down onto him, taking everything she could get.

She wasn't just looking for pleasure, the tingle of orgasm, but she was chasing away the lingering pain. The harassing thoughts that Elijah didn't need her, he just needed pussy. Crying out as cool heat of release washed across her skin, she rode him harder, up, down, in, out, up, down. She just wanted to feel, to feel him hard and moving inside her. Didn't want to think about what this would mean, or what would happen between them.

Elijah's hands settled on her hips, his body lifting from the cushions, his breathing labored. And with a firm touch, he thrust upward on her downstroke and held her with her clit pressed against him, his balls against her ass as climax hit hard.

"Oh gawd," she cried, her body clamping down, her pussy grasping him in shuddering waves of release.

"Aw…hell, Shortie." And then he was shaking too, hot sticky cum spurting into her. His fingers tightened on her hips as he convulsed, emptying into her welcoming pussy.

Gasping for air, Simone curled into him, resting her forehead against his shoulder, her thighs aching, her body sated. His half-hard flesh was still buried inside her, still drumming the beat of climax. If she didn't feel so damned good right now, she'd have ridden him again, because that erection of his was still hard enough to give her plenty of pleasure and she bet it wouldn't take long to get him all the way rocked again.

As if thoughts alone controlled his body, she felt him begin to swell. Giggling, she lifted her head, then pressed her mouth to his. She playfully nipped at his lips as she smoothed her palms over his brow, wiping away the slickness of his sweat.

"I like that."

She laughed again. "I betcha do."

"You smiling, Shortie. I like to see you smile."

"You make me feel good."

"I make you feel *damned* good, girl. Don't get it twisted." He flicked his fingers across her hard nipple just to prove his point.

She nipped his bottom lip, then soothed it with her tongue. "Yeah, Elijah, alyight."

"Alyight." He smacked her ass. "Better than that, girl."

Elijah watched Simone's face as she lifted on her knees, then shifted off his lap. He knew she'd had fun, gotten off during their quick hard screw on the sofa, but he wanted to see her emotional reaction to being with him. Wanted—hell, needed—to know this was more than sex for her.

She was smiling as she adjusted her dress and then reached for his carton of orange chicken and took a bite—apparently deciding to eat rather than reply. Reaching for his pants, he yanked the boxers and sweats over his hard-on, adjusting himself so the strain of wanting her again wouldn't be so painful.

"What were you doing?" she asked between mouthfuls of food, her gaze sliding to the table and the box of pictures and papers he'd been going through.

"Just going through some stuff." He leaned toward her. She laughed and put a piled forkful into his mouth. He chewed a minute. "Just trying to decide to do with Mami's things. With the house."

She nodded solemnly. "Are you going to sell?"

"Nah." Hell no, this was his house—the home he wanted to share with her. The place he eventually wanted to raise their children. The problem was he was having one hell of a time getting a read on Simone.

She fucked with emotion, but the sex seemed to be something that just happened between them. God knew it wasn't something he'd planned, no matter how many recovery hours he'd spent in fantasy. It wasn't something they'd talked about, and afterward things just slipped so easily back into friendship that he had to wonder if that was all she'd ever wanted.

And shit, he was a coward, because though he could brave gunfire and bomb-throwing enemies, he couldn't deal with—didn't want to think about—life without Simone. Without having her beside him daily and sharing his bed each night.

"Nah, boo, I'm not selling, but maybe you can help me go through some stuff." He leaned over for another bite and grinned when she read his action and filled his mouth with the sweet chicken.

"Anything, Elijah. I'll do anything to help."

Right now, sitting with a half-naked, sexy-as-hell woman, feeling sexually satisfied and being fed was exactly what he needed. He lounged back on the sofa. For now, he'd enjoy the moment. There was always tomorrow to find out where he stood.

* * * * *

Simone filled a plate with scrambled eggs and added a lump of butter to the grits. She'd slept well beside him, secure in his arms and body heat, just as she had for the last eight days. It was hard to recall the last time she had slept in her own bed, hard to remember when she hadn't fallen asleep after sexing him, when she hadn't awoken each morning in his arms.

But something had happened last night that had made her restless and sleep elusive. Every time she took him between her legs, every time she accepted him inside her body, she tried to tell her this was sex for sex's sake. And she'd taken pleasure in giving Elijah the release he needed, felt good that she was the one he'd turned to ease the ache of months gone by of warfare and backed-up nuts.

But last night, amid moans and whispered sensual praise he'd muttered something else, something that hinted of the future.

As he'd driven his hard cock into her, as his hand worked against her clit, as he made her cry out for him, he'd put a claim on her pussy. "This is mine," he'd said, thrusting powerfully into her wet flesh. "Only mine."

And when she'd screamed, "Yes!" he'd come, his body shaking fiercely before he collapsed rolling them to the side and said, "Damn right, boo. Mine."

He'd spent the last eight days making her cream. Making her cream. He'd petted her, whispered bed-play in her ear, stroked her in all the right places, but not once—not once—had he said a thing about being her man.

And so she'd spent the rest of the night tossing and turning, replaying his words over and over again and trying to make them make sense. Then she'd left the bed early, looking for a little distance. Taking a deep breath, she brushed the moisture from her cheeks and gave herself a warning to not read too much into his pre-orgasm words.

Catching her lip between her teeth, she wondered what Elijah would say when he woke up. If he'd even remember what he'd said, or the claim he'd made. Whether he'd regret the night before, dismiss it as emotion run amok.

Shaking off the apprehension, she filled a glass with milk and added a couple heaping tablespoons of chocolate, then carried breakfast back to his bedroom.

He was awake when she came through the door — lying on his side, supporting his weight on a forearm. The bed sheet draped over his hip, sending shadows over his defined ab muscles. Her mouth watered, remembering how she'd slid her tongue along his sculpted body.

Sometime during their foreplay last night he'd removed his T-shirt and she could again see the angry gashes where he'd been injured, tarnishing his prefect skin but doing nothing to mar his beauty.

"Mornin', Shortie."

"I made you breakfast," she said softly, wanting to be near him again, but worried he'd think they made a mistake. Worried that he'd remember his words and take them back. She wanted to belong to him, to have all this sex be about something.

"Smells good." He patted the bed beside him. "Come here."

He grinned, and her pulse shot up. She moved to the bed, putting the dishes on the side table before she sat down and folding her hands on her lap to keep from reaching for him. To keep from pushing him on his back and mounting the morning erection she knew he was sporting beneath the sheets.

His warm palm settled on her naked thigh, the shirt she'd snagged from his closet falling just below her ass. He drew small circles with his thumb, shifting higher to the tender skin between her legs but stopping short of offering the pleasure of his caress to her wetness. The touch had her nipples puckered. Had her ready in an instant, like all the times before.

He was drawing circles against her inner thigh, his touch light and alluring. "I need to tell you something, boo." He sounded serious.

She lifted her gaze from his hand on her skin to his eyes. She held her breath, her heart aching in her chest as she prepared herself. This was the end. He'd gotten what he'd needed from her and was ready to call it quits. To return things back to the friendship. A hands-off relationship.

Tears burned behind her eyes but she shoved them back, lifted her chin and squared her shoulders. He may have needed her strength when he'd returned. But she needed it now. After loving Elijah so physically, so intimately she'd never be able to go back to how things used to be.

She let out a long, slow breath. She'd talk first, unable to bear hearing his excuses. "It's okay, Elijah. I know you needed the release. I know it'd been a long time since..." She took a deep breath. "I don't expect you to—"

"Don't expect me to what, Shortie? Don't expect me to want more than a set of pretty legs wrapped around my waist? To want more than sex?"

She shrugged. "You're a man. You were gone, hurt, alone. I know you needed to."

"Is that what you think? That I didn't mean nothing by making love to you?"

She missed the warmth of his hand as he lifted it from her leg, but he took her fingers and twined them with his. The circles he'd done along her thigh he now did against her palm.

"You just got back. You've got a lot to take care of, with Mami's house and all... I just don't want you saying it was a mistake." Simone closed her eyes tight for a moment, praying he wouldn't. She loved him. Wanted him. Wanted to be with him. But he had enough to deal with that she just couldn't pressure him. She'd take the eight days and cherish them.

He squeezed her hand enough to get her attention. She opened her eyes and looked at him.

"You've got it wrong, Shortie. I didn't come back here for Mami's house."

"Why then?" she said quietly.

He tugged her hand forward. Lifting it to his mouth he kissed her skin gently, kissed the sensitive skin on her wrist. "I'm—" he kissed her again, longer, "back for you."

About the Author

ℰℭ

Multi-published author Renee Luke believes in keeping-it-real erotic romances that feature funky urban characters who get their groove on and give up their hearts. She strives to write stories that both stimulate physically and satisfy emotionally. She believes in happily-ever-afters and found her own in California with her fine-ass man and their four damn-cute children.

Renee welcomes comments from readers. You can find her website and email address on her author bio page at www.ellorascave.com.

Tell Us What You Think

We appreciate hearing reader opinions about our books. You can email us at Comments@EllorasCave.com.

I WAS AN ALIEN'S LOVE SLAVE

By Charlene Teglia

Trademarks Acknowledgement

The author acknowledges the trademarked status and trademark owners of the following wordmarks mentioned in this work of fiction:

ET: Universal City Studios, Inc.

Maglite: Mag Instrument, Inc.

Tony Lama: Boot Royalty Company

Valium: Hoffmann-La Roche Inc.

Chapter One
🔊

"The problem—" Micki Sloane began, but broke off with a frown of distraction at the sound of her own voice. Rusty with disuse at the best of times—her occupation didn't require a great deal of vocalization—it now not only rasped in the low register that accompanied a cold, it also had a distinct slur from the combination of tiredness, cold medicine and the purely medicinal brandy she'd consumed.

With a mental command to her vocal cords to shape up, Micki began again, enunciating as precisely as a professional drunk. "The problem," she informed the silent bartender, "is that there aren't any more heroes."

She waved an expansive hand at the few customers in the Starlite Lounge. They weren't any more impressive as specimens than any of the other men she'd found in any of the other bars she'd looked in that night, and Seattle boasted an impressive number of bars to choose from.

"Look at them," Micki urged. "How am I supposed to get inspired? How could anybody get inspired?"

Defeated, she slumped lower on her stool and toyed idly with the slender glass stem of her snifter. "How am I supposed to make anybody believe in love when I don't? How am I supposed to find a hero when there aren't any heroes anymore?"

The bartender eyed the slender brunette with professional calculation. She spoke clearly. She'd seemed composed when she came in, and she'd only had one drink. Still, her wild, rambling speech spelled one thing only to him.

"Lady, that was last call. How about I call you a cab?"

Startled from her thoughts, her attention and her wide blue eyes fixed fully on him. For a moment, he wondered uneasily if she was going to lunge across the bar at him. Under the influence, people could be unpredictable.

The longer she stared, the more nervous he got. So it was with relief as well as masculine appreciation that he watched the slow, sweet, sad smile that spread over her delicate features.

"A hero for today," she murmured. And drained her brandy snifter after raising it to him in a silent toast. "I'm not drunk. If I were, at least one of those men would look better to me. But please do call me a cab. And don't worry about me. I can always change careers. I know how to type."

Micki waited outside for the cab. It was winter and the chill in the air wouldn't help her cold if she walked home. A warm, dry cab ride would be just fine. And she wouldn't be outside long enough to feel much worse. Inside was just too depressing, with every man in the Starlite Lounge that much more evidence that her career was over.

Thirty-two years old and washed up. Pitiful.

One more book, one lousy book, that was all she had to come up with to fulfill her contract. Unfortunately, it couldn't be a book about killing her landlord for not fixing the broken light in the foyer of her building, forcing her to go up the stairs to her apartment in the dark.

No, it had to be a book about true love, blazing passion, happily ever after. And she'd been staring at the blank screen of her laptop day after day, week after week, as the months to complete the manuscript and fulfill her obligation crept past until desperation drove her out into the streets looking for some star of inspiration to hitch her imagination onto and ride to The End.

She was nearly out of time. If she couldn't do it, she really would be in trouble. She would get a reputation for not being dependable and she wasn't good enough to be labeled difficult to work with. She was replaceable. Especially if she missed her deadline.

Maybe a hypnotist could cure her writer's block.

Maybe, as her friend Angie was always advising her, she should just get laid.

"Get your oil changed, girlfriend," Angie would say. "Go do some hands-on research."

There were always lots of jokes about the kinds of books she wrote and the research involved in them. The joke, however, was on her, because the only experience she'd had lately was in her vivid imagination. Not so much due to lack of interest in the idea as a lack of real-life heroes to do hands-on research with.

And now the lack of real-life heroes had led to her wellspring of fictional heroes drying up like the Sahara.

"Stop it, Michelle, you're getting depressed and that will not help," she muttered to herself. She huddled into her black wool jacket and shoved her hands deep into the side pockets. "You can do this. You can write twenty pages a day from now until the end of the month and make that deadline. You just have to focus."

Focus. On believing in the impossible, a heroic man, true love and happy endings. Think happy thoughts and her fingers could fly.

She needed fairy dust to fly, didn't she?

Or maybe she only needed to make a wish.

She turned to look at the neon sign that hung above her, a tilted cocktail glass with a multiple-pointed star on the rim and the words Starlite Lounge spelled out below.

Why not? Nothing else was working.

If it didn't help, she would get hypnotized. Or laid. Or both. Anything to keep her word, make her deadline, earn her next advance and avoid going back to being a secretary. She'd been a lousy secretary.

"Star light, star bright," Micki chanted, "First star I see tonight. I wish I may, I wish I might, have the wish I wish tonight." She closed her eyes and wished, fiercely, passionately, with all the feeling she could summon.

I need my hero. I need to believe in true love and happy endings. Please.

Micki opened her eyes again. The neon sign was flickering and it was starting to rain again. There was no sign of her cab.

So much for wishes. So much for heroic bartenders.

She started walking.

On the bright side, by the time she got to her apartment she would probably be late enough to avoid her neighbor. Larry was kind of jumpy and had a tendency to think Visitors were waiting outside in the dark hall when she went past, mistaking her for something paler, thinner and with bigger eyes. If she was late enough, he'd be asleep and wouldn't hear her go by his door on the way to hers.

If she wanted to put her own problems into perspective, she only had to think of Larry. She just needed to meet a deadline. He probably needed lithium.

Keeping it in perspective was the key. No need to dramatize her situation. Nobody was going to die if she never wrote another book, including herself. She also didn't have to take it as a given that her problem was unsolvable just because time was getting short and she was feeling the pressure.

Writers got blocked. There were ways to get unblocked. Ways that didn't involve fifteen years of psychoanalysis while she dredged out every early childhood memory in search of the cause of her current problem. She didn't have fifteen years. No editor on the planet would extend her deadline that far.

An extension of a few weeks was possible, though.

Micki expelled a breath. "Tomorrow," she decided. "If I don't have a solid beginning tomorrow, I'll admit I need an extension and ask for more time."

As soon as the decision was made, she felt calmer. More in control. She had a plan. Try again tomorrow, ask for more time if things didn't go well, make an appointment to see a hypnotist.

Getting laid was a much more attractive cure for writer's block, but a good hypnotist was probably easier to find than a good man. For all her advice on Micki's sex life, Angela didn't have any prospective heroes lurking around her, either.

Although heroes didn't lurk. Did they?

Occupied with her musings, Micki punched in the code that unlocked the door to her building, switched on the Maglite attached to her key chain and went up the stairs to the second floor she shared with Lithium Larry. At the top she attempted to tiptoe to her apartment.

To no avail. His door swung open as she went past and he shined a bright flashlight into her eyes.

"Ow! Cut it out!"

"Sorry." Larry swung the flashlight beam up to the ceiling so that light bounced off the surface and illuminated the hall without blinding either of them. The increased visibility meant she could see a weird-looking helmet on his head. It vaguely resembled Snoopy's flying hat when he pretended to fight the Red Baron.

She shouldn't ask. But she couldn't help herself. "What is that thing on your head?"

"It's my Velostat helmet. It blocks alien mind control," Larry said. "The Visitors have been really active lately, so I made myself one. I made one for you too. If you keep it on at night, it will protect you from their mental commands."

"Thanks," Micki said. "But it looks kind of uncomfortable to sleep in."

"You should take it." Larry's earnest face wrinkled up in concern. "You know what time it is?"

"No. I don't wear watches."

"See, I noticed that about you and that's why I made you a helmet too. People who fritz out electronics are at high risk for alien abduction. Those people are usually psychic, and open to alien telepathic contact."

"It's not a big deal," Micki muttered. She hated any mention of her weird inability to wear a watch. Every time she tried, it ran fast, then ran slow and then stopped running altogether. So she'd given up on watches, big deal. And she wasn't psychic. She just had good instincts. "Lots of people can't wear a watch. It's not that unusual."

"Lots of people get abducted." Larry nodded vigorously at her. "You ought to be careful."

"I will," Micki assured him. Anything to end this conversation and get inside her own sane, quiet apartment without an alien-thought-control-prevention helmet. "Bye."

She slid past Larry and his helmet and unlocked her door. "Thanks for the light," she called back to him. "I really hate having to grope for the lock in the dark." Her tiny Maglite made a really inadequate substitute for the hall fixture the damn landlord ought to fix before somebody got hurt.

"No problem." Larry pointed the flashlight suspiciously around the hall, up, down, checking for signs of Visitors, apparently.

While he was occupied, Micki sidled inside her door and closed it behind her. She leaned back against it and let out a long breath.

Helmets. Geez. She didn't know if she should be amused, alarmed or touched that Larry had gone to the trouble to make one for her. She didn't need a helmet to block alien transmissions. She could use one that channeled Nora Roberts though. Did anybody make helmets like that?

Probably not.

Well, at least she was home. She could take more cold medicine, put on her warm fleece socks and her flannel nightshirt, cuddle up under the covers. Tomorrow she'd feel better.

Micki kicked off her shoes, stepped away from the door and headed for the kitchen. She mixed a mugful of lemon-flavored cold medicine and microwaved it until it steamed. It tasted awful, but since she had a cold her sense of taste was greatly reduced, so what the hell. At least the hot liquid was soothing to sip.

She sipped it, feeling soothed, while she went down the hall to her bedroom and the fleece and flannel that would warm her outsides to match her insides, which still had a warm glow from the brandy.

Too late, she remembered the warning not to mix cold medicine with alcohol. Oh well. She was going to bed, not operating heavy machinery. She'd just sleep really, really well.

Maybe the combination would help her dream up a really terrific hero. She perked up at that thought while trading her wool coat, jeans and sweater for a gray-and-white-striped flannel nightshirt and gray fleece socks.

The discarded clothes got piled on a handy chair in her bedroom. The elastic on her panties irritated her, so she stripped them off and tossed them on top of the pile too. Micki downed the last of her bitter mugful of lemon-flavored cold cure and debated grabbing a book to read. She gave up on the idea almost immediately. Reading would take too much effort right now.

Bed was all she needed. And sleep. Micki padded back to the kitchen to leave her empty mug in the sink, double-checked that her apartment door was locked, switched off lights and returned to the bedroom to climb under her comforter.

Her last thought as she drifted off, was that if she had to make a career change, she could always start by interviewing Larry about his history of alien visitations, and sending the results to the tabloids. She was not going to ask him about anal probes though. Forget journalistic integrity.

No need to despair. No matter what happened with her last book, she wasn't washed up. If she really couldn't believe in heroes and happily ever after anymore, she could still write something.

Aliens seemed more believable than true love, anyway.

The light woke her up.

It was really bright. Seattle didn't get that much sunlight in the winter. Not in the summer either, actually. What the hell? Was there some sort of searchlight on her building from a police helicopter?

Micki flung one arm over her eyes to protect them from the glare. Or tried to, anyway. Her arm refused to move.

That disturbed her much more than the light and brought her fully awake. Why couldn't she move her arm? She looked at it to confirm that it was still attached to her body. It was. Still covered with striped flannel too.

Good. All normal. Except she couldn't move.

She tried moving her legs, her hands, wiggling her toes. Nothing. Maybe she'd overdosed on cold medicine and brandy and the side effects had paralyzed her.

Micki couldn't see anything except the brilliant light that seemed to only wrap around her body—the rest of her bedroom was in darkness.

The light seemed to be pulling at her, swallowing her, and she couldn't resist because she was too dumb to read warning labels on over-the-counter drugs and had gotten herself paralyzed.

The light swallowed her completely. A sensation of nothingness followed, total sensory deprivation, no sense of anything touching her or even the feeling of soft flannel on her skin. And then she was disgorged onto a hard surface in a brilliantly lit room.

Good. An emergency room. Somebody had found her, they were going to pump her stomach, and she'd live to warn others not to abuse cold medicine. And dammit, her mother was right. She should've worn new panties in case of medical emergency instead of going commando. Micki made a mental note to never make that mistake again. Too late now, the doctor would know the awful truth any minute.

Except the doctor seemed awfully thin, with awfully large eyes.

If she'd been able to move, Micki would have screamed.

It had to be a nightmare. Larry's nightmare.

Wake up, she commanded herself sternly. *This is not even your damn dream, so wake up right this minute.*

It didn't work.

She was not in an alien operating room about to be the victim of some bizarre experiment. She hadn't just been abducted from her own bedroom by Visitors. None of this was real. And when she woke up, she was going to get that helmet from Larry so she'd never have this nightmare again.

While she watched, the thin, big-eyed creature lifted her nightshirt, made an incision in her abdomen, installed some tiny device and then approached her head with something in its impossibly long-fingered hand.

The thing touched her temple.

What if it was an alien mind-control device and this creature was putting it inside her brain?

Micki did what any self-respecting independent modern woman would do under the circumstances. She passed out.

Chapter Two

∞

When she opened her eyes next, she immediately closed them again tightly. If she couldn't see them, they weren't there, right?

Micki opened up one eye cautiously to see if this argument had any validity.

It didn't. They were still there, both of them. One of the pale, big-eyed, thin aliens, and one Norse god who'd escaped from his pantheon.

This had to be a dream. It was too big a coincidence that she was seeing an alien right after her conversation with Larry and after falling asleep thinking about them.

She'd also been thinking about a hero. Maybe the god was a hero and he would save her from this scary place.

"I will take her now," the god said. He had his muscular arms folded across a broad chest, his stance clearly that of a man who considered himself in charge.

Well, that was good. Maybe.

Micki let her eyes wander over him, cautiously sizing him up. He had a big, square jaw, brown eyes, a hawk nose, blond hair that fell below his shoulders, more muscles than a Charles Atlas contest. No, she wasn't dreaming this. He was built in a way her imagination had never stretched to.

He wore some sort of blue leathery vest that outlined those amazing muscles and left his arms and a great expanse of his chest bare. Intricate tattoo designs decorated each bulging upper arm. The same leathery fabric in a slightly darker hue hugged his hips and thighs until it met the top of a pair of boots that looked like a cross between Tony Lamas and a bondage fantasy.

That sidetracked Micki temporarily. Cowboy bondage boots? The mind boggled.

He didn't look very friendly. He looked commanding. He looked like the kind of guy nobody argued with very much, actually.

Micki mentally lowered her chances of heroic rescue by an order of magnitude. He was taking her, but where, and for what? And would she like it?

Come to me, he ordered her. Without moving his lips. The words appeared in her head, and with them came a blinding pain. She clapped both hands over her ears and shrieked.

"What is the matter with her?" the god demanded of the clichéd alien.

"She is one of the sensitive ones," it answered.

"As I told you. You have not modified the implant? Do so immediately. You should have done so already."

He looked impatient, as if having to tell the big-eyed alien how to do its job irritated him no end.

"If I modify it, you cannot control her with it."

The god made an impatient gesture with one hand, cutting the air with nearly palpable force. "I will control her without it. I need no device to enforce my commands. She must have it to understand me and form the necessary bond with me, but I will not have it harm her."

The big-eyed alien stood near Micki's head with something that looked like a Star Trek tricorder and made some adjustment with it.

The pain in her head turned off abruptly. She panted with relief.

"What of the other implant?" the god wanted to know now.

"Standard, of course, my lord."

145

"Neutralize it until such time as I desire you to engage it again."

The big-eyed alien, who must actually be a doctor, used the tricorder-like device to make another adjustment over her abdomen.

"It is as you command, my lord." The doctor alien stepped back.

"Good. Come to me now," the god said, holding a large hand toward Micki.

She sat up hesitantly and frowned at a pulling sensation in her midsection when she moved. "Doesn't your surgery come with anesthetic?"

"Yes. The discomfort is temporary. Your body will soon adjust to the presence of your contraceptive implant and it will cause you no pain," the doctor alien informed her.

"Contra-what? The one you just shut off?" Micki shrieked.

"It is not necessary," the god informed her. "You are my own personal slave. If it were otherwise and you were for the use of any who desired to enjoy you, the implant would be needed."

He took in her horrified look.

"I tell you this to reassure you, but I will not explain myself to you in future. A slave is owed no explanations. Your duty is to please me. I have said that it is not necessary. The matter is settled. Now come to me."

Go to him. The man who obviously had plans for her and who considered being her private owner something that she would find reassuring.

Should she be reassured that he didn't think birth control was a priority? Was she supposed to have an alien's love child? Was this some sort of horrible experiment?

In his favor, however, he had told the doctor not to turn her into a mind-controlled zombie who had no choice but to obey. That was something.

Maybe she was leaping to wild conclusions. Maybe he just wanted a slave to polish his boots. Maintaining that glossy sheen had to involve some real effort. And for all his air of command, he didn't look cruel.

She'd seen cruel, and it usually showed around the mouth and eyes. If he had a vicious streak, he hid it well.

Micki slid off the table and put her hand into his larger one, which seemed to swallow it whole.

It didn't strike her as a positive omen. She had the fleeting thought that he wanted to swallow all of her whole, somewhat like a boa constrictor enjoying a leisurely meal. Or maybe it was just the reptilian pattern on his clothing that gave her that idea. This close she could see that it looked more like snakeskin than leather.

His hand didn't feel alien. Not that she'd really had any sort of expectations about what alien flesh felt like. It felt warm. Strong. Masculine. Engulfing.

His engulfing alien hand pulled her inexorably closer, until she was plastered against him. She struggled to pull back and put some space between their bodies.

"Stay," he commanded as if she were a wriggling puppy instead of a grown woman. "The closeness is necessary. You must become accustomed to my presence, my touch."

That so did not sound reassuring, in light of the disabled contraceptive device.

The doctor alien looked at the god intently for a minute and then left.

"What was that about?" Micki asked.

"He says that you hurt his ears and you are bound to be louder soon."

"I didn't hear anything."

His species dislikes speaking thoughts aloud. They prefer to communicate by mental touch. They dislike noise.

"I heard you in my head." Micki frowned, remembering the pain that had accompanied that mental intrusion.

So you did. So you will. The words formed in her mind without his lips moving, but they didn't hurt her this time. "No, little slave, it does not hurt. The pain came from your refusal to obey the control unit. You resisted. Mental force against force caused the controller to punish you. The sensitive ones may become broken in this way."

Broken. Micki felt sick, imagining what that meant.

"You will not be broken. The unit remains in place so that language is translated between us, not to cause you harm. It is a crime to break the mind of a sensitive one, they are too few. No sane being would do such a thing."

"You keep using that word, sensitive. What do you mean by that?"

"Sensitive." He frowned at her as if suspicious that she was being deliberately obtuse. "It is as it sounds. Able to sense. Send and receive. You sent your mind to touch mine from the surface of your planet. I received your call. Now you are here and you are mine."

Sense? Send and receive? He was saying that she'd called him, like E.T. phoning home?

"Uh. No offense, but I didn't call you." Micki licked her lips nervously. "Somebody made a mistake."

"No mistake." He was arrogant confidence personified. It practically oozed from his pores, and given the sheer quantity of bare skin exposed, there was a lot of it permeating the air around them. "You called to me."

Great. She had writer's block, she was in danger of missing her deadline and going even broker so that she'd lose her lousy apartment with its lousy slumlord owner, she'd been kidnapped by aliens who performed medical procedures on her without her permission or knowledge. And now she was owned by an insane Norse god.

"Enough. We waste time." The god folded her into his arms and carried her bodily out of the alien hospital area. "You must be properly protected when we enter the singularity."

"The what?" Micki shrieked. Singularity was another word for black hole, wasn't it?

"The Yehlihnn was correct." He didn't slow down. If anything, he stepped up his determined pace. "You are a loud one. I will soon give you cause to be loud for better reason. That will please me much more than these outbursts."

"You've kidnapped me, planted alien devices in my body, made me a slave, and now you're going to kill me by dragging me through a black hole!" she howled. Her dignity was already shot, since she'd also been dragged away in her nightshirt and socks and nothing else, so she had nothing to lose by kicking and screaming like a toddler having a tantrum. "I want to go home! Right now!"

"Hush."

The word was more than a command. He did something to her with it, like flipping a switch inside her mind. It didn't hurt, like the control device. It flooded her with peace, relaxation, comfort.

All was well. She was safe. She was protected. This was where she belonged, where she had always wanted to be.

"What are you doing to me?" Micki managed to ask.

She wasn't frightened by the fact that he'd overridden her body and her emotions, and she should have been. But all she could feel was peace and a deep sense that for the first time in her life everything was right.

"I give you calm. For both our sakes." He smiled down into her eyes and the smile suddenly made him seem warmer, younger, more approachable. "It is well, little one. You will see that there is nothing to fear soon. On your world the term for this fear is white-knuckle flyer, yes?"

"It isn't just the idea of the black hole that scares me. But you're right, that's what put me over the top."

Micki cuddled into his chest, glad that he was holding her so close. She needed to be close to him, to feel his warmth, to have his scent wrapped around her like a fuzzy blanket with a spicy sachet. The leathery vest he wore felt nice, too. She had the vague thought that it would be nice to wear, a sensual all-over body caress.

"It is. I will dress you as you desire and you will see for yourself." The god plucked her thoughts from her head without effort, or maybe he'd planted them in the first place.

"It is your own thought. I have not taken over your mind, only shut off a switch. You have a term for it. Fight or flight."

Oh. That made sense. He'd turned off her reflexive burst of adrenaline and given her mental Valium instead.

The thought crossed her mind that he might be able to do other things with that sort of mental connection. Like trigger the pleasure center of her brain.

No sooner had she thought it than she convulsed in orgasm. Her vaginal walls spasmed violently, liquid coated her sex and shock waves flared out to her extremities as if from the epicenter of an earthquake.

The relaxation that followed spread even more peace through her body.

"Better, yes?"

"Yes," Micki agreed wholeheartedly. "Can you do that any time you feel like it?"

"Only to one who is sensitive."

"Can I do that to you?"

"When you have formed the bond to me, yes."

"Whoa. Alien sex is cool," Micki sighed. She melted into him, feeling boneless and limp and incredibly satisfied. "On

Earth there are all sorts of books about how to do that to a woman, not that most men bother to read them. And you just think 'orgasm' for me to have one."

"This is not sex." He seemed to find her amusing, but she was too relaxed to care. "It is a side effect. A benefit." He brushed his lips against hers, and a strange buzz spread from the point of contact. Or maybe it was more of a humming feeling, like a vibration.

"Sensitive." He touched her mouth again but with the tip of one finger this time, holding her weight easily in the cradle of one large, muscle-bound arm. The finger buzzed against her mouth like his lips had. "It is the harmony you feel. You are strong, as I thought."

"Strong?"

"You must have great strength to call me from such a distance. It is a sign that we will be greatly harmonious." The god frowned. "You do not understand that word rightly. Compatible."

"No offense, but I think we have very different ideas about compatibility," Micki said from her well of drowsy contentment. "And I didn't call you. Really."

"You did. You had no male, no bond. You sent the call for bonding."

"Bonding or bondage?" she mumbled. "I'm your slave, according to you, not your girlfriend."

"This is no matter." He brushed off her objection, which to Micki sort of underscored the point of it.

They apparently had reached their destination. She was suddenly lowered into some sort of padded coffin. Gently, to give him credit, but it still looked far too much like a coffin for comfort.

A vague hysteria stirred under the layer of induced calm. In a culture where slave and girlfriend where interchangeable terms, was it okay to bury one alive?

He must have picked up her thought, because he gave her an exasperated look. "It is not a place of death. It is for sleep. I cannot sleep with you, I command this vessel. I must be at my station. So you will await me here for a time." He stood back and did something that resulted in a hard, clear cover coming up from the sides to seal her inside the padded not-a-coffin.

Micki had the weird sense of being inside a confused fairy tale, the princess sleeping inside a glass coffin until she was awakened by a kiss.

Except her slave-owning Norse god wasn't exactly Prince Charming.

She did have some stirring of memory about Norse mythology and a sleeping woman and a warrior who woke her. The ring cycle? In the story, she seemed to remember that the sleeping woman was a Valkyrie and her punishment was to be bound to the man who broke her enchantment, although to even things up only a fairly heroic sort of male could find her in the first place. Had that couple ended up living happily ever after?

While she tried to remember how that story ended, a strange smell like the heavy perfume of Easter lilies mixed with antiseptic filled the pod she occupied. Micki breathed it in and then slept.

Chapter Three

❧

"Wake."

At the command, Micki's eyes opened automatically. She saw a face above hers that was becoming familiar. There should be a name to go with it, though. Shouldn't there?

"I have a name. It is Keelan Os'tana."

"Keelan," she repeated, letting the strange syllables roll off her tongue. "My name is Micki."

"I dislike the name you go by," Keelan informed her. "I see a large black and white rodent of that name in your mind. I will think on what name I will give you."

"You could just call me Michelle." Her tone was deceptively mild. Kidnapping, enslavement and strange devices planted in her person weren't enough, now he had to take away her name, too? He was good-looking, if you liked the Norse god-type, but he was really starting to piss her off.

"No. I will give you a new name to use between us, what you call a pet name. One fitting to your new life. Your new life is here and now." He folded his arms on his chest and nodded as if to emphasize his statement. Mr. Large and in Charge.

"My new life is slavery," Micki snapped. The artificial calm was going away fast now that she was awake.

"You are angry." Keelan seemed amazed.

"Duh."

A crooked smile formed on his face. "Ah. I see the reason for your foul temper now. Your world has no males for you to please, they do not read these books you mention so they have no knowledge of the giving of orgasm, and so you have been greatly deprived of the sex you mentioned."

"You mean the sex you mentioned," Micki shot back.

"No, it was you who said, 'alien sex is cool'," Keelan reminded her, quoting her words back exactly.

Since he had her there, Micki abandoned the argument temporarily and climbed out of the coffin. She looked around the room without the distraction of his mental blanket of calm damping down her curiosity.

The first thing she saw was a view of stars against a blanket of utter darkness from what had to be a long, horizontal window. "Holy shit," she said. "That's space. We're in space."

Probably she should have come up with something deeper to say than "holy shit", but words seemed to have deserted her. Micki stared and stared and then she shivered in her flannel nightshirt. Space was so deep. So dark. So cold. So far from home.

Keelan frowned at her. "This is now your home. You are cold. Come to me and be warmed."

She stayed rooted to the spot. Space. She was in outer space, on the other side of a wormhole if she understood Keelan correctly. Maybe not even in the same galaxy Earth occupied.

Lost. She was truly, completely lost.

She would never find home again, even if she got away, and that might be difficult because Keelan seemed determined to dog her steps continually with all that talk about needing his constant presence for bonding.

Hard hands closed on her shoulders and yanked her back against his body. "You will not get away. You are mine. You will cease these thoughts of escape. You will accept your destiny."

Micki's mouth trembled. A sob escaped her. Tears tracked down her cheeks.

"Your weeping displeases me. Cease immediately," he growled at her.

"I'll cry if I want to, you insensitive alien male." She flung the term at him as if his gender was an insult. Her heart wasn't really in it, though. She was too lost, too full of grief to work up any anger. She felt so helpless and alone, and all she could do was stand there and look at the vast expanse of space and cry.

"You grieve because it is so distasteful to be mine?" he roared at her. "Do you prefer to belong to no male, for the use of any and all who desire you at whim? Perhaps you would prefer that since you are so deprived of the sex!"

Sheer terror gripped her at the very thought. He was some sort of alien pimp who was going to whore her out to alien rape gangs?

Her fear seemed to get through to him where tears hadn't. "Hush."

The calm spread through her again. Keelan's voice was warm and soothing in her ear. "I apologize, little one. I was wrong to speak so. I spoke foolishly, out of anger that you might prefer another male. I have searched long for my bondmate and never did I anticipate that she would not be pleased by my claiming. I have said that you are mine for the bonding. The bond is for life. You will not be discarded. I will not tire of you. This whoring you think of in your mind is ugly. Had I known your world had such things, I would not have spoken so."

"You can't say your world doesn't have it if slaves can be forced to have sex with anybody and don't have a choice," Micki whispered, feeling ill at the thought of mass rape happening all around her, potentially being a victim of it herself.

"You will see for yourself that it is no such thing as that. It is a service performed to mutual agreement, that is all."

Keelan stroked her shoulders, spreading circles of buzzing, humming vibrations that added to the sense of calm from his mental interference. Unfair that he could manipulate her from the inside and the outside both.

"I speak the truth. It is not our way to mistreat. You think of this as a class system, yes? I am one of the warrior class, slaves are of another class. All classes have their place, all have their duty. If it is one's duty to be a slave, what shame is there in that? And a warrior who satisfied himself with a slave would not cause harm in the doing. Such would be beneath him, not worthy of his position."

"You're saying it's not rape because everybody's willing?"

"All do their duty, yes. It is an honor to perform one's duty well. If it is one's duty to please any male who desires you, a slave is honored to do so. But your duty is to please me."

"I think your logic is terribly convenient for you," Micki muttered. "It sounds like you could rape me and call it doing my duty. And if I don't cooperate, I'm not honorable. I don't see how this duty and honor business benefits me."

"Perhaps I should have the controller reset," Keelan answered. "You seem most noncompliant. You refuse to warm yourself against me as ordered. You have not yet even been brought to my bed and you are resistant to your duty."

"So it's my duty just to please you in bed and the rest of the time I can ignore you?"

"It is your duty to please me at all times. It is my duty to control you and see that you obey all the laws. You are my slave until we are bonded, therefore the responsibility for your actions is mine. You are not from an allied world, you have no citizenship. There must be law and order upheld on this ship at all times."

Micki closed her eyes and groaned. "I just knew I wasn't going to like this place." Although she hated to admit she could see his point. Even on Earth, naval vessels couldn't allow anarchy or chaos. In space it would be even more crucial. She could honestly understand that some system had to keep people in check or everybody on board could be endangered.

So, Keelan was the only thing between her and sexual servitude to warrior masses. If she didn't please him or if she broke some law, like refusing to do her duty, would he release her to that fate? Worse, if she didn't do her duty, would he be forced to release her to that fate, whether he wanted to or not?

Even under the calming mental influence of Keelan's interference, Micki felt ill at the prospects. Rock, hard place, none of it looked like an attractive future. She had to get out of here.

"You upset yourself for no reason. You will form the bond to me and then you cannot be parted from me as you fear. As my bondmate you will share my status. Your term is green card? And you will cease to fear me also." Keelan's lips brushed against her cheek as he spoke, and his arms slid down from her shoulders to fold her back against him, cuddling her from behind.

How could he cuddle her as if he cared and still force her into slavery? And what did he mean, green card? If she bonded with him, she became a free citizen?

"You are the most confusing man," Micki said.

"You are confused, but this is to be expected," he answered. "You are new to this life, new to our ways, and all females find it an adjustment to belong to a new male. You will soon adjust."

"I'm glad you think so." Doubt was palpable in her voice. "And what do you mean about belonging to a new male? I thought this bondage thing was forever. Do you guys swap bondmates or something?"

"You do not understand the bond, so I will not punish you for this insult. But never speak so again, not in any person's hearing. The bond is sacred."

He actually sounded as if her question bordered on blasphemy. She nearly expected the wrath of God to strike her.

"Sacred. Right. Got it," Micki said. "By the way, what do you mean you won't punish me this time? Would you normally beat me, lock me in my room, put me on bread and water, or what? It would be nice to know what to expect."

Keelan let out a low sigh. "Never have I heard such dramatics. You are not to be deprived of sustenance, or of my company, and I would not raise a hand to harm you. But if you persist in defying me, I would have you recall what you termed alien sex."

It took her a minute to get it, but she did. He intended to keep her in line and get his way by stimulating her to orgasm with a mental touch whenever she resisted his orders.

Well, that was certainly novel. And probably effective, she was forced to admit. How much of an argument could she put up if she was busy letting her eyes roll up in her head while her body convulsed in pleasure? How could she yell protests when she was more likely to yell out, "Oh God, yes"?

"That is so not fair," Micki informed him.

"What is not fair? Form the bond to me, and not only will I never have need to punish you in this manner, you will be able to respond in kind." His voice was matter of fact, as if there were absolutely no problem with this plan.

He turned her around to face him. "For now, it is enough for you to know that you belong to me. You will not be cast off, you will not be harmed. And if you fail to please me at all times as is your duty, I will inspire you to obedience with the mind touch of pleasure. You will accept your new life. You will accept me and you will accept your position."

Micki looked down at her feet instead of looking back at him. Gray fleece socks. No ruby slippers to click together and take her home. Look where thinking happy thoughts and wanting to fly got her. She was in Neverland, all right. Never, never, never was this going to work.

Which was too bad, because Keelan so looked like hero material. Felt like it, too. His arms were big and strong and comforting. His voice was confident and reassuring, if she ignored what he was saying and just listened to the sound. The timbre of his voice had a vibration that set off a response, just like the vibration of his touch.

He seemed very devoted to honor and duty and seemed deeply insulted at the very idea that he would ever harm her. Fairly heroic qualities.

But there were some terribly non-heroic issues she just couldn't get past. Slavery, for one. Then there was his ability to manipulate both her mind and her body to get his way.

No wonder everybody was so willing around here, Micki thought. Forget honor and duty and being pleased to serve as a sex slave. It would be darn hard to say you weren't a willing participant while you were having an orgasm. Pleased to serve, indeed.

Which led to another awful thought. If Keelan gave those mental orgasms to her one on top of the other, how long would it take before she was willing to do anything at all he commanded?

"Speak your thoughts to me." Keelan gave her a light shake, prompting her to return her attention to him. "We may communicate without words, but you do not aim any of your thoughts at me. This does not please me. If you would say something, then have your say."

"You scare me," Micki said bluntly. "Does this bond thing mean that you take over my brain? I stop being me, I just turn into your sex doll and I get so brain-damaged from orgasm overdose that I like it?"

"I do not know how to explain the bond. I begin to think your world has nothing like it." Keelan studied her intently as if pondering the mystery she presented him with. "How can one who senses not instinctively seek the bond? It is well for you that I have taken you for my own. To be forever alone, no joining of the minds, I would not leave you on that world to suffer so."

"So naturally out of the goodness of your heart, you rescued me from my cruel fate and graciously enslaved me." Micki shook her head. "You know, all your explanations sound very one-sided."

"I should not explain at all. You should accept my word and my will without question. That is your duty. Yet I would relieve your fear of me. It is a hindrance to the bond."

Keelan lifted her up by her elbows until her eyes were level with his. The movement slid her torso along his, causing that humming feeling to throb in her nipples. "You will go to my bed now and see that it is nothing to fear."

Micki gulped audibly.

"But first we will engage in a ritual of your people. We will have a drink and talk together."

She stared at him. "You want to take me to a bar? I think I've spent enough time in bars tonight. Look what it led to."

He smiled at her. "Yes, it led you to me. Come, are you not curious?"

She had to admit, at least silently, that she was. What would it be like? The bar scene from *Star Wars*? All kinds of aliens drinking alien drinks?

Chapter Four

❧

It wasn't anything like the bar scene from *Star Wars*. If the Kama Sutra had had a bar scene, what met Micki's eyes when the door to their destination slid open would have been it.

Couples, threesomes and moresomes stood, sat and reclined in various positions and states of undress, in various stages of erotic play, from mere cuddling to mild foreplay to full-out group sex. One group that Keelan led her past really captured her attention. A naked woman in the center of the group was bent forward at the waist, her lips wrapped around a warrior's cock, while another warrior thrust into her with deep, even strokes from behind. A third stimulated her nipples and presumably her clit from a kneeling position underneath her.

While Micki watched, the three men switched positions as if following some mental signal. The man receiving oral pleasure took up the rear position and slid his engorged penis into her waiting cunt. The warrior who had been kneeling beneath let her nipple slide out of his mouth and stood to thrust his cock into her mouth. The warrior who surrendered the rear entry position took up the kneeling station and began pinching the woman's nipples as her breasts swayed with the impact of the rear warrior's thrusts.

"Some enjoy play in full view of others, finding it heightens their pleasure. Some enjoy watching, either while they begin their own play or to build their anticipation of what is to come," Keelan informed her.

Another of the tall, muscular, Nordic-looking warriors strode into the lounge and paused by the coupling foursome. "Ah, Zette, you are fully occupied?" he asked.

The woman, who Micki realized must be Zette, slowly slid her mouth all the way off the warrior's cock, seemingly reluctant to let it go even for a moment in order to answer. "Lord Danek, you honor me. But I fear I am too occupied to give your magnificent cock the concentration it deserves. Do you wish for me to come to you later?"

"No need. You may be busy for some time." He smiled at her, tweaked one of her nipples and left the group to continue.

"She said no," Micki blurted out.

Keelan raised a brow. "This surprises you? It is as I told you. She is not mistreated. She is valued for the service she performs. And because she is valued, she is not to be overworked or made to provide any service she finds distasteful. We have different classes, but all people have value. Zette is very well-liked by the unbonded warriors. All treat her well. And all understand that she cannot be everywhere at once. To mistreat another because they are not of your class is not honorable."

"Huh." Micki thought about the implications. Maybe slavery was a term that didn't translate well here. "She doesn't seem like a slave. More like, I don't know. Somebody who sets her own appointments, like a hairstylist. Who really likes men. A lot."

Zette was now moaning and shuddering, obviously in the throes of orgasm. The warrior who had been enjoying a leisurely blowjob withdrew his spent penis from her lips, kissed her and then left the lounge. The kneeling warrior stood to face her and drew her into an upright position. With the standing woman sandwiched between them, the warrior behind her withdrew his cock and spread her ass cheeks as he positioned himself for rear entry. Then the two of them began to double penetrate her, with her vocal encouragement. Getting an alien anal probe looked like a hell of a lot of fun if Zette's reaction was anything to go by.

The erotic scene had Micki squirming in her seat. She pressed her thighs together and hoped Keelan wouldn't notice the effect the bar's ambiance was having on her. The flannel should be thick enough to hide her erect nipples and if she managed not to make a wet spot on her nightshirt...

"Do not become too fond of what you see," Keelan said, watching her watch the tandem fucking Zette was getting and thoroughly enjoying. "I will not share you in that manner."

Before Micki could say anything to that, the warrior who had asked if Zette was busy joined them. "My lord." He bowed formally to Keelan. "May I join you?"

"Please." Keelan indicated the seat across from him, and pulled Micki into his lap. His arms closed around her as if caging her off. *Private, keep out,* Micki thought irreverently.

"Who is your fair companion?" Danek smiled at them both and took the proffered seat.

"She is my lady Michelle."

The smile vanished from his face. "You have taken a bondmate?" he asked Keelan. To Micki he gave another formal bow with the greeting, "My lady."

"Yes," Keelan answered. "She is from the unallied world we stopped at. Very sensitive. Very strong. She called to me and I heard her."

"You are very fortunate." In fact, Danek looked as if he envied Keelan his fortune. "Congratulations, my lord Keelan, my lady Michelle."

"She is *my* lady," Keelan said. "Find your own. Begin now, in fact."

"Ah, like that, is it? You will have no time for anything but your bondmate for days," Danek sighed. "If such fortune has come to you from that world, perhaps I should chart a return course and see if it harbors any other sensitive ones who are unbonded."

"My lady cannot be the only one among her people," Keelan answered. "There are too few sensitives in all the worlds to overlook any possibility."

Danek nodded. "As you say. I will indeed chart a return course and store it in my private ship's navigation system." He stood and bowed to them both. "I wish you joy of each other."

"A moment." Keelan studied Micki's face with its betraying flush of arousal. "The sight of you pleases my lady. She thinks you are a stud muffin. She was disappointed that she did not get to see you pleasuring Zette."

"What?" Micki said, feeling defensive. Then she realized how useless it was to try to hide her thoughts or reactions. The man was a mind reader. Even if he didn't see it on her face or notice the dampness in her crotch, he knew what flipped her switches because her thoughts gave everything away. "Okay, fine, I admit, for a second I wondered how Danek here would look naked and if he—" she broke off, blushing in embarrassment and unable to say it out loud.

"If he was skilled in oral pleasure," Keelan said calmly. "You wondered how it would feel to have two men pleasure you. You imagined yourself in Zette's place, with Danek's cock in your mouth while mine took you from behind and others watched."

If Keelan hadn't been holding her, Micki would have bolted. Since she couldn't, she simply closed her eyes and fervently wished a giant hole would appear and swallow her up before she died of embarrassment.

Keelan cupped her breasts with his hands and began to toy with her nipples through the flannel as he continued to speak. "You do not understand the bond. You do not understand our ways. I brought you here to make you at ease, to remove the barriers you have in your mind that would prevent our bonding. I said I will not share you fully, but this I will do. I will invite Danek to be a part of our foreplay this once so you will see that you have nothing to fear from me or from others of my class. Also, you must understand your choice. If you refuse to bond with me, you must know the true alternative and not the fears you harbor in your so-active imagination."

164

Micki opened her eyes to see Danek grinning at her.

"You honor me," he said. He sounded sincere. He wasn't leering at her. He just looked pleased to hear that she found him fantasy material.

"I make my living off my so-active imagination," Micki informed Keelan, but without any heat. What he was doing with his hands felt too good. And his words were making her warm in an entirely different way. Warm on the inside at his unexpected consideration. Warm from arousal at the idea of living out a fantasy.

"Let me see if I have this straight. I can choose to bond with you and what, become a citizen with all rights and privileges that entails? Or I can choose not to be your bondmate, and decide which intergalactic stud muffins I want to do and be done by instead? And you want me to fool around with both of you so that I can make an informed decision?"

"Yes." Keelan's hands were making her nipples hum, Micki thought in distraction, that strange buzzing sensation, as if some kind of harmonics were at work. He'd said harmony and maybe that wasn't a poor translation. "You must make the bond freely."

It truly was her choice, Micki realized. And he was actually willing to risk her choosing not to bond. She felt her resistance melting away at the possibility that she could truly trust him, that he wouldn't keep her by force.

"Would you send me back home if that was my choice?" Micki asked.

He laughed and nuzzled her ear. "Do you not feel it in my touch? You are mine already, but your mind must admit what your body has acknowledged."

Cocky, she thought. But maybe he had reason. Her body did respond to his on a level she'd never imagined. She was hot and bothered and halfway hoping he'd slide her nightshirt up and do her right there in the booth with no further preliminaries. She felt his arms tighten around her in a possessive hold and knew he'd caught that wish.

"You are mine, and I will make you mine in all ways. But I will say this to remove your fear. If you truly did not want me, if you rejected me as your bondmate and your wish was to return to your home, I would send you back."

So, her potential career as a tabloid journalist awaited her if she didn't want to marry a telepathic alien or remain an alien love slave. But first she was going to get a taste of both options. "Yippee," Micki said, feeling giddy and wondering how much mixed brandy and cold medicine were still in her system.

Then Keelan stripped her nightshirt off and lifted her naked onto the table. Before she had time to feel stupid, Danek stepped forward and put his hands on her thighs, pushing them slightly apart to expose her swollen and slick sex. "She has beautiful tits, does she not?" Keelan asked, moving behind Micki to support her back with his chest. His hands returned to her now-bare breasts, circling, squeezing, cupping and displaying her to the other man. "Perhaps you would like to take one into your mouth."

Danek leaned over her and ran his tongue around one hard nipple. Micki felt dizzy and not from any aftereffects of cold medicine. One gorgeous man was behind her, another in front of her, and both of them were focused on her. Then Danek's mouth closed over her breast with gentle suction and a lot of heat and she gasped at the sensation. Keelan flicked her other nipple with his forefinger, sending a charge along her nerve endings that shot straight to her clit.

"I think she likes that," Keelan murmured.

She liked it a lot, but couldn't find the words to say so. Although she noticed the difference between her response to the two of them. Danek's stimulation of her nipple felt very, very good, but Keelan's made her body sing. When he pinched her nipple, she thrust her hips in reaction, needing something between her legs.

"Who do you wish to have licking your luscious cunt?" Keelan asked. "Should Danek get to suckle your clit and thrust his tongue into you first?"

"Yes," Micki said, her tongue feeling thick in her mouth. That seemed right. It was a test of something important, although she couldn't exactly say what. It was difficult to hold on to any thought just now.

Danek kissed his way down her belly, taking his time in reaching his objective. She liked having him kiss her bare skin, but it was Keelan holding her, Keelan's hands working her breasts that made her melt, made her molecules shift and dance. Danek circled her clit with his tongue and Micki let out a groan. He traced the outline of her labia, licked inside her, lapped at her clit, sucked gently, then thrust his tongue into her all the way.

"Come for him," Keelan commanded her. "Let him give you pleasure. Feel his mouth on your sex as his tongue prepares you for my cock. Come while others watch you spread your legs for him to devour on the table like a tasty dessert."

Micki felt the pressure building. She felt Danek suck on her clit again as Keelan's hands molded and squeezed her breasts and his fingers pinched down on her distended nipples. She felt Keelan give her a mental nudge, permission, approval, encouragement and then she felt her back arch and her head fall back as she came hard.

As she gasped and panted and waited for the stars that danced in front of her eyes to disappear, the men switched places. Danek supported her while Keelan took his place between her thighs. At the first touch of his mouth on her sex, Micki closed her eyes and sagged into Danek's hold. She melted for him. There was no other word for it. His lips moved over her sex, his tongue teased and tasted, he nibbled, licked and nipped and her body hummed for him, buzzed, sang and...called?

"What's happening?" Micki whispered, or thought she did, but no sound escaped her lips except sighs and moans.

The harmony, Keelan answered in her mind. It was a statement full of triumph and male satisfaction. *You are mine. Your mind called to me and I answered. Your body calls to mine and I will answer. I will make you mine in full and you will bond with me.*

What, from an orgasm? Micki thought, even as she teetered on the brink of another one so soon after the first. And this one was going to be a doozy.

In part. But not like this. I must be inside you, you must take my seed. It is why the contraceptive implant was neutralized, you must be completely open and without barriers to form the bond.

Since it wasn't going to lead to anything life-altering and since she couldn't hold out any longer anyway, Micki abandoned any pretense at control and came screaming while one man held her and another took her with his mouth, and who knew how many others watched.

Chapter Five

❧

"Now you are ready to form the bond with me." Keelan lifted his head from between her thighs and gave her a look so possessive Micki almost expected a "sold" tag to appear on her bare belly. He cupped his hand over her sex and squeezed her mound. Micki made a strangled sound and no intelligible response. "You have seen for yourself that you would not be abused if you refused my bond. You have also felt the difference between one whose psychic wavelength matches yours and one whose does not. Danek gave you pleasure but he could not make you feel what I make you feel. In all the worlds there is only one mate, one match who can bond with you in full."

"Nngh," Micki said. She would have tried to say something in English or any language that made sense, but Keelan was rubbing the heel of his hand into her sex, pressing into her clit, and something was building under her skin that was making her shake with the force of it.

"She is close," she heard Danek say. "You will have to carry her to your quarters now or do it here."

"I will take her home," Keelan said and Micki's mind screamed in protest until his quieted her with the thought, *I am not letting you go. Your home is now with me.*

She felt Keelan's arms close around her, felt herself being lifted, cradled and carried while her head flopped against his chest and her body throbbed with some alien rhythm. Micki knew it should bother her that a bunch of strangers had just seen her naked in a bar and a few more were now seeing Keelan carry her naked through the ship's corridors, but it

169

seemed incredibly distant and irrelevant. Nothing mattered but the touch of Keelan's skin against hers.

That gave her something to hold on to, quieted the urgency in her body, but not by much. She needed him. Needed him inside her. Needed him to fuck her, take her, make her his.

"Yes, all that," Keelan said as if she'd spoken out loud. "I will give you all that you need."

Her sex clenched in reaction and she closed her eyes. "Hurry," she whispered. Then he was lowering her onto something soft and stripping away his leatherlike clothing, boots and all. She realized dimly that she still wore her wool socks and nothing else. She started to giggle but the sight of Keelan's naked body drove the laughter away and all the air out of her lungs.

He really did look like a Norse god, one with defined muscles, inviting skin and an erect cock that looked very capable of fucking her to Valhalla. Micki had a split second to contemplate that possibility and then he covered her body with his, held her face between his two hands and took her mouth with his while he drove his cock into her slick, ready sex, filling her with one stroke.

A shock wave ran through her. Keelan, on her, in her, holding her. Taking her breath and her body. Taking. Giving. Demanding. He drove into her again, hard, fast, deep. Her body shuddered and her sex clenched convulsively around his cock as the thing building between them racked her. She had to do something, had to, or it was going to split her in half. She let out a sob as Keelan thrust into her over and over, taking her, felt her body shift, felt her mind shift. And then it was happening. Her body vibrated in tune with his. Her mind hummed in harmony. She felt his thoughts, his feelings. She was so beautiful, she felt so good, she pleased him so utterly. He had searched so long for her, her very presence delighted him.

The two become one, she thought, just before all coherent thought spun away as they merged, spasming in a joint orgasm that seemed eternal. She couldn't differentiate her pleasure from his, couldn't tell where her body left off and his began. All she knew was that no barrier existed between them. She was no longer alone in her mind or in the universe. She sensed that she would never be alone again.

When Micki opened her eyes again finally, she looked into Keelan's and felt something burst inside her. Love. Love was the bond. And they were truly bonded now.

Their bodies were still locked together, Keelan's cock was still buried as deep inside her as he could go, but the psychic bond they shared would remain, no matter where they were. They could never be apart again. A sense of wonder flooded her at the knowledge that he would always be a thought away. That no matter where she was, he could touch her with his mind.

Her earlier fears, her outright panic over becoming an alien's love slave, made Micki laugh out loud.

Keelan's eyes danced with answering humor. "You see? All is as I said."

Micki sighed. "You're going to say 'I told you so', aren't you?"

"No." Keelan's eyes darkened. "I am going to say that I love you, my bondmate. My one, my heart. In all the worlds there is no other but you and I thank all gods that may be that you called to me."

"I love you too." She smiled at him, feeling shy all of sudden. Which was dumb, considering all the things she'd just done with him. Some of them in public. With a third party. And what was there to feel shy about, when he could read her every thought?

"It is not foolish to feel vulnerable when you give your heart and your all to another." Keelan gave her a long, deep kiss. "You honor me, my bondmate."

"My hero," Micki whispered. She hugged him close and kissed him back with all her heart. She had her hero after all. True love, a happy ending. And she thought she really might be able to fly among the stars now.

"My Astrea," he answered. "That is my private name for you. My shining star. Does it please you?"

Nothing could be more perfect, she thought, but didn't speak out loud because her lips were very busy.

* * * * *

Ten days later Micki removed the earbud that had become her new best friend, "folded" her virtual display, peeled a strip of electrode-studded tape from her throat and stripped off the gloves that allowed her to manipulate blocks of text by electronic touch. "This interface is incredible," she told Keelan for about the hundredth time. "No carpal tunnel or repetitive motion issues, software that writes as fast as I can focus my thoughts and subvocalize, adaptive customized editing functions so intuitive they practically know what I'm going to do before I do it. I'm in love."

Keelan gave her a mock scowl. "I do not like having a machine for a rival."

"You have no rival in all the galaxy, and well you know it." Micki grinned at him and tickled his bare chest with one discarded glove. "You're my hero. And now you're not only mine. You're about to star in reader fantasies all over Earth."

"So you have finished?" He moved closer and pulled her out of the floating chair that conformed to her body when she occupied it and smoothed itself into a neutral shape when she left it empty.

"I finished." She nuzzled his throat and wrapped herself around him. "In record time, too. I must've been inspired."

"I found assisting you with your research inspirational as well," Keelan said.

172

Micki laughed, not needing to read his mind to know he was thinking about the night she'd woken him from a sound sleep to ask if zero-g sex was physically possible and if so what difficulties it might present. He'd turned off their room's gravity and demonstrated every possible variation before she could say another word. By the time he finished, she'd been beyond speech.

"I don't know how I ever managed without a research assistant," she said.

"You do not have to manage without one ever again."

No, she didn't. Micki burrowed closer and breathed him in, feeling the harmony of their bodies, in tune with each other, completing each other. "I really don't know how I managed without you." She wasn't talking about the book or research anymore and Keelan followed her thoughts, his arms tightening around her.

You are mine and I am yours. We are together. His voice in her mind was full of love and reassurance and Micki felt tears sting the back of her eyes.

Show me, she answered him.

Keelan turned and sat in the floating chair, reclining with her in his lap as it shifted to accommodate them. *My pleasure.*

And mine, Micki thought, giddy with anticipation. His hands moved over her, releasing the fastenings to her vest and pants, peeling them off her. Hers tugged impatiently at his waistband, and he assisted her efforts, stripping away every barrier that separated them until they were skin to skin. Her heart skipped a beat as heat and need raced through her. Keelan's mouth found hers and she kissed him back with all the urgency she felt coiling inside her, shifting on his lap so that she straddled him. Her breath caught in her throat as her sex, already slick for him, made contact with his hard length.

In a hurry?

Yes. I waited a long time for you.

You do not have to wait now. Keelan's promise filled her mind as he filled her with himself in one slow, sure stroke. Micki felt the heat of him inside her, felt her sex adjust to the alien invasion and gave herself up to the moment.

Also by Charlene Teglia

❧

Dangerous Games
Earth Girls Aren't Easy
Ellora's Cavemen: Legendary Tails II (*anthology*)
Love and Rockets
Only Human
Wolf in Cheap Clothing
Wolf in Shining Armor

Also see Charlene's non-erotic stories at Cerridwen Press
(www.cerridwenpress.com):

❧

Catalyst

About the Author

෨

Charlene Teglia writes erotic romance with humor and speculative fiction elements. She can't imagine any better life than making up stories about hunky Alpha heroes who meet their match and live happily ever after, whether it happens right next door, in outer space, or the outer limits of imagination. When she's not writing, she can be found hiking around the Olympic Peninsula with her family or opening and closing doors for cats.

Charlene welcomes comments from readers. You can find her website and email address on her author bio page at www.ellorascave.com.

Tell Us What You Think

We appreciate hearing reader opinions about our books. You can email us at Comments@EllorasCave.com.

SUNSHINE FOR A VAMPIRE

By N.J. Walters

Chapter One

ॐ

The moon was a huge golden orb floating in the night sky with a sprinkling of stars hovering around it. But it wasn't full. Not yet. By her reckoning, it wouldn't be truly full until tomorrow night. She wished it were already here because that would mean tonight was already over.

Sunshine DeMarco strolled through her garden, admiring the night-blooming flowers. Her fingers lovingly stroked the bell-shaped angel's trumpet before trailing across the moonflower that she loved so well. There was a profusion of evening primrose and four-o'clocks. Each plant bloomed only at night and either had a unique fragrance or was white in color, drawing the otherwise quiet insects to them after dusk settled.

Her garden was much like her — only opening up to the world after the sun had gone down. Sighing, she lowered herself onto a stone bench, which sat directly in the center of her garden. Her sanctuary. Here she could be herself without worrying about the censorious glances that she received when she was around others of her kind.

Vampires.

She just didn't fit in. Never had. Her family line was old, part of the upper class of society, and everyone knew that the aristocracy prized the purity of their bloodlines more than anything. They bred true — tall, dark-haired and dark-eyed, except for the occasional redhead with witchy-green eyes, which was exotic and erotic. Sure, they all had the occasional human in their family trees, but no one talked about it. Vampire genetics were almost always dominant...except that hadn't happened in her family. By some stroke of fate, the recessive family genes had surged forward when she was born, making her forever an outcast among the ruling elite. A short, blonde-haired, blue-eyed vampire was almost unheard of, especially among her peers.

Her mother had claimed that Sunshine represented a precious part of the world that none of their kind could inhabit and had named her appropriately. As a small child, she'd felt special. But when she'd ventured out among her own people, she'd felt like a freak, a genetic anomaly, an aberration.

Beyond that, she didn't fit into the whole vampire lifestyle. Most of them enjoyed opulent, rich surroundings, overindulging in everything from food to drink to blood. They laughed a little too loudly, gossiped way too much and were incredibly bored with life, always searching out the next adventure to keep them entertained. Personally, Sunshine thought they'd be much better off just finding something constructive to do with their time. After all, what was the point of living forever if you weren't going to do something useful?

So she kept mostly to herself, enjoying her garden and her work, venturing out into the world only when she had to, or when she wanted to be with the handful of truly close friends that she possessed. It was a satisfying life. One she'd painstakingly built for herself over the past fifty or so years. For the first fifty years of her life, she'd lived at home in upstate New York on her family's estate with her aloof father, her doting mother and her beloved brother, Rainier. But after her mother died in childbirth, along with her unborn son, their father had changed. Home became a place that Sunshine just didn't want to be anymore.

She'd left the estate and moved around for the first thirty years or so before settling here in her quaint stone cottage about an hour outside Boston. It was secluded, which she liked, but close enough to visit the galleries and bookstores in the city, which she craved. The only visitors she had were her brother and her two close female friends, Cereus and Gemma.

The water in the large stone fountain that dominated the center of the garden tinkled merrily as a light breeze carried the perfumed scent of flowers to her nose. She loved her garden and found immense comfort just sitting here amidst the peace and quiet. Unfortunately, she knew it couldn't last.

Sometimes even she was forced out of seclusion, and tonight was one of those nights. With the untimely death of her father a year ago, only she and Rainier remained to represent their family line. Vampires were immortal, but exposure to sunlight, beheading and starvation due to lack of blood could kill them. The females had the added possibility of dying during childbirth. Pregnancy and birth were hard for vampires. Sunshine always believed it was Mother Nature's way of keeping the growth of their species in check. In her heart, she truly believed her father had walked into the sun because he hadn't wanted to live without her mother any longer. Since her brother was on the other side of the country on business, it was up to her to attend tonight's huge celebration at the Kasmarek estate just outside Boston.

The Kasmarek clan was the oldest in the United States, and as a result they usually hosted the bigwigs from the European clans when they deigned to visit. And tonight one of the biggest of the big was flying in from Romania. The Rusnak clan had all but ruled the European Council for hundreds of years and the firstborn son of the head of the Council was coming to visit. She couldn't remember if she'd heard his first name or not, but she wasn't really interested. She'd go to the celebration, put in her hour watching them all fawn over the European prince and then come home. She wanted to try to get a few hours work in before dawn.

Photography was her passion and she had discovered that she was actually quite good at it. She specialized in night shots, both black and white as well as color. Her work was now shown in several galleries around the country and paid her very well. Not that she needed the money. She came from a very wealthy family and her brother had taught her how to

181

handle her own investments. It was easy to make money when one had the time to wait and the money to invest. She preferred not to touch the bulk of her fortune, but she did use the interest it accrued, dividing it among several charities that were near and dear to her heart. So while she technically didn't need the money from her photographs, she did indeed live off it.

Her father had never understood her interest in the humans who had persecuted her kind over the millennia. He hadn't understood that she felt more at home with them than she did amongst her own kind. One of her best friends, Gemma, was a human and she felt closer to her than she did to anyone.

She'd much rather be spending a quiet evening curled up watching a movie with Gemma. She really didn't want to put on a fancy dress and spend an hour with people who looked down their noses at her, but duty called. Sighing, she drew her feet up onto the bench and wrapped her arms around her bent knees as she stared up at the sky. No, her wants and dreams were much simpler, yet so elusive. She was a hundred years old, and though she was content with her life, she longed for a life's companion to spend the rest of her years with.

Most of the male vampires she knew just weren't interested—not that she had any interest in any of them either, but it did limit her possibilities. Getting involved with a human wasn't really viable—not because she had any prejudices toward them, but because she didn't want to love someone who would only live for such a short time. Unlike what books and movies portrayed, you couldn't make someone into a vampire. They either were one or they weren't. Vampires were just a different species. Half-breeds, those children born of a union between a vampire and a human, did exist. Not many half-breed vampires survived, but those that did were incredibly strong. They weren't immortal, but they could live for hundreds of years.

Sunshine stared at the moon, imprinting the glowing orb on her brain so that when she closed her eyes she could still see it. She dreamed of a man sometimes, a man who loved her for what she was, wanted her in spite of her odd ways...

~ ~ ~ ~ ~

He slid onto the bench behind her, his arms wrapping around her waist. She could feel the heat of his body as he pulled her back against him. She released her hold on her legs, letting her feet touch the ground again as she leaned back, wanting to get closer to him. "What are you doing out here alone?" His low, gruff tone sent a shiver running down her spine.

"Waiting for you." Her voice was husky, almost unrecognizable.

His laugh, soft and sexy, made her womb clench with need. His breath was a whisper on the nape of her neck as he nuzzled closer to her ear. "Hmm," he murmured as he traced his tongue around the sensitive shell. "I'm glad."

His hands slid up from her waist, stopping just below her breasts. They felt heavy and aching, craving his touch. Her nipples were puckered tight, pressing against the thin cotton of her top. "Touch me." She placed her hands over his and slid them higher, until they covered her breasts completely.

He laughed again. "So eager. So willing." His thumbs traced the hard nubs before pinching them gently between his thumb and forefinger. "Is your pussy hot and wet, my love?"

Her core felt swollen, pulsing with a savage rhythm only he could sate. At his words, she could feel cream, hot and thick, sliding from within her, softening her sex and preparing her body to take his. "Yes." She felt no compulsion to protect herself from this man. Somehow she knew that he could quench the fires that burned within her, appease the loneliness buried deep in her heart.

His hands slipped from her body and she cried out, not wanting to lose that precious contact with him. But they weren't gone for long. He grabbed the tail of her top and yanked it over her head, tossing it to the ground. He shifted her suddenly, lowering her so that she was lying back on the stone bench. She squinted upward but for some reason couldn't make out his features. Worry began to tickle the back of her brain, but she forgot it when he removed her sneakers and socks and then reached for the opening of her jeans.

Quickly, he flicked open the button and pulled down the zipper. The jeans were skimmed down her legs and thrown aside. "You are so beautiful." His tone was almost worshipful as he skimmed his hands up her calves and thighs. "Pale as the moon, vibrant as the sun."

Sunshine felt as if the heat of the sun were flowing through her veins. She'd had several lovers in her life, but she hadn't had one in a long, long time. She'd never found sex all that appealing. But now, for the first time in her life, she understood the need, the craving that drove people to mate. She wanted him with a fierce yearning that came straight from the depths of her soul.

His thumbs traced the crease at the top of her thighs and she moved her legs, restless for more of his touch. Her panties were wet, her core empty. Still, he seemed in no particular hurry. Sliding her hands over her torso, she covered her breasts, trying to ease some of the ache.

He groaned, his hands pushing hers aside, tracing her distended nipples though the covering of flimsy lace. Growling, he grasped the fabric in his hands and tore her bra open, exposing her naked flesh to the night air and his burning eyes. She could see him better now as he leaned over her. His hair was dark and thick, falling over his face as he bent lower. She caught a flash of red-rimmed green eyes and then his mouth was on her breast.

He didn't waste any time, but took her nipple into his mouth and sucked hard. Sunshine cried out as desire flooded her body. Her blood surged through her veins, demanding more. She wanted his body joined to hers, wanted to feel his cock pounding into her as they both climaxed. She craved the taste of his blood, wanted to feed from him even as she wrapped her legs around his waist as he fucked her hard.

While his mouth continued to devour her breasts, traveling from one to the other, he hooked his fingers in the band of her panties and pulled downward. She lifted her behind, helping him. A sheen of sweat covered her body. Her lungs were struggling to pull enough air into them. She'd never wanted anything so much in her life as she wanted him.

He tore his mouth away from her breast and kissed his way down her stomach. Hot, openmouthed kisses that made her insides quiver. "Spread your legs." His voice was low, almost a guttural growl. She felt wild and wanton, pleased that his need was as great as hers. She shifted her legs, making space for him. His shoulders were incredibly broad, opening her thighs wider as he settled between them. "Your scent is sweeter than every flower in this garden."

She could feel heat on her cheeks and realized that she was blushing. She was spread naked on a stone slab waiting for him to pleasure her and yet it was his words that made her blush. "Taste me." She'd meant her words to be seductive, but instead they were a plea.

"With pleasure, my love." His thumbs spread the slick lips of her sex wide, exposing her totally to him. She dug her toes into the cool stone and wrapped her fingers around the edges, desperate for something to hold on to.

He dragged his tongue up one side of her sex and down the other, barely brushing her swollen clitoris at the apex. She shivered and cried out, the sound echoing in the garden. "Delectable," he murmured before he did it again.

The jagged edge of the stone dug into her palms. Her chest rose and fell as she gasped for breath. Her teeth ached and slowly her fangs began to lengthen. "Yes," he crooned as he glanced up at her face. She could see the faint smile teasing the hard edges of his mouth. "I shall feed you and you shall feed me." His two elongated teeth gleamed in the moonlight.

She cried out as he dragged his teeth lightly over her swollen sex. A long, thick finger slid inside her and she arched her hips upward to draw it deeper. He withdrew it and inserted two fingers this time. They stretched her swollen inner muscles in a delicious way, making them spasm. Spreading his fingers wide, he slowly pulled them out. At the same time, he flicked her clitoris with his tongue. Her entire body tightened. She was so close.

Tilting her head back, she closed her eyes and concentrated on every sensation flooding her body. "Look at me," he commanded. She opened her eyes and met the fire in his green-eyed stare. "Watch me." Unable to resist, she lowered her gaze to watch as he thrust his fingers deep into her core and buried his face between her legs.

It was too much, pushing her over the edge. Her body convulsed, every muscle pulsing. Tangling her fingers in his hair, she held him close, not yet ready to lose the feel of his tongue and teeth teasing her clitoris. She cried out as her orgasm washed over her...

~ ~ ~ ~ ~

The ringing of a phone jolted her out of her daydream. Shocked, she could feel the wetness between her legs, feel the clenching of her inner muscles as they continued to contract and relax. Oh God. It had been so real!

The phone rang again.

Her hands shaking, she reached into her back pocket and hauled out her cell phone. "Yes?" She pushed her long hair out of her face and took a deep breath. "Hello."

"Sunshine?" She recognized her brother's voice on the other end and straightened up immediately, trying to bury the remnants of her sexual release. She knew he couldn't see her, but he was very sensitive to her moods.

"I'm fine, Rainier. You just caught me daydreaming in the garden." *Some daydream.* She shook her head, desperately trying to clear the sensual haze from it.

She could almost hear him pondering her words, weighing them to see if she was telling him the truth. The man was too perceptive for his own good. "Did you want anything in particular?" Distraction was her only course.

"I wanted to make sure you didn't forget the party at the Kasmarek estate tonight." Sunshine muttered a pithy reply beneath her breath, but her brother heard her and laughed. "I know you don't want to go." His tone sobered. "I wouldn't ask you to go if it weren't imperative. But Rusnak is too important for our family not to be represented."

"I know." Rainier gave her so much and asked for so little in return. "I'll go for an hour and represent our family well."

"You always do." His words were filled with pride. Her brother was the only person, other than their mother and her two friends, who made her feel as if she were indeed special — or at least normal.

"I have to hang up now if I'm going to be ready in time." She glanced at her watch and winced. She only had a half-hour before she had to leave. Thank heavens she'd already laid out her dress. She needed a quick shower as well, thanks to her phantom lover.

"I'm sending Angelo to pick you up in the limo."

"You didn't have to do that."

Rainier laughed. "I figured it was the only way to ensure you didn't detour at the last second. Besides, it'll make it easier for you to make a quick getaway." She could hear voices in the background and Rainier's attention was momentarily pulled from her. "I've got to go. I've got to get ready for a meeting."

"Take care."

"You too." Then he was gone. Sunshine closed her cell phone and took one last glance around her garden. Her sense of peace was shattered. Obviously she'd been too long without a lover if she was having daydreams that real. Hurrying into the house, she left the garden behind her. Right now, she had a party to go to.

Chapter Two

🔊

Silvestru Rusnak gazed around the opulent room filled with vampires who were here specifically to pay homage to his family. He was utterly bored. Conversations flowed around him, and with the innate skill honed by hundreds of years of practice, he followed most of them, filtering out the inane but always alert to the possibility of picking up some tidbit of information that might be useful to himself or his family. They hadn't ruled the European Council for hundreds of years by being stupid or lax.

"I don't know why she came." He ignored the condescending tone of the female voice not far from his left, allowing his hearing to drift onward.

"I suppose someone in her family had to show." Her female companion was just as spiteful. Silvestru felt a twinge of pity for whomever they were currently tearing to shreds with their words. Beautiful and polished, the two female vampires exuded an underlying malice.

He decided he'd better try to circulate. After all, this party was in his honor. He cut through the room like a shark amongst minnows. Some of the older vampires tried to catch his attention while others just tried to stay out of his way. He hid his impatience with the whole event beneath a bland façade. He knew how to play politics, but that didn't mean he enjoyed it.

Perhaps when he was younger, he'd found some pleasure in the posturing and the jockeying for power that went on between families. But now that he was older and wiser, he disdained it even as he saw the necessity. They were a small, select community and to ensure their continuation, a certain control had to be maintained. It wouldn't do for the human population to discover their existence.

He didn't know how his father did it—how he managed to maintain interest in ruling the Council century after century. His father always credited his mother, telling his sons that there was nothing like having the right woman by his side to share the burdens of the position, to put everything else in perspective. He thought his father might be right, but he'd never come across a female of his race that he'd wanted to be tied to for eternity.

His grandfather had retired about four hundred years ago and now spent all his time enjoying his hobbies as well as meddling in his children's and grandchildren's lives. Silvestru adored his grandfather and, as a child, had loved listening to his stories. His grandfather had watched the pyramids spring up across the deserts of Egypt. His father had walked the earth the same time as Christ. He, himself, had been around for the great crusades that had flooded into the holy lands centuries ago. Silvestru was one thousand years old and his mother despaired of his ever finding a mate. Thankfully, he had a brother only a few hundred years younger than himself. She hounded Mathias as much as she did him.

"Do you think the European Council will support the latest venture proposed by the American Council?" Braden Kasmarek, the eldest son of his host, had ventured up beside him, crystal goblet in hand.

Silvestru shrugged. "Who can say?" He wasn't about to give any of his thoughts away this soon. Not until he'd seen the full proposal and talked with his father about it. "The financial aspects look acceptable. It will be the chance of unnecessarily exposing ourselves that will concern the Council the most." The Americans wanted to open a chain of hotels and casinos that catered to the rich and famous. While he was not opposed to the idea in principle, did the world really need another playground for the wealthy?

Braden sipped his wine and studied him. Silvestru kept the bland expression on his face. "Don't give much away, do you?"

Silvestru shrugged. "You give me too much credit, my friend. I am simply waiting until I hear all the facts."

Braden snorted. "I'm sure my father will believe that, but I don't. I think your mind is already made up."

"What do you think of the proposal?" Silvestru turned the question back on the other man. He kept his posture relaxed, one hand loose by his side, the other casually tucked in his pocket.

He shrugged. "Doesn't matter what I think. Not yet." With that cryptic statement, he walked away. There would be problems there in the future. Silvestru made a mental note to mention it to his father. Obviously there was trouble among the ranks of the Kasmarek family.

He whiled away another half-hour watching as couples took to the dance floor, their bodies swaying provocatively to the heavy pulse of the music. Several females tried everything short of throwing themselves at him to get his attention. He ignored them all.

The hands of the clock moved slowly. All Silvestru wanted was to get five minutes of peace. It had been months since he'd had a day to himself. Council business had all but taken over his life. He'd promised himself some time off after this trip was over.

Working his way around the room, he slid silently out onto the balcony. The night was warm, the air redolent with the perfume from the roses that climbed a nearby trellis. The garden, like the home, was cultivated to present an image of grandeur and wealth. Still, he was alone. Or so he thought.

A faint sound had him turning toward a shadowy corner of the balcony. He all but stopped breathing, unable to believe such a vision of beauty stood before him. It was as if there was a halo of sunlight around her. Intellectually he knew it was the

191

glow of the moon shining on her pale hair, but still he couldn't shake the feeling that she might disappear if he blinked.

She was standing with her hands braced on the edge of the iron railing that ran around the balcony. Her blonde hair was piled on her head in an intricate knot and secured with some kind of fancy pin, leaving her nape bare. It gave her an appearance of vulnerability that had the predator in him growling to life.

His fingers itched to pluck out the pin to see just how long her hair was. He longed to touch her flesh to see if it was as silky as it appeared. She was wearing a dress that hugged her curves. The material was soft, probably velvet, and the color was a light sky blue. He'd seen pictures of the sky that color and, combined with her hair, it gave her the appearance of a summer day. Her fingers dug into the metal so hard he knew it had to hurt them. She was obviously upset about something.

He strolled closer, not wanting to do anything to alarm her or frighten her away. As if she sensed him, her head swung toward him. Her eyes were luminous with unshed tears, making him unaccountably angry. He wanted to find out who or what had upset her and make everything all right.

He stopped in his tracks, unable to believe his own thoughts. She was nothing to him. A complete stranger. Yet, deep inside a voice was telling him to claim her. She was his. She just didn't know it yet.

"I'm sorry." Her voice was low and husky. "I didn't know anyone was out here." His entire body clenched with need. His cock began to swell. He hadn't lost control over his body in centuries. Intrigued, he moved closer.

She made as if to leave, but he stopped her by laying his hand on her arm. Her skin was as soft as it looked. He stroked one finger up and down her warm flesh, pleased when goose bumps rose beneath his touch. "It is my fault." He slid his hand down her arm and gripped her fingers gently in his. Raising her hand slightly, he bent his head, placing a light kiss on her knuckles. "You were here first. It is I who must beg your forgiveness."

She tugged on her hand and he reluctantly released it. "You must be with the Rusnak contingent from Romania." Up close, she was even lovelier. Her eyes were the same color as her dress and possessed an innocence he rarely saw anymore. When she blinked, her long, pale lashes fanned out across her cheeks, which were tinged with a faint pink blush. Her lips turned up at the corners. They were rosy and full and he longed to taste them. "You are forgiven. If you will excuse me." She tried to go around him, but he stepped in front of her, blocking her path.

"Please. Stay and talk with me a moment." He motioned toward inside. "I think that you do not like the party any more than I do."

She smiled and Silvestru felt as if he was seeing the sun for the first time in his life. His heart clenched, his cock pulsed with need as it pressed again the zipper of his pants and his teeth ached to nip at her neck, to drink from her. Her blood would be sweeter than any he had ever tasted, he was sure of it.

"Just for a minute and then I'm leaving."

"You do not plan to stay for the buffet supper at midnight?"

She snorted. "I wouldn't be here at all if my brother wasn't away on business, but someone has to represent the family." She groaned. "I can't believe I said that. Please forgive me. I know you're with the Rusnak family. I've got nothing against them. Don't even know them. It's these parties that I dislike."

"Why?" This mysterious lady had piqued his curiosity. Unlike many of the others, she seemed to have no idea who he was. Her honesty was incredibly refreshing and utterly captivating.

"Why?" she parroted. "Just look at me."

He ran his hot gaze over her body from the top of her lovely head to the tip of her small toes that were showcased in silver-colored sandals. Her toenails were a pale pink. As he moved back up again, he paused at the juncture of her thighs and again on her breasts. She was short and curvy rather than tall and lean, which was the norm among their kind. Her breasts were full and lush and would more than fill his hands.

Her cheeks were stained a rosy pink as she took a step away from him. He smiled, trying to keep his predatory nature under wraps. From the way she took another step away from him, he could tell he hadn't been as successful as he'd hoped. "You are absolutely beautiful. Like a ray of sunshine."

Her head jerked up and she studied his face, as if checking to see if he was mocking her or being sincere. What was wrong with these American males that this exquisite creature did not seem to understand her own allure? All the better for him if they were too stupid to notice the treasure beneath their noses.

"Thank you." There was a finality in her words that told him she was on the verge of leaving again. He could not allow that to happen.

Strains of music drifted out onto the balcony from the room within. He held out his hand to her. "Dance with me. Please," he added. "Take pity on me and don't make me go back inside just yet."

She laughed and seemed to relax. "Somehow I don't think you lack for dance partners."

"But none of them interest me the way you do."

Shaking her head as if she wasn't sure she was doing the right thing, she slipped her hand into his. Savage pleasure filled him as he pulled her closer. He kept her hand tight in his as he wrapped his other arm around her, bringing her body close. She started when she felt his erection pressing against her stomach, but before she could pull away, he twirled her around, executing several turns that left her breathless.

The top of her head barely came up to his chin, so it was easy for him to hold her close. This is what it must be like to feel the heat of the sun against one's body, he thought as he continued to whirl her around to the soft, sensual sounds of the music.

Sunshine had never felt as alive as she did at this moment. Swirling around the dark balcony in the arms of a handsome stranger was like something out of a dream. She'd never danced with a man before, other than her brother, and this definitely was not the same. Whenever she'd been forced to come to these kinds of gatherings, all the males had avoided her, asking the darker, more exotic females to partner them. She couldn't have danced inside in front of all those who disdained her, but out here, under the light of the moon, it was easy to shift and sway to the music.

And he was aroused. That had shocked her. Never had a male of her kind been so blatantly aroused by her, but there was no mistaking the hard-on poking her in the belly. Maybe it was because of the daydream she'd had earlier this evening. Maybe it was the moonlight and the music, but whatever the reason, she wanted him too.

Like the daydream, this was a moment out of time, a chance to experience something special. She knew that this man wanted more from her than just a dance. If she allowed it to happen, he would lead her down into the garden and make love to her.

No. They would have sex together. There was no love because they didn't really know each other. Furthermore, she wanted to keep it that way. She knew he was from Europe, so chances were she might not see him again for years after tonight, if ever again. She kept to herself and rarely went to these celebrations anyway. He'd find out soon enough what the people inside thought of her. There was always someone ready to gossip about her. But by then it would be too late — she'd have had her one magical night with him. It would be a wonderful memory to tuck away and pull out on nights when she was lonely. His face would be the one her fantasy lover would wear.

His hand shifted lower, massaging her behind, pressing her closer. His erection, long and thick, pressed against her stomach. Her breasts ached, so she rubbed them against him. She wished that his suit jacket and shirt were gone so that she could see and feel the hard planes of his chest. He groaned and pressed her even closer. Cream seeped from her core. She felt empty. Needy.

He released her hand and placed a finger under her chin, tipping it upward. Her eyes fluttered closed as his mouth moved closer to hers. His lips skimmed over hers ever-so gently. She wanted more and went up on her tiptoes, threading her free hand through his hair. Soft and midnight black, it flowed through her fingers, coming to rest back on his shoulders. She dug her fingers into the fabric of his suit as she tried to steady herself. He pulled away and stared at her for a brief second before swooping back down and claiming her mouth as his.

This was what she'd wanted. Heat and desire melding into one as his tongue thrust into her mouth. She parted her lips and tilted her head to one side, wanting to get closer to him. He tasted faintly of wine, spicy yet sweet. But underlying it all was the hot taste of male.

He hooked his arm beneath one of her thighs and pulled it up around his waist. The movement brought her pelvis in tighter contact with his. She moaned, grinding her sex against his erection.

This wasn't like her at all. It was if she'd been possessed by some moon madness. Her blood pumped wildly though her veins and her heart sang with joy. This was what she'd been missing—this untamed sense of desire, this unquenchable need that only he could slake. One night. She deserved to have this, to take what she wanted, to have what she'd only dreamed about.

It was here for the taking and she wanted it.

He pulled his lips from hers and she cried out at the loss. "Not here," he murmured. "Come." Releasing her, he wrapped his long fingers around her wrist and tugged her behind him.

She hurried, trying to keep up with him as he all but dragged her down the balcony steps to the garden below. When she stumbled, he swooped her up into his arms, barely breaking his stride. He muttered an apology as he strode toward the intricate maze in the middle of the garden. Clasping her arms around his neck, she hung on tight as the tall shrubs swallowed them up and the sounds of the party faded away.

Chapter Three

ဆ

Silvestru admonished himself to slow down even as he picked up speed. He'd had women before—everything from the most practiced courtesans from the pleasure palaces of the east to the most innocent of maidens ensconced in a medieval castle, and every other class and type of female in between. But never in his one thousand years had such a craving come upon him as he had for this woman in his arms. She was a song in his heart, a fever in his brain, as necessary to him as the blood he had to consume to survive.

He wished he could read her mind, know what she was thinking at this moment. But vampires had strong shields that guarded their thoughts from others. Only after they shared blood could they read each other's thoughts, and not always then. But Silvestru was certain he'd be able to know what was in her mind after he'd taken her blood. He was stronger than most, able to push past barriers that would keep others out.

Still, he would never take what she would not willingly give.

"What are you thinking?" He entered the maze, striding confidently through the twisting, winding path.

She sighed and her arms tightened around his neck. "How perfect this night is. A time out of time."

"What is your name?" He wanted to know. Needed to know.

Her small hand came up to cover his mouth. "No names. There is only now."

Every part of him shouted his denial. She was mistaken if she thought he'd let her escape him. But he had not risen to a place of power within the vampire ranks without knowing when to take a step back. He would wait for his opportunity. At this moment, he had the most fascinating and delectable woman he'd ever met in his arms and she wanted him. He planned on making the most of the situation.

He snaked his tongue out and licked the fingers that were still covering his mouth. Her hand jerked away and she laughed. She closed her fingers into a fist as if capturing his touch. He smiled at her. "Since you will not tell me your name, I will call you Sunshine." He finally broke through to the center of the labyrinth, which was little more than a grassy square. There was no bench or seating of any kind. Damn! He'd have to make do.

She stiffened in his arms as set her down beside him. "Why did you choose that name?"

He reached behind her and plucked the jeweled pin holding her hair in its elaborate twist, sucking in a breath as the mass of blonde hair cascaded all the way to her hips. "That is why." His voice was husky as he slipped the pin into his coat pocket. "You are like a ray of sunshine in the darkness that is our world."

"What should I call you?"

He wanted to tell her his name, wanted to hear her call it as she cried out in ecstasy, but he didn't know if she'd recognize it or not and he was loath to break the easy companionship of the moment. He gave her a wicked grin. "You may call me 'my prince' or 'my love'. I will answer to either." She laughed, even though he was deadly serious. He was a prince in his homeland and he longed to make her his princess.

The thought stopped him cold. Was she the one he'd been searching for? Only time would tell. For now his throbbing cock was insisting he get down to the business of pleasure. Slipping out of his jacket, he hung it over one of the thick branches that surrounded them.

Sunshine had averted her gaze, twisting her fingers in the material of her dress. He framed her face in his hands, tilting it upward. "There is no need to be nervous. I will stop if you do not wish this." His body cried out in denial, demanding he toss her to the ground, mount her and claim her as his. He felt more like a barbarian warlord than a sophisticated modern man. In many ways the first was his true self, the second a façade he wore when he faced the world. Still, he would not do anything she did not wish.

"No." His heart all but stopped as he took a step backward. He swore inwardly at himself, damning his latent sense of chivalry. "No," she whispered again as she stepped closer to him. "I want you to touch me." Her nimble fingers slipped up his chest and quickly began to slip the buttons free from their holes. "I want to touch you."

It was one of the hardest things he'd ever done to just stand there and let her remove his shirt. She had some difficulty with the buttons at the cuffs, but she persevered. She looked absolutely adorable, her tongue caught between her teeth as she concentrated on freeing him. When the last button was undone, he shrugged out of his shirt, letting it fall to the ground.

"My turn," he murmured and her head jerked up. Her eyes were impossibly blue. He could spend all night just staring into them. His hands went around to the nape of her neck and he caught the tab of her zipper, slowly sliding it down her back. His fingers grazed over the supple flesh as he exposed it. She was so soft, so very lovely.

She also wasn't wearing a bra. Every cell in his body was on alert. His blood pounded though his veins, his cock throbbed and his balls felt incredibly heavy as they hung down between his legs. His teeth ached, demanding he taste her.

He slipped his hands inside the material at her waist and he gripped her lush ass, pulling her close and rubbing her hot pussy against his straining erection. He groaned, unable to suppress his growing need for her.

Wanting more, he pushed his hands beneath the lace of her panties, teasing the dark cleft between the mounds of her bottom. She sucked in a breath and then moaned. He stroked his finger over the puckered opening of her ass before pushing further. Her sex was hot and damp and it was all for him.

With a growl of need, he removed his hands, grabbed her dress and peeled it down her arms. The only reason he didn't tear it from her body was because some semblance of sanity whispered that she'd need to have some clothing to wear home. When the fabric bunched around her waist, she gave her hips a shimmy and it fell to the ground to pool at her feet.

"Beautiful." He'd been right. Her breasts were high and firm and generous enough to fill his hands. He cupped both mounds with his palms and stroked his thumbs over her puckered rosy-beige nipples. He was thankful for his perfect night vision, which allowed him to see every exquisite inch of her body.

She was so different from other vampire females—shorter and curvier with long, light hair. He could spend years—no, decades—just stroking her soft flesh, discovering all her secret fantasies and fulfilling every one of them.

She moaned, pushing her breasts more firmly into his hands. He growled and took a step back. "Take off your panties."

He almost came in his pants when she smiled at him, hooked her fingers through the lace band of her panties and pushed them down her legs. When they fell to the ground, she stepped away from her clothing and kicked off her sandals. Totally naked, she resembled a picture of a pagan goddess he'd seen centuries ago.

"Like what you see?" Her voice was sultry. Inviting.

He knew his eyes were tinged with red, could feel the bloodlust rising within him. He struggled to control it. He wanted to fuck her first. "Show me. Spread your thighs and show me your pussy." His voice was little more than a guttural snarl. The suave, sophisticated man was gone. In his place was the ancient warrior.

She was his.

Sunshine knew she should be afraid. The man before her was a commanding presence, and not just physically. It rolled off him in waves, demanding she do as he asked. Standing naked before him, she felt more powerful than she ever had in her entire life. She felt sexy and erotic. She wanted to tease him and entice him until he lost all remnants of control.

Licking her lips, she dropped her hands between her legs and stroked her inner thighs as she parted them. She could see his green eyes glittering with desire and it pushed her own need higher to know that he wanted her so badly. She slid her fingers over the damp, slick folds of her sex and parted them, knowing he could see every pink inch of her in the dark.

He growled as he dropped to his knees in front of her. His long hair tickled her thighs as he dipped his head between her legs and licked. His tongue was slightly rough but incredibly thorough as he stroked up one side and then down the other, leaving no part of her labia untouched. She could feel the sweat on her body in spite of the cool evening air. Her toes curled into the grass and her thighs quivered.

He was so like her phantom lover—dark and dangerous, nameless. She longed to know his name and had to bite her lip to keep from asking. If she knew his name then he would be entitled to know hers.

She ceased to think and worry when he caught her swollen clitoris gently between his teeth, stroking his tongue over the tight bundle of nerves. Sunshine cried out, her hips jerking forward.

He stroked up her legs and slipped one hand between them, pushing two long fingers inside her. The pressure was delicious as he stretched her swollen muscles. His other hand massaged her behind before sliding down the deep cleft. He coated his finger in her cream before brushing it over the tight opening to her bottom. No man had ever touched her there before, but it was incredibly arousing.

Forgetting everything except the man kneeling in front of her and the sensations he was kindling in her body, she gave herself over to the moment. With his fingers stroking in and out of her pussy and his tongue teasing her clit, she thought she might explode at any second.

When he inserted the tip of his finger into her ass, she knew she wouldn't last much longer. The tight band of muscles resisted at first, but he was persistent, pushing deeper. She sucked in her breath, squeezing the muscles of her behind tight. It hurt, yet it was pleasurable. The two conflicting sensations made her head spin.

"Relax, my love. You can take even more of me." His thumb continued to stimulate her clitoris as his fingers slid easily in and out of her core.

"I can't," she groaned even as she forced herself to relax. His finger slipped deeper and she cried out. She was panting hard now, her chest rising and falling quickly. She couldn't breathe, she couldn't think. All she could do was feel.

"You can." He pulled his finger almost out of her behind before pushing it deep again. Sunshine's entire body shook, every muscle coiled tight in anticipation. "That's it," he crooned. "Come for me."

She tried to resist, tried to hold out longer, but it was no use. Her vaginal muscles clenched hard and then began to spasm. Pleasure flooded her body. She cried out and clutched his shoulders, needing something to hold on to. He didn't stop touching her, but continued stroking until her legs finally crumpled beneath her. He caught her easily, lowering her to the cool, dew-laden grass. She lay there, sucking in breaths, her body shaking as tiny aftershocks of pleasure shot through her.

After a few moments, she managed to push her hair out of her eyes and open them. He knelt alongside her, his face a hard mask of desire, his eyes glittering, fangs bared. He hadn't come. As she watched, his hands went to the opening of his pants, quickly undoing them. When he pushed the fabric and his underwear aside, his cock sprang forward, hard and thick and ready. The bulbous head was red and moist and the blue vein running down the side was pulsing with need. As she watched, a bead of liquid seeped from the tip. She licked her lips, longing to taste him.

Sunshine started to sit up, reaching for him, but he grabbed her and flipped her over onto her stomach. "Not this time," he growled. "I won't last ten seconds if you touch me."

Pride filled her. She wanted him to lose control just as she had. Coming up onto her hands and knees, she wiggled her behind seductively. "What are you waiting for?" she all but purred.

His hands were firm yet gentle on her hips as he pulled her back toward him. He spread his thighs wide, pushing hers farther apart. The head of his cock stroked over her damp, swollen lips, teasing her. "You want me, don't you?"

"Yes!" she cried. There was no thought of holding anything back from this man.

The head of his cock slid just inside her core. She tried to push back, but he held her hips in a firm grip. He'd penetrate her only when he was ready. She arched her head back, gasping for air again. Unbelievably, she was on the verge of coming again. This time she wanted more. Her fangs lengthened as another need pulsed through her body. This time she wanted his blood.

"Yes, my love," he whispered as if he could read her mind. Then he pushed forward suddenly, seating himself to the hilt in one quick thrust.

She sucked in a breath. Her inner muscles were still swollen and sensitive from her orgasm and he was so big. But it felt amazingly good. She closed her eyes, absorbing every sensation. The grass was damp on her knees and her hands — her long hair pooled on the ground around her face. Every nerve ending in her body seemed alive in anticipation, and she could feel every inch of his cock inside her pussy. It was incredible.

He shifted his hands, sliding them up to cover her breasts. Her nipples stabbed the center of his palms as he squeezed and massaged the heavy mounds. She tipped her head downward so she could watch. The sight of his large hands on her breasts made her vaginal muscles clench tight, almost sending her spiraling over the edge.

Slowly, he pulled back until just the head of his cock was still inside her. Flexing his hips, he slammed forward. Tilting her head back, she cried out, "More!" She wanted him harder, deeper.

His hips picked up speed as he hammered into her. If he hadn't been holding on to her so tight, she would have collapsed onto the ground. She tried to push back every time he stroked forward, but it was impossible to keep up with the pounding pace he set. Her body tightened again. She could feel her orgasm rising from the very tips of her toes and spreading throughout her body. He pushed deep one final time. His body began to jerk and she could feel his hot cum flooding her core. It pushed her over the edge, sending her rocketing to the stars. Her body shook as she came. Her inner muscles clamped down hard on his cock, milking every last drop from him.

Her head fell forward as she tried to catch her breath. But he wasn't finished. With his cock still buried deep inside her, he caught her long hair in one hand, pulling on it until she tilted her head back. His breath was hot on her nape and her inner muscles spasmed in anticipation. He groaned even as she felt the tip of his fangs slide through her flesh. He locked onto the back of her neck and began to suck.

Sunshine started to orgasm again. Bolts of lightning shot through her body. She shivered, she shook and she cried out. The feeling of him sucking on her neck, feeding from her while he was still buried deep inside her was as intimate as it was arousing. She'd never experienced anything like it in her life.

It scared her and she began to fight him. He tightened his grip on her, but withdrew his fangs. His tongue slid over her nape, sending shivers down her spine as he closed the small wounds. He slid his softening cock from her and she had to bite her lip to keep from crying out at the loss.

Lifting her easily, he settled her in his lap, pulling her face close to his neck. "Drink," he commanded. She couldn't deny him—didn't want to. Opening her mouth, she sank her fangs into him. Blood, sweet and potent, filled her mouth. She swallowed as she tugged him closer, curling her body around him. More! She'd never tasted anything so fine. She drank until he pulled her away. She wanted to protest, but was shamed that she'd taken so much. Swiping her tongue over the marks to close them, she buried her head against his chest, not wanting to face him.

But he wouldn't let her hide from him. He moved his arm so that her head fell back and she was staring up at him. The reddish glow was fading from his eyes, and as she watched, he licked the last remnant of her blood from his lips and his fangs receded. She shuddered at the sight, need starting to thrum through her body again.

"That was incredible, my love." He sifted his fingers through her hair. "Tell me your name?" There was a hint of command, of compulsion, beneath his request. She withdrew immediately, resisting.

"We agreed, no names." She tried to climb out of his lap, but he tightened his hold on her. It was like being trapped by velvet bars. He wasn't hurting her, but there was no way for her to escape.

He opened his mouth to speak, but closed it quickly, his head canting to one side. He swore under his breath and shifted until they were in the shadows of the maze, hidden behind a high shrub. Reaching out, he grabbed her clothing and his shirt, pulling it behind them. Sunshine could sense raw power swirling around them and realized he was erecting a mental shield to keep them from being detected.

"I know he went outside." The female's voice was loud, her irritation obvious. "I saw *her* go out on the balcony too."

"I'm sure it was nothing but a coincidence," a male voice assured her. Sunshine thought she recognized it as Braden Kasmarek.

The woman snorted. "I'm not worried about that freak, but I would like to find Silvestru Rusnak." She gave a sultry laugh. "I've decided to let him seduce me."

Shame filled Sunshine as the other woman's mocking words penetrated her worry about being discovered in such a compromising position. *Freak!* For a few moments, she'd forgotten what others thought of her.

"How kind of you, Celestine, but he might have other ideas." The male voice held a hint of mockery.

"Your father asked me to entertain our exalted guest. Help him to maybe see his way toward supporting our cause with the European Council." Celestine's voice quavered with excitement. "I can't wait to fuck him."

"I'm sure," Braden agreed. "But he's obviously not here. Perhaps we missed him and he's back at the house."

"You're probably right. There's nothing out here."

As the voices faded into the distance, Sunshine relaxed and more of what the unexpected guests had said seeped into her muddled brain. "You're Rusnak." She jumped from his lap, grabbed her dress and yanked it over her head.

Sighing, he stood and gave her a short bow. "Silvestru Rusnak at your service."

Reaching behind her, she pulled up the zipper as far as she could, then she reached over her shoulder and dragged it up the rest of the way. Her hair was a mess and she couldn't remember what had happened to her hairpin. She grabbed her sandals and shoved her feet into them.

While she'd been dressing, Silvestru had pulled on his shirt and buttoned it. As she turned to face him, he plucked his jacket off the branch that it hung from and slipped it on. One quick drag of his fingers through his hair and he looked no different than when he'd stepped outside. She, on the other hand, looked like a woman who'd been tumbled in the garden. Her hair was loose, her dress was wrinkled and she had grass stains on her hands and probably her knees as well. And she couldn't find her panties.

God, she was so embarrassed. He was the guest of honor and she'd all but told him she didn't want to be here. Why had he singled her out? Had the others mentioned her to him? Was this some kind of cruel joke? She didn't think so, but it wouldn't be the first time a male had tried to seduce her so that he could tell his friends he'd had sex with the freak. But it was the first time one of them had succeeded.

She had to leave. Needed to go home where she felt safe and secure. Even though she felt sure he'd been sincere in his wants, she didn't belong here and she definitely didn't belong here with him. She thought back to what he'd said she could call him earlier. "My prince," she muttered.

Silvestru inclined his head in acknowledgement. "I did not lie." His words were clipped, his expression one of annoyance. "I am a prince in my country."

She ignored him and began to walk. She had to find her way out of the maze. To hell with her underwear—she wasn't staying at this party. Silvestru joined her, saying nothing as he gripped her arm and guided her out of the labyrinth. She stopped at the bottom of the stairs, digging in her heels when he tried to keep her moving.

"We can't go in there together. Everyone will know."

"I don't care." He looked very imperious, the epitome of the arrogant male.

"Well, I care. It won't do your reputation any harm, but it certainly won't help mine."

He scowled but slowly released her arm. "What do you suggest?"

"You go in first and I'll follow in about five minutes."

He hesitated. "You will have supper with me?"

She nodded even as she knew she was lying. He stared at her for the longest time and she began to get nervous. She wouldn't put it past him to just drag her back inside behind him. Finally he nodded. "I will be waiting for you." He dropped a hard, possessive kiss on her lips, turned and stalked up the stairs.

She touched her fingers to her lips as if she could capture his kiss forever. She watched until he disappeared from sight and then she turned and fled toward the parking lot, thankful that Angelo was waiting there for her.

Chapter Four

∞

Sunshine sat on the stone bench in her garden, staring up at the moon. It was full tonight. Her thoughts kept returning to last night in the Kasmareks' garden. She still could hardly believe she'd been so uninhibited with a complete stranger. Except that Silvestru Rusnak hadn't seemed like a stranger, even before she'd known his name.

She leaned her hands back on the bench, letting her hair flow down behind her as she closed her eyes, reliving every single moment of the night before. She'd been doing it ever since she'd run from Silvestru and the party. Not only had she not gotten any work done last night, but she hadn't slept at all today either.

She sighed and rubbed her hand over her face as she sat forward. There was no going back to change what had happened. What was done was done. And she wouldn't change a moment of it for anything. Okay, maybe she'd have stopped it before she'd had to overhear the conversation between Celestine and Braden, but other than that...

Her thoughts trailed off as she heard a noise. She turned, knowing that someone had invaded the peace of her garden. Her heartbeat picked up, and even before she saw him, she knew it was him.

Silvestru.

He stood like a statue carved from the finest stone as he watched her. "How long have you been there?"

"Not long." He strolled toward her, his hands in his pockets. He looked different—but no less intimidating—tonight, dressed casually in jeans and an expensive linen shirt. "Your name is truly Sunshine?"

She nodded. "My mother named me." Somehow she'd known he'd come. Had been expecting him.

"It suits you." He stopped in front of her. "You did not return last night." There was the slightest tinge of hurt beneath his bland statement.

"I could not." How could she make him understand that being amongst that crowd was an ordeal for her even when she was at her best?

He nodded. "I understand." His entire body tightened and she could feel the anger emanating from him. "There were many people who were more than willing to tell me about the woman with the sunshine hair."

She tilted her chin up. They might make her feel uncomfortable, but she was not ashamed of who she was. "Then you know what they all think of me."

"They are idiots." His quiet-spoken anger was scarier than if he'd roared. Sunshine clasped her hands in her lap, not quite knowing what to do or say next.

"Well, yes. I think that most of them are." She nodded. "Is there anything else you wanted?" She still wasn't sure why he was here. Was he looking for a repeat of last night? If so, he was mistaken. Last night was a one-time deal. Moon madness.

"What do I want?" He withdrew his hands from his pockets and moved closer to her until their feet were touching. "My father once told me that I would know I'd found my proper mate when I met a woman who fascinated me on every level—physically, mentally and emotionally. A woman who I could spend time with and study for centuries and still be surprised. I'd never met such a woman until last night."

She shifted to the side and stood, not willing to let him tower over her any longer. "What are you saying?" Butterflies fluttered in her stomach. Surely he wasn't saying what she thought he was. That was crazy. Wasn't it? Her mind said *yes*, but her heart cried *no*!

He lifted his hands, framing her face. "I'm saying that I found such a woman in a garden last night when I least expected to find her." He grinned and she found it utterly boyish and endearing. "I all but announced that I was claiming you at the party last night."

"You didn't?" She groaned.

He shrugged, totally unconcerned. "Be glad that was all I did. I wanted to cut short the existence of some of them." His gaze turned lethal. "Many of them were singing a different song about you by the time I left."

"Oh my God." She buried her face in her hands. "They all know that we had sex in the garden last night, don't they?"

She peeked through her fingers and caught Silvestru's predatory smile. "They know that you are mine and that I plan to keep you."

"What are you saying?"

He traced his finger down her cheek. "You are mine. Now and forever. Will you be my mate?"

Sunshine swallowed hard. "This is so sudden. You know nothing about me. I know nothing about you. I don't want to leave my home." There were so many seemingly insurmountable problems.

"You are close only to your brother, Rainier, and keep to yourself. You are a photographer by profession and use most of your wealth to help others. You have several close female friends, including a human. I find you fascinating, admirable and incredibly sexy."

He continued, addressing her next concern. "I am the firstborn son in my family. I am close to my grandfather, my parents and my younger brother. I work hard and do not indulge in the excess that you also seem to disdain in many of our kind. But more than that, I am a man who sees your true worth and will cherish you for the rest of your life."

Silvestru smiled at her as he stroked his finger down her throat. She knew he could feel the pulse pounding there. "I know you love your home. We shall live here most of the year and travel to Europe occasionally. My family is dying to meet you and you will love Romania. I will be staying here as an ambassador of sorts — more of a liaison between the old country and the new."

"What do you mean your family wants to meet me?" Sunshine's head was spinning with how quickly he countered her arguments. How had he found out so much about her?

As if he'd read her mind, he offered her a soft smile. "I spent the rest of last night and a good part of today finding out everything about you. It is easy when you have the resources that I do at your disposal. I also called my family and told them everything."

He leaned down and nuzzled his nose against hers. She inhaled his unique scent and fought the urge to jump on him. Just his presence had her breasts aching and her sex becoming damp and slick.

"I talked to your brother."

"You what?" Sunshine pulled away, put her hands on her hips and glared at him. Silvestru tried to hide a grin, but he wasn't quite successful. That made her even madder. "You had no right."

His grin disappeared and he scowled at her. "I have every right. Your father is dead and Rainier is your closest male relative. You might be surprised to find out that he gave me his blessing." Only after several hours of interrogation, but Sunshine didn't need to know that. He'd go through it again in a heartbeat if it cleared his path toward claiming her.

His happiness began to fade. Perhaps she did not feel as he did. "Did last night mean nothing to you?" He reached into his pocket and touched the hairpin that was nestled carefully in the folds of her lace panties. Both were talismans that he'd kept close to him during the long day when he could not venture outside.

Her eyes widened. "Of course it meant something to me. I don't usually sleep with complete strangers." Her face softened and once again he was struck by her ethereal beauty. "It meant something." She tilted her head to look up at the sky, exposing the slender column of her neck. He longed to lick it, to taste her once again. "I'm odd, Silvestru, but I like myself. I'm not likely to change."

"I don't want you to change." He curled his fingers into fists to keep from reaching out to her. He needed her agreement first. "I love you as you are. Join with me. Be my mate for all eternity."

"You love me?" There was wonder and a touch of doubt in her voice.

Unable to keep his distance any longer, he pulled her into his arms and claimed her mouth. She groaned, parting her lips as his tongue slid into the moist cavern. He sucked on her tongue, savoring her unique flavor and reveling in every single moan of pleasure. He pulled away, almost breathless with need. God, he wanted her. "Yes, I love you. My father always told me that I would recognize my true mate, and he was right. I knew from the moment we made love, when I tasted your blood, that you were meant for me."

She gave a cry of pleasure, wrapping her arms around his neck as she pulled his mouth back down to hers. "I felt it too, Silvestru. I love you." He heard her pledge just before she locked her lips with his.

When they broke apart again, he scooped her up into his arms and headed for the house. This time he wanted to take all night to claim her. He wanted her spread across the bed, naked, while he discovered every hill and valley of her body. He wanted to touch her, taste her, feed from her. Then he wanted to fuck her hard. When they were both sweaty and sated, he wanted to begin again, this time making love to her slowly and gently.

"Yes," she whispered, clinging to him. "I want that too and more." Until she spoke, he hadn't realized he'd voiced his desires aloud.

"Tell me you'll be mine for eternity." He wanted a formal joining ceremony with her. In fact, his mother had probably already begun making plans. He shouldered his way in through the back door, kicking it shut behind him. Unerringly, he walked through the dark, carrying her straight to the bedroom.

Sunshine clung to Silvestru's wide shoulders. She no longer doubted that he truly wanted her. There was no other reason for him to say anything about her to his family or the rest of their people at the party last night. Even if someone had found out they'd slept together, no one would have thought anything of it. He was male and he'd claimed an interesting female as a novelty. Everyone would have shrugged and forgotten about it.

He certainly hadn't needed to call her brother. She suspected there was more to that conversation than she'd ever know. Rainier wouldn't have gone easy on him. Still, he wanted her and not just for today, but forever.

The full moon shone in through her bedroom window, illuminating the room. Even though she didn't need the light to see, it made the space look more romantic. It was another detail she would add to the story that she'd tell their children in the centuries to come.

He stood with her still clutched tight in her arms. She could feel the heavy thump of his heart against her cheek. He was still waiting for her answer.

She raised her head and stared at him. In one short night, he'd become the most important person in her world. He was her future. His love for her shone from his eyes. Was evident in every word he spoke.

"Yes. But I have one condition."

"Anything," he vowed.

She smiled at him, licking her lips in anticipation. His arms tightened and she could feel a rumbling growl low in his chest. Last night she'd barely gotten to touch him. "Tonight I get to taste you too."

His eyes widened and then he began to laugh. He tossed her lightly onto the bed and began to tear at his clothing. "Anything, my love." Tossing his shirt aside, he came down on the mattress beside her, hauling her into his arms.

He rolled her beneath him and proceeded to kiss her senseless. She didn't mind. She knew she had eternity to have her way with him.

Also by N.J. Walters

❧

Anastasia's Style

Annabelle Lee

Awakening Desires: Capturing Carly

Awakening Desires: Craving Candy

Awakening Desires: Erin's Fancy

Awakening Desires: Katie's Art of Seduction

Dalakis Passion 1: Harker's Journey

Dalakis Passion 2: Lucian's Delight

Dalakis Passion 3: Stefan's Salvation

Drakon's Treasure

Ellora's Cavemen: Dreams of the Oasis IV *(anthology)*

Ellora's Cavemen: Legendary Tails IV *(anthology)*

Heat Wave

Jessamyn's Christmas Gift

Tapestries: Bakra Bride

Tapestries: Christina's Tapestry

Tapestries: Woven Dreams

Three Swords, One Heart

Unmasking Kelly

About the Author

ဢ

N.J. Walters worked at a bookstore for several years and one day had the idea that she would like to quit her job, sell everything she owned, leave her hometown and write romance novels in a place where no one knew her. And she did. Two years later, she went back to the same bookstore and settled in for another seven years.

Although she was still fairly young, that was when the mid-life crisis set in. Happily married to the love of her life, with his encouragement (more like, "For God's sake, quit the job and just write!") she gave notice at her job on a Friday morning. On Sunday afternoon, she received a tentative acceptance for her first erotic romance novel, *Annabelle Lee*, and life would never be the same.

N.J. has always been a voracious reader of romance novels, and now she spends her days writing novels of her own. Vampires, dragons, time-travelers, seductive handymen and next-door neighbors with smoldering good looks all vie for her attention. And she doesn't mind a bit. It's a tough life, but someone's got to live it.

N.J. welcomes comments from readers. You can find her website and email address on her author bio page at www.ellorascave.com.

Tell Us What You Think

We appreciate hearing reader opinions about our books. You can email us at Comments@EllorasCave.com.

A MAN OF VISION

By Kate Willoughby

Trademarks Acknowledgement

⁓

The author acknowledges the trademarked status and trademark owners of the following wordmarks mentioned in this work of fiction:

Chanel: Chanel, Inc.

Versace: Gianni Versace, S.P.A.

Author Note

I would like to thank Alfredo Croci for his invaluable assistance. The man deserves a medal for putting up with my endless requests for Italian translations.

Chapter One

✂

"If I may be frank," Alessandro Rossi said after lighting his cigarette. "*Signore* Valtieri requires sexual release. Often."

American expatriate Delphine Alexander sipped her wine. "If you're trying to shock me," she said, "it's not working."

The two of them sat at a café on the Rue de Vaugirard, pleasantly removed from the busy Champs Elysées. The late afternoon sun graced the street with golden light.

Delphine had just finished a six-month stint with a Parisian stockbroker who decided that he could no longer keep a mistress now that he was getting married.

How ridiculously un-French of him.

As a result, she discreetly put out the word that she was without a patron. The very next day, Rossi had called with a lucrative proposition from the world-renowned sculptor, Cristoforo Valtieri of Florence, and she immediately scheduled a meeting. She adored Florence. Nestled in Tuscany with its russet rooftops and historic soul, the city called to her like a lover. She could learn a new language, add some Italian pieces to her couture wardrobe and earn a hefty fee if what Rossi said on the phone was to be believed.

"You are a true professional, *Signorina* Alexander," Rossi said, exhaling smoke. "I expected nothing less."

"Then let's talk terms, Mr. Rossi. You mentioned that Valtieri is willing to offer money above my usual fee. How much more, and why? Did you send him a copy of my standard contract?"

"Yes, *Signore* Valtieri agrees to your terms. He was actually shocked at some of the items on your taboo list. He wants only the basic services and has already undergone the tests you require." Rossi pulled out papers that guaranteed Valtieri was free from sexually transmitted disease and laid them on the table. "The reason he offers so much extra is that he wants you on call twenty-four hours a day."

"*What?*" Looking up sharply from the medical forms, she couldn't mask her surprise. "That's unheard of."

"He was adamant. He requires you to live in the villa. You'll have your own rooms, but he needs you to be available at a moment's notice. As I said before, his needs are great."

Delphine reached for her wine and took a controlled sip, even though she wanted a gulp. "That's impossible. That's slavery. I need time to myself."

"He understands that, of course, but he works extremely odd hours and wishes for you to accommodate that. You would start with three months. Then, if both of you desire it, he is willing to extend the contract."

"And the compensation?"

"Thirty thousand a month."

Delphine only just stopped her jaw from dropping open. She'd spent countless hours in the bars of upscale restaurants studying the wealthy patrons and observing how they interacted with one another. She'd scrutinized *femmes fatale* in old movies with an attention to detail that had so far stood her in good stead. As a result, she now had a sizable nest egg in the bank, and because of the advice of a top-notch financial advisor, planned to retire before she was forty—still young enough to pursue whatever caught her fancy, whether it be life on a yacht in Cannes or in a quiet house in Nantucket. How many women could boast such an array of choices? Not many.

"Euros or dollars?" she asked Rossi.

"Euros."

To cover the fact that her hand was shaking, she swirled the wine in her glass. Thirty thousand a month would buy a lot of Versace.

"Twenty-four/seven availability is an outrageous demand. I've never committed to anything that even comes near that."

Rossi inclined his head in agreement. "*Si*, but thirty thousand Euros is more than fair, *signorina*."

Delphine took a deep breath. "I need a day of rest every week. One complete day with no demands."

"I will have to speak to him about that."

"I also want the first month's pay in advance. And the trial period is to be reduced. Three months is too long. I'll try it for one."

"This I will also confirm with him, but I believe he will be amenable."

"One more thing then, and we have a deal."

Though her heart pounded with anxiety over what she was about to do, Delphine flipped her customary braid over her shoulder and regarded Rossi with a cool expression.

"Tell *Signore* Valtieri that I won't accept a penny less than thirty-five a month."

* * * * *

A week later, Delphine arrived at Valtieri's country villa. A brisk afternoon breeze caused the hem of her Chanel dress to flutter around her legs as she viewed her home for the next three weeks. Grand and sprawling, the two-story complex spread atop the Impruneta hills like a reclining monarch. The stone and stucco buildings were a warm golden brown with dark shutters flanking the windows. Acres of olive trees and vineyards surrounded the villa, and she wondered how much property Valtieri owned.

The door of the main building opened and a solidly built older woman appeared, eyeing Delphine like a general would a new recruit. With a raised brow, Delphine returned the stare.

"*Mi chiamo Antonella*," the woman said haughtily. "I am housekeeper."

"A pleasure to meet you," Delphine said.

Antonella just pursed her lips as if she'd eaten something distasteful. Apparently she didn't approve of Delphine and the services she was to render. Or perhaps she was upset that another woman was invading her territory. Whatever the reason, Delphine kept her cool as always as the housekeeper led the way to her rooms.

Despite the fact that the villa appeared to be quite old, it had all the modern conveniences, and her suite of rooms had a breathtaking view of Florence. Temporarily awestruck, she stood at the picture window and drank in the rich vista as if it could nourish her. Amidst the red roofs, she could easily make out the Duomo and the utilitarian gray stone tower of the Uffizi Gallery. In contrast, the Arno River snaked its way through the landscape like a discarded hair ribbon.

On a table near the window she found a vase of fresh flowers, a chocolate bar and a note from her new patron. Inhaling the fragrance from the bouquet, she mentally gave the man points for style and thoughtfulness.

Delphine, welcome to my house. I work all day and night, so we meet tomorrow.

Cristoforo

After unpacking, Delphine explored the compound. The main house fronted a lovely winding avenue at the crest of a hill. Behind the house and back garden stood the warehouse that served as Valtieri's studio, from which sharp rapping could be heard. Intense bursts of banging were interspersed with brief pauses. This pattern of noise continued for hours.

When she sought her bed at eleven, tired from her travels, Valtieri was still working.

Later that night, the bedside lamp clicked on, waking her from a sound sleep. Through the open window, the night breeze brought in the faint aroma of the Tuscan countryside and the soothing sound of crickets. As she blinked to adjust to the brightness, she saw Cristoforo staring down at her like a forbidding gargoyle.

Gaunt and apparently exhausted, he looked quite different from the glamorous pictures she'd seen of him. He had been one of Europe's most eligible bachelors for years. Invariably the photographers captured him with a dashing smile as brilliant as a beacon, but he had fallen off the paparazzi radar in the last year, mysteriously retreating from the public eye.

Tonight he was clad, not in a tuxedo, but in dusty jeans and a t-shirt. Purple shadows under red-rimmed eyes proved the man needed a good night's rest more than sex, and yet behind his obvious fatigue, raw desire lurked.

Delphine reached for the lamp to turn it off, but he grasped her wrist and shook his head. A lock of midnight hair fell in front of his eyes.

"No," he said in heavily accented English. "I want to see you."

"Of course," she said, drawing the sheet away from her naked body. Her job was to please him, and if he wanted the lights on, so be it. She raised her arms above her head, arching her back a little to show her figure to its best advantage.

His gaze was a hot caress. It swept over her face and down to her breasts, lingering there so long that her nipples puckered in anticipation and heat spread through her to throb insistently between her legs. Her eyes were drawn to the bulge in the front of his jeans, and her breath came more quickly when she imagined freeing his cock and curling her fingers around the unyielding shaft, which was odd. Usually the initial encounter with a patron required a good amount of acting from her, but for some reason, she felt extremely attracted to Valtieri.

As he pulled off his shirt, she looked him over, thinking that perhaps his appearance had something to do with it. He had highly defined arms and shoulders—a result, no doubt, of his profession—and his hands possessed an arcane power and beauty. She also noted with pleasure that, unlike her last patron, his taut abdomen held little fat. No, Valtieri was very handsome, but looks alone didn't explain her attraction to him.

Then, naked, he sat on the edge of the bed and caught her gaze. That did it. It was his eyes. His deep-set, dark brown eyes seemed to capture hers, making it impossible to look away until he allowed it. With them he communicated his need so fully that her body thrummed with a primitive insistence. Longing pulsed within her, moistening her sex. As his thumb scraped her cheek, she shuddered, wondering how he kissed. But then he curled his hand around the back of her neck and she didn't have to wonder anymore.

He pulled her close, and as he slid his tongue inside her mouth, she tasted the rich tang of red wine. The heady aroma of sandalwood and cinnamon filled her nostrils.

"Ah, Delphine," he said against her lips, "I need this very much."

His English was rough, but the delicious rhythm with which he spoke more than made up for it. When he said her name, he added another syllable to the end—*Del-phee-nah*.

More urgently now, he kissed her neck, her ear, her shoulder, then bent to take a taut nipple between his lips. His unshaven cheeks abraded her, but she didn't care. Each strong pull of his mouth commanded her body to respond, and respond it did. Her breasts ached, the tips contracting almost painfully. Her swollen sex bloomed, wet and ready to be filled with a hot, hard cock.

Awash with unaccustomed pleasure, Delphine abandoned herself to the moment until he tried to undo her braid. With her hand on his, she stopped him with a brusque shake of her head. This one part of her body she kept private. Everything else could be used by her benefactors as they pleased, but her hair was hers alone.

His brows drew together, but he didn't argue or force the matter. Instead, he urged her down on the mattress, one hand snaking to her mound. When he felt how slick she was, he made a gruff noise of approval. Then, hurriedly positioning himself between her legs, he thrust into her hard. The rush of sensation encompassed her entire body and she arched against him, but he seemed intent on his own pleasure. As if desperate, he pounded into her with long, almost violent strokes, and in a matter of moments, he cried out, grinding his pelvis against hers.

Well accustomed to sex without orgasm, Delphine thought that perhaps this assignment wasn't so different after all.

Cristoforo gasped for breath as the last spasms of pleasure faded. His new American mistress gazed up at him, her cheeks flushed, her lips curved in a smile. With a rough sigh, he withdrew and rolled off to collapse beside her on the bed.

As if posing for a portrait, she lay with the sheets in artful folds around her nudity. She had long hair worn in a plait that she would not allow him to loosen, which was a shame. If he were to paint her, he would need an entire palette of shades just for that hair—crimson, cadmium yellow, copper, sienna. And her eyes were the most unusual shade of blue-green. Like the Aegean when the sun hit it just so, or perhaps a blending of a green meadow meeting a cloudless sky. She truly was as beautiful as God could make a woman.

He heaved a deep sigh. He was so tired. After twelve straight hours of work, he had finally remembered to eat, but before he made it to the kitchen, he also remembered his mistress had arrived that afternoon. Curious and half-aroused at the thought of sex, he went to her room. When he saw her asleep, he had felt a strong surge of lust. The night was warm and she had left the windows open and lay with only a thin sheet covering her. Many months had gone by since he'd had a woman and, gripped with an overriding hunger for her, he had decided to end his celibacy at that moment and not wait until morning. Thankfully, she'd welcomed him with an eagerness that had not appeared to be feigned.

"I am Cristoforo," he said now, belatedly.

"Antonella told me you wouldn't need me tonight," she said in a soothing contralto. She spoke English, not with the usual brash American accent, but with careful pronunciation, perhaps having taken elocution lessons.

"I make a change," he replied.

Dio, he longed to remain in bed with beautiful Delphine all night. He knew she'd been cheated of any pleasure. Their encounter had been entirely one-sided. Would that it could be otherwise. He would have welcomed the chance to perhaps kiss her awake and then make love to her all day, but his lust had been appeased and his wish for companionship had to be set aside. Those lazy days of indulgence with women were over. He had no time for that anymore. His work ruled his life, and time was against him. He could not waste any more of it tonight.

When he forced himself out of bed, she looked at him in surprise. No doubt she expected him to stay at least five minutes.

"Where are you going?" she asked.

"I must work." He had already pulled on his pants.

"But it's four in the morning."

"I am sorry." Sighing heavily, he pulled on his shirt and then brushed his lips across her hand. "*Grazie, zuccherino*," he said.

Minutes later, he was walking across the courtyard to his studio. Needing energy, he devoured a chocolate bar as he went. As he swallowed the last bite, he consciously redirected his attention to his unfinished sculpture before him. He could not afford to lose focus, so, picking up his tools, he located the area he'd been working on earlier and brought mallet to chisel with a resounding blow. *Crack.* Chips flew. *Crack.* Reposition. Again and again his arm came down, and he lost himself in the familiar rhythm of creation. So absorbed was he with his work that he barely noticed Delphine, clothed in a silk dressing gown, slipping into the studio to watch him. He worked tirelessly until just after dawn, when he muttered a request that she wake him after an hour and collapsed on the nearby sofa.

Concerned, Delphine ventured to the kitchen and gathered food and coffee. The man clearly needed more than an hour's rest. He needed a month-long vacation. Yet, to defy him so soon after arriving seemed unwise. Perhaps in time she could convince him to take better care of himself.

When she woke him as requested, he wolfed down the food.

"Delphine," he said between bites, "when I see you in the studio I am very surprised. You no sleep?"

"I wanted to watch you," she replied.

Many considered Valtieri to be the modern-day Michelangelo. His carved panel, *Hancock's Signature*, adorned the White House, and some of the world's most influential people owned his work.

"It is good you here. I want to say some things." He took a gulp of coffee. "I do not want much from you, except you be here when I need you. If you want to go from the house, please ask me. I mostly say yes because I work all of time. Sometimes all day. But when you are here, you wait me to call.

"All things in the house are yours to use. If you want to drive, you take what car you want. All the weeks you find envelope with Euros for you. Go shopping, get face treatments," he said, gesturing with a dusty finger at her cheek. "Spend it how you want. It is not part of fee that we talk about. That amount I put into your...mmm...account at bank."

"Thank you. You're very generous," she said, meaning it.

He downed some more coffee and then stood up. "*Grazie*," he said. "I forget sometimes to eat."

Then, as if he'd used up his word quota for the day, he returned to his work and said nothing more.

Chapter Two
From the personal journal of Delphine Alexander
1 May

ॐ

After almost three weeks, I think Antonella has accepted me — maybe because I'm trying so hard to learn Italian, even if it is at her expense. I follow her around, practicing every day. And I'm improving. She corrects my pronunciation less and less, and once in a while her mouth even twitches in approval.

I also think she likes that I've been able to get Cristoforo to eat more regularly, an accomplishment in and of itself. The man is a workaholic of heroic proportions. He's in his studio day and night with only sporadic breaks. Most of the time he inhales his food. Sometimes he doesn't eat at all, subsisting only on espresso and/or chocolate. He sleeps only a few hours every night, which explains the omnipresent circles under his eyes.

As agreed, I stay on the property in case he wants me. I don't bother wearing underwear because we have sex four, maybe five times a day. He is always quick, always intense, and I don't think it's because of a problem with premature ejaculation. I think he just needs the release and doesn't have the time to spare for anything more, not even my pleasure.

Not that I'm complaining. I'll take thirty-five thousand Euros a month over a paltry orgasm any day. What intelligent woman wouldn't?

Chips of marble flew in all directions as Cristoforo hacked away at the commission from the German embassy, a life-sized statue of Ludwig von Beethoven. He wore protective eyewear, but Delphine could still see the concentration furrowing his forehead and the sheen of sweat on his face.

Wary of the flying fragments, she wandered toward the other end of the studio so she could peruse her Chanel catalog in peace. She adored all things Chanel and was trying to decide between two outfits when the clatter of Cristoforo tossing aside his tools echoed in the vast building.

"Delphine!"

So intent was he on his carving that she hadn't thought he'd noticed where she'd gone, but he had. He was already striding purposefully toward her, opening his pants as he walked.

"I need you," he said, just before taking her into his arms and fusing his mouth to hers.

He pushed her back against one of the stone slabs, kissing her hard. She gasped as he smeared kisses over her neck and shoulders while gripping greedy handfuls of her derriere. Around them the sunlight streamed in, illuminating the dust motes in the air, and with his hammering gone, she could hear birdsong outside.

He bent his head and sucked hard on her breast right through her clothing. As usual, his burning impatience fanned her own desire. She made no protest when he spun her around to press his erection against the cleft of her bottom. He bit the back of her neck as he rubbed his hard shaft between her cheeks. Then, groaning, he lifted her dress and his hand batted at her thigh, urging her to open for him. She obeyed. Anticipating his entry, she raised up on her toes and braced her hands against the stone just as he shoved inside with a grunt.

Delphine gasped as he filled her with his thick, hard cock and began thrusting at a feverish pace. The slap of his flesh against hers imitated the repetitive sounds his hammer had made just moments before. As usual, the sensations built quickly, but before she could come, he seized her hips and cried out.

"*Dio*, Delphine, *si*," he exclaimed between harsh breaths. His cock erupted deep inside her and Delphine used her inner muscles to milk every last drop from him until at last he sagged against her, limp and empty.

Cristoforo sighed heavily as he withdrew from her body. "That was good, *zuccherino*. Very, very good."

But not for her, he admitted as he tucked himself back into his pants. Every time he availed himself of her body, his conscience needled him. It went against his nature to take his pleasure without giving any back in return, and yet this was what he had hired her for. They had an understanding, a business arrangement.

So, murmuring more endearments in Italian, he took her hand, pressed a kiss on it and then walked back to his work area, mercifully relieved of his tension. He had always had an enormous appetite for sex, magnified when he sculpted. He'd read that men experienced heightened levels of sexual excitement after physical combat and likened that to what he felt when sculpting. Energy flowed to every part of his body, especially his cock. Much of it he expended carving the stone, but the rest built up until he began to lose the focus. Loss of focus meant error, and errors on marble could not be fixed.

His muscles hummed. His fingers itched to hold hammer and chisel, but before he could return to his carving, a knock sounded at the door and Antonella's nine-year-old grandson dashed inside clutching a shoebox to his chest.

Antonella bustled in, waving a dishrag like a flag. "Brizio! I told you not to come in here. *Il maestro* is not to be disturbed!"

"It is all right, Antonella," Cristoforo said.

Delphine came over and gasped with delight when she saw what was in the box. "Kittens!" she exclaimed, scooping up a wriggling calico fuzzball.

She took a seat on the couch and rubbed her cheek against the soft fur.

"Oh, it's purring!" she exclaimed with delight.

From his pocket, Brizio pulled a bit of string with a bell on the end and got the kittens to chase after it. Soon Delphine was tugging it along the floor herself, laughing as the kittens stalked and pounced on it. Cristoforo watched as she began to swing the string in a circle, slowly at first, but gradually gaining speed. Eventually the kittens chased the bell in earnest and Delphine and Brizio hooted with laughter.

"Are they boys or girls?" Delphine asked.

"Brothers," Brizio replied. "And they are very sad when they are not together, but Mama says we must get homes for them."

"It'll be hard to find someone who will take them both," Delphine said, letting the kittens catch the bell. A twinge of regret tinted her voice.

Cristoforo surprised himself by saying, "I take them both."

There was a brief silence as three pairs of eyes swung toward him, and then Brizio whooped in triumph. Antonella clucked her tongue, a slight smile curving her mouth, but it was Delphine's approval Cristoforo wanted.

"You'll keep the kittens?" she asked.

"*Si*," he said with a begrudging smile. "I keep kittens."

Delphine's answering smile struck him like an arrow from *Ermes*. She walked toward him, her head cocked to the side, appreciation glowing in her eyes, and although his body still hummed from fucking her just a few minutes ago, Cristoforo wanted her again. His cock stiffened as he thought about taking her on the sofa, but unfortunately the Beethoven wasn't going to carve itself.

Antonella clapped her hands briskly at her grandson and urged him toward the door with her dishrag.

Delphine smiled ruefully, fingering the end of her braid. "Yes, well. I'd better let you get back to work."

As everyone headed toward the exit with Antonella waving them through the door, Cristoforo's ardor settled into a contentment he had not felt in a long while. His decision to keep the kittens had pleased Delphine, and her pleasure, the way it had shone in her eyes, made him feel as if he'd accomplished something important.

With a lightness in his step, he went to take up his tools and get back to work, but Antonella paused at the door to say in Italian, "I almost forgot to tell you. The doctor called to confirm your appointment tomorrow."

And as quickly as that, his good mood disappeared.

* * * * *

Around two in the morning, Delphine awoke when Cristoforo crawled into bed with her. Although half-asleep, she felt a strong throb of arousal. It amazed her how quickly her body responded to just his presence. Her breasts ached, the nipples tightening in anticipation, and her skin hummed as if from a low charge of electricity.

But murmuring softly in Italian, he merely hooked a strong arm around her waist, pulled her close and promptly fell asleep. Delphine lay there, puzzled and a little disappointed. As his breath warmed her neck, she told herself she should welcome a respite from her duties. Besides, he would likely wake up in a few hours, hot and hard, probing her pussy before she was fully aware of his intention.

And yet, the next morning he wasn't there.

Assuming he was already working, she left the kittens— whom she had named Rafael and Donatello—asleep in her room and ventured downstairs to have breakfast. As she sipped her coffee, she realized the persistent clatter of Cristoforo's work was missing, but he wasn't in the studio sipping espresso, nor was he in his bedroom sleeping. She stood on the landing at the top of the stairs, baffled. Finally, she tracked down Antonella and asked, "*Dove è Cristoforo?*"

The gray-haired woman pursed her lips and said, "*Dal dottore.*"

"*Perchè?*"

Antonella's face took on a pained expression as she rattled off an explanation in Italian Delphine had no hope of understanding.

"In English, *per favore*," she pleaded.

The housekeeper struggled for a moment as if searching for the words and then just pointed to her eye. "He have problem. He do not see soon."

Delphine felt as though she'd been punched. Cristoforo was going blind? Suddenly it all made sense. His preference for full light during sex. His obsessive drive to work, forcing himself to go, go, go until he dropped from exhaustion. Without his sense of sight, he would not be able to sculpt. His art would be lost to him forever.

Sick inside, Delphine waited all day for him to return. She kept vigil on her balcony as she completed more Italian lessons on her computer, but no car came up the road, and by the time she went to bed he still had not come home.

* * * * *

Delphine woke in the middle of the night to the sound of a door slamming. Relief washed through her as she pulled on a wrap and hurried downstairs. When she didn't find him in the house, she headed out back.

Despite the warmth of the night, the brick of the garden pathway felt cool against her feet. She had almost reached the studio when a bellow of rage cut through the night, followed by a crash, then a harsh, repeated *crack, crack, crack.*

Filled with dread, she raised the hem of her nightgown and ran the rest of the way.

When she burst into the studio, she saw Cristoforo with a heavy hammer in his hand and the statue for the German embassy on its side in ruins. Beethoven's marble face, still whole and unmarked, stared up for a split second before Cristoforo smashed the high forehead. Chips of marble flew like shrapnel and fractures appeared in the skull just before it fell apart.

Delphine ran and grabbed his arm. "Cristoforo, stop!"

"*Lasciami stare!*" he snarled, turning. A twisted mask of rage distorted his face, and he was obviously drunk. His breath smelled foul.

"Stop it! Please, stop it!" she cried, hanging on to his arm with all her might.

Unfortunately, she was no match for his superior strength, and he wrenched his arm from her grip. In doing so, he lost his balance and fell onto the rubble, grunting as the jagged chunks of marble bit into his skin.

"Oh God!" she cried.

She struggled to help him to his feet, but he would not get up. Instead, he rolled over onto his back, arms flung out to either side, his body stretched over the debris. His shirt had torn in several places and was stained now with blood from numerous cuts.

"*Sta capitando tutto così in fretta,*" he moaned as he lay there. His hands were clenched so hard the veins in his forearms stood out in relief. Tears escaped his closed eyes to roll down into his hair.

"God, Cristoforo, you're bleeding. Let me help you. Please."

Mindful of her bare feet, Delphine crept closer and reached for his hand. Thankfully, he gripped it tightly and allowed himself to be helped up. Chips of marble stuck to his skin. She wanted to get him back to the house to see to his cuts, but instead he pulled her close. Instantly, she put her arms around him. He let much of his weight fall on her, but she was expecting it. Hot tears dampened her neck.

"Delphine," he cried. "*Voglio morire!*" His words were muffled against her skin and his anguish reached in and clutched her heart. "I want God to kill me."

"Don't say that."

"Why God punish me? Why give me gift of sculpting and then take away?"

The way his voice cracked brought tears to Delphine's eyes too.

"Shhh, shhh," she cooed softly. "Everything will be fine. Shhh…come with me. Come back to the house. Let me clean you up."

Chapter Three
From the personal journal of Delphine Alexander
9 May

ℰ

It has been over a week since the Beethoven incident and Cristoforo has not worked at all. He's gotten plenty of sleep but wanders around the house like an abandoned child. I don't think he's going to try suicide, like he'd hinted that night, but the fire has gone out of his eyes.

Not only that, but he hasn't shown even the slightest interest in sex. That alone is cause for worry. This respite has made me realize that I always allowed him to take me, but I have never given myself. Not surprising, of course. Ours has been a strictly business relationship. But even though I've extended the contract for another two months, things have changed. I care about him, more than I should, but he seems so lonely and full of despair.

Antonella is having a birthday party for her husband in a couple of weeks and she told me to bring Cristoforo. She hopes a party might cheer him up. If this goes on much longer, I'll need cheering up myself. She also told me he has eye drops that he is supposed to be using daily, but probably isn't. Stupid man. I'm going to get him to use them if I have to sit on his chest and administer them myself.

Cristoforo slumped on the oversized sofa, looking up at the ceiling of his study where a captivating scene from Roman mythology had been painted. At one time he would have marveled at the skill required to layer color upon color with brush and palette, but now the winged cherubs, seated god and soaring trumpeters left him utterly unmoved.

Delphine came in. Today she wore a sleeveless dress with a layered skirt of turquoise and teal. Her honey-and-amber braid lay over her shoulder, the tapered tip brushing her waist.

"How do you feel today?" she asked. "You look rested. The circles under your eyes are gone."

He shrugged. "I have no feeling, Delphine. I am empty. Dead."

She looked at him a moment, then, taking a cushion from the couch, tossed it at his feet. "Well, I can help you feel...something."

As she settled herself between his spread legs and tugged down his pants, he raised an eyebrow. He had planned to take a nap, but he did feel a sluggish interest at the prospect of fellatio, especially since so far he had not asked anything of her but straight intercourse.

Cristoforo watched as, with a smile, she lowered her head and took his flaccid cock between her lips. The wet heat enveloped him and a muted surge of pleasure rolled through him. Her tongue undulated rhythmically against his stiffening shaft, but when he was fully hard, Delphine let him slip out of her mouth. He frowned but couldn't muster the energy to protest.

She nudged his knees wider apart and licked at the spot where thigh met groin. Then, smiling, she traced a wet path with her tongue along that crease, up to just under his testicles. He made another reluctant sound of enjoyment, but when she took one of his testicles in her mouth he couldn't stop himself from growling. He stared down at her, desire rekindling. She teased the small globe with her tongue, caressing, tickling, and need built inside him, making him want to shove himself deep inside her.

Finally, breathing hard, he gripped his cock and nudged her cheek with it. "*Dio, si, per favore...*"

His words melted into a ragged groan as she wrapped her lips around the swollen head, stroking the shaft and lightly scratching his thighs. Had he thought about refusing her earlier? What a foolish idea. To deprive himself of such consummate pleasure...

His thought was cut off when she slowly lowered her head and took him all the way in. All the way. Balls-deep, his cock lodged in her throat. At the same time, she took his hands and placed them on either side of her head.

He reacted instantaneously. He couldn't have stopped himself if he'd wanted to. Planting his feet flat on the floor and gripping her head tightly, he held her immobile and jerked his hips upward. Mindless with lust now, he fucked her mouth like an animal. His deep thrusts surely cut off her air, but she made no protest, did not pull back. He drove his swollen cock between her lips again and again while guttural grunts burst from his throat.

Suddenly, a shout tore itself free.

Delphine braced herself. With a week gone by since his last orgasm, she expected a larger than normal explosion. She wasn't disappointed. His pungent essence flooded the hollow of her mouth. Delphine gulped and swallowed, struggling to keep up, but some of the fluid escaped the corner of her mouth to trickle down her chin. Sitting back on her heels, she dabbed up the dribble and sucked it off her finger.

As his orgasm finally subsided, Cristoforo sighed deeply and rubbed his thumb against her cheek.

"You are very good," he said, a rumbling, physical satisfaction in his voice.

"I try."

Nodding, Delphine got to her feet. The rush of power that came from pleasuring a man with her mouth lingered inside her like a sustained echo, and yet she felt oddly ill at ease. They never embraced after sex. Typically, he returned to work, but today, of course, he did not. Uncertain, she turned to go, but he took her hand, regarding her with a thoughtful expression.

"Wait," he said. "I am selfish with you before. I do not make you feel good like you make me feel."

Perching next to him on the couch, Delphine delivered her rote reply. "But my pleasure comes from yours."

"*Stronzate*," he said with a frown. "Come, Delphine. I make you feel good now."

Surprised by his reversal in attitude, she made no protest as he slid lower on the sofa and pulled her so that she was poised above him with her pussy over his face.

As he cupped her bottom with his strong hands, his tongue snaked out, and with a long, slow lick, he opened her. Delphine hissed and gripped the arm of the couch. She only vaguely remembered the last time she had felt the silken sensation of a tongue there. He nibbled, pulling on her soft lips, sucking on them, and a warm flush of arousal throbbed between her legs. She moaned softly. He was very good at this. Very good. Her body's wetness added to the humid heat created by his breath as he lapped at her under her dress.

Delphine felt dizzy, perhaps because it had been so long since she'd had sex for her own pleasure. As she pulled the dress off over her head, she abandoned herself to his rough hands as they roved over her bottom and hips, pulling her closer to his demanding mouth. He explored each hidden fold, each dusky crevice with his tongue, coaxing sounds from her that she loved making. Her hips moved to and fro and she became selfish. As the sensations built upon themselves, she delayed her climax, drawing out the feelings for as long as possible, and Cristoforo patiently obliged. He followed where she led, obeyed her silent pleas for more.

By the time she reached the point where she could hold back no longer, her swollen sex dripped juice like an overripe plum. So much fluid had flowed from her body that her inner thighs were slick with it. God, she was close, so gloriously close.

Cristoforo sensed the imminent approach of her orgasm and her unspoken surrender to it. He gripped her hips and kept her still while his tongue lashed at her clit relentlessly, demanding culmination, propelling her toward an explosive climax.

When it finally came, Delphine arched her back and cried out as pleasure burst inside her. Heedless of anything but her own gratification, she ground down on Cristoforo's face, wrenching every spark of satisfaction from him that she could.

After the last glimmers had waned, she slid down to lay upon him. He kissed her and she tasted the spicy, sweet tang of herself on his lips. Limp with fulfillment, she gave a long, contented sigh. Satisfying sex with a virile, accomplished man was an indulgence she had greatly missed.

"There. I do my job. You feel good," he said. "You pay *me* now, eh?"

Amazed that he had made a joke, Delphine laughed softly. "Are you expensive?" she asked.

"*Si*, but for you," he said, the corner of his mouth curving upward, "I work for free."

Then he actually laughed. A reserved *eh-eh-eh*, but a laugh just the same.

Hopeful that his mood was on the upswing, she said, "I hear your birthday is coming up next month."

Cristoforo cocked his head at her. "How you know this?"

"A little bird told me."

"Birds do not talk, Delphine," he said with a chuckle.

"A bird named Antonella. And I'm going to make you a cake," she declared, deciding at that moment. "No, I'm going to make you a chocolate soufflé."

"You know chocolate is my favorite. But a soufflé is very fancy cooking. Your mother teach you to cook for men?"

"My mother?" Delphine shrugged. "My mother taught me a lot of things," she said blandly. "Cooking for a man was one of them. But she cooked for one man. I broadened my skills to please many."

"Was also your mother a companion to men?"

Delphine smiled humorlessly. "Yes and no. She was a mistress like I am, but she liked to pretend Elias was her husband."

"Ah. That is not a good thing," Cristoforo said, shaking his head.

"No," she agreed, "not good at all."

Worse, her mother had made Delphine pretend as well. Delphine had spent the latter half of her childhood living as if Elias was her stepfather, explaining to her friends why he was never home, making up excuses why she wasn't at the father-daughter dance and hating herself for wanting his attention when he *was* around. Delphine sighed. She hadn't thought about him in years, nor did she want to. That life was behind her.

"I won't ever do that," she declared, forcibly pulling herself from her memories.

"Be with a married man?" Cristoforo asked.

"Oh no," she scoffed. "I've been with married men before. I meant I'll never pretend I'm something I'm not. Or make up excuses for what I am. Her mistake was thinking she could have the fairy-tale life. She always believed he'd leave his wife for her. We have a saying in America. 'Fake it 'til you make it.' That's what she did. But she never did make it."

Delphine sat up and tossed her braid over her shoulder. "It's a waste of time to want something you'll never have."

"I waste time wanting to see your hair," he said. "I thought you do not let me see it ever, but maybe you change your thoughts now you know about my eyes." His expression begged for sympathy, but Delphine felt none.

"Shame on you for using your illness as a bargaining chip. Especially," she said, getting his eye drops from the pocket of her discarded dress, "when you're not doing a damn thing to keep things from getting worse."

He scowled. "Where you find those?"

"It doesn't matter where I found them. You need to use these every day."

He waved a hand in irritation. "I forget."

Delphine rose up on her knees and unscrewed the cap. "I'll help you remember," she said firmly.

Chapter Four
From the personal journal of Delphine Alexander
23 May

℘

Cristoforo has been reborn. Gone is the driven, tortured artist, and in his place is a slap-happy sex fiend. He spends as much time in bed with me as he can, but it is different than it was before. Now he makes sure that I enjoy it too. And my God, I have never been so sexually satisfied. I doubt any woman ever has.

That's not all. He laughs, he smiles, he jokes. I find flowers on my pillow and he gives me gifts. Perfume, small trinkets, and when he found out Chanel is my favorite, a pair of their sunglasses.

I now spend every night in his bed with him and go to my own rooms only to change clothes. The past two Sundays I spent my day off with him. We walked and picnicked in the countryside one Sunday. The other we spent cooking together. Cristoforo is quite a chef. He showed me how to make pasta from scratch. We also made his great-grandmother's Bolognese sauce, which took hours to cook but not very long to eat. Long after the food was gone, we talked. We talked about art, his family, cities we've both visited...oh, pretty much everything under the sun. But as much fun as this has been, I still worry. I don't know how long it will be until his vision deteriorates completely, or if it will only get very bad. He won't discuss it with me. Antonella says the doctor has recommended surgery, but Cristoforo won't schedule it. He's like an ostrich burying his head in the sand.

Antonella's large and boisterous family gathered on the brick patio of her home where two long trestle tables groaned with rustic largess—*pasta al sugo, polpette, lasagna* and numerous bottles of rich Tuscan Chianti. After Gaetano opened his gifts, people fetched their instruments — a concertina, guitars and even a tambourine. Then, under trees festooned with strings of lights, young and old alike danced and laughed and sang.

Delphine sat with Antonella's infant granddaughter cuddled in her arms. Delphine's aquamarine eyes radiated such joy Cristoforo wished he had a sketch pad with him.

"You're the most precious, most beautiful thing I've ever seen," she cooed, brushing the baby Carina's cheek with her fingertip. She looked up at him when he came near. "Isn't she beautiful?" she asked in Italian.

"Very beautiful," Cristoforo agreed, crouching next to her chair.

"Oh, and she smells very good. Smell her."

Chuckling, he obliged.

"Do you want children? Yours would be gorgeous," the baby's mamma said, looking at them both expectantly. Obviously Antonella had not explained to her family the nature of his relationship with Delphine.

Cristoforo found himself at a loss for what to say.

But after only a brief pause, Delphine said, "Cristoforo and I are good friends."

"That's a pity," the young mother said, smiling. "You are a beautiful couple."

Later, Cristoforo watched Delphine dance by. She caught his eye and laughed as the hem of her dress swooped and fluttered like a festival banner. How young and carefree she looked. Seeing her like this made him realize the gradual change that had come over her. So unlike the composed sophisticate that arrived on his doorstep a month and a half ago.

Remembering his behavior when she'd first arrived, his face heated with shame. He'd been an animal, fucking her whenever the urge took him and with no consideration for her pleasure. Even as his paid mistress, she deserved more respect

247

than he'd shown. So now when they had sex, her orgasm was his goal. Whenever she shuddered in his arms, crying out as the pleasure overwhelmed her, the self-recrimination eased just a fraction. He didn't know how much time had to pass before he felt he'd atoned, but he would continue to see to her needs, spoken and unspoken, until the slate was clean.

The dance ended and Brizio's father, Giancarlo, delivered a gasping Delphine to him. Her cheeks were flushed pink, her smile warm.

"*Grazie*, Giancarlo," she said in Italian, "but I want to dance with Cristoforo now."

Cristoforo didn't particularly like dancing, but whatever made her happy, he would do.

"But wait," she said, her hand around the end of her braid. "I have to fix my hair."

"Let it go," Giancarlo said. "It's a crime to hide such beauty."

"Oh no."

Delphine shook her head, but Giancarlo's nimble fingers set hers aside. Other voices encouraged him as, grinning, he began to unravel the braid.

Seeing Delphine's look of distress, Cristoforo reacted without thinking. He grabbed Giancarlo's wrist a little too hard and said in as calm a voice as he could manage, "She likes her hair braided."

Delphine looked up sharply, surprised, and Giancarlo's smile faltered.

"I'm sorry. I didn't know," he said, letting go of Delphine's hair.

"This is no problem," she assured everyone. Then in English she said, "Cristoforo, really. It's all right."

Delphine was relieved when Cristoforo nodded and shook hands with Giancarlo. As the musicians struck up a lively tune, she followed Cristoforo to the gift table where he picked up a piece of discarded ribbon and proceeded to retie her hair. When he was done knotting the strip around the end of her braid, their eyes met. Without any warning whatsoever, emotion welled up inside her in a sudden rush. She was alarmed to feel tears threatening.

Blinking them away, she asked in a small voice, "Can we go home? I think I've had enough partying."

An enigmatic smile on his face, Cristoforo cupped her cheek. "*Si, zuccherino*, we go home."

* * * * *

A short while later, the two of them undressed by the light from a table lamp on the far side of the room. Still unsettled by the incident at the party, Delphine took her time. As she slipped out of her clothes, she realized with dismay that she was trembling like a virgin and mentally scolded herself. This was Cristoforo, for heaven's sake. She couldn't count how many times they'd had sex. Tonight was like any other night, offering nothing more than mutual satisfaction. They were just two people giving each other pleasure.

But then he said, "Come, *zuccherino*."

Frowning slightly, Delphine turned to see him standing by the bed, naked and waiting for her. As he held a hand out to her, his black hair fell over his forehead and he smiled with a tenderness in his gaze that made her realize she loved him.

For a moment she couldn't breathe. When had she let down her guard enough to let him in? Silly question. Every moment they'd shared since his breakdown in the studio. After she'd seen him so vulnerable, she hadn't been able to keep herself from slipping into the role of lover, not mistress. And now, here she was, hopelessly in love with him.

Oh God. She closed her eyes. Love changed everything. Everything.

Cristoforo must have seen her distress. He frowned slightly. "What is wrong?"

She couldn't let him know. Unwittingly, she'd given him too much power, but he couldn't hurt her if he didn't know he had it.

"Nothing is wrong." She drew on her years of experience as a courtesan and painted a smile on her face.

"If you're too tired..."

She summoned a bigger smile and closed the distance between them. "Never," she said.

He looked at her a moment longer, then apparently took her at her word. Cupping a hand along the back of her head, he kissed her. As always, desire unfolded inside her. He bestowed kiss after kiss on her mouth, gently drawing her into a place where nothing mattered except showing him with her body what she felt. She told herself that sex with him tonight would change nothing and that she was obligated by her contract in any event.

So she abandoned herself to his lovemaking. As his lips caressed hers and his tongue slipped inside, she welcomed it with her own. She fitted herself to his body, rubbing against his erection, reveling in his groan of pleasure.

This would have to be the last night, she realized. She had to leave for her own emotional safety. If she didn't, she'd be in danger of falling into the same trap her mother had made for herself.

Perhaps because of this, every caress of his hand over her skin felt magnified. The roughness of his chest hair against her breasts inflamed her, and when the ribbon slipped off her braid, trapped between their bodies, she said impulsively, "Leave it."

Chapter Five

ဆ

Cristoforo's eyes widened. He couldn't believe what he was hearing. "You let me see your hair?"

Delphine nodded.

"I feel like I am winning the jackpan."

"Jackpot," she said with an odd laugh.

He took her braid in his hands and smiled. "That is what I meant." Then he put a hand over his heart. "I feel honor from this, Delphine. Your hair is special to you."

"It's just hair," she said lightly.

"No, you are wrong," he said, beginning to unravel the braid. "Your hair is you. You give me your hair, you give me you."

Bewildered, Cristoforo tried to catch her gaze, but she wouldn't look at him. Her dismissal of the act was just that—an act. Again he wondered what lay ahead for them, but he would think about it afterward. Now was for pleasuring Delphine as she deserved and enjoying the gift she had given him.

He turned his attention to her hair. Taking his time, he began loosening the hanks. Like silk it spilled through his fingers, unraveling on its own as if eager for him to see it loose and free. Slowly but surely, he worked until at last she was undone.

His tongue felt thick in his mouth and he stared. Cristoforo had visited the most prestigious museums in the world. His position in the creative community afforded him invitations to homes where he'd viewed priceless *objets d'art*—many of them illegally obtained and kept secret—and living in

Florence, he often took visual magnificence for granted. But here stood Delphine, more beautiful, more soul-stirring than any work of art he'd ever seen. He wanted to etch the image of her into his brain and tuck it away like a keepsake.

Her hair cascaded around her breasts in a drape of shifting hues that almost defied description—molten gold and honey, sienna, ginger and copper sunlight. Layer upon layer of color glinted in the uncertain light as he combed his fingers through the softly curling mass, savoring the sleek slide of it against his skin. He wanted to wrap it around his cock and stroke himself with it. He wanted her astride him so he could feel it brush against his face and chest as she rode his body to orgasm. If he had needed evidence of God's existence, he had only to look at this woman and know that nothing less than a divine artist could create such perfection.

"Delphine," he said, his voice hoarse. "You steal my breathing."

Finally, she raised her eyes to his, and so shy and vulnerable did she seem that he suddenly felt as though nothing could be more important than protecting her from ever being hurt. Overwhelmed, he took her face in his hands and kissed her. Her mouth tasted as sweet as ever, but different. Richer, warmer, more exquisite. The stroke of their tongues stiffened his cock and heat pulsed through his body in a steady thrum. He felt as if everything in his life so far had led up to this moment with Delphine pliant and willing in his arms. She yielded to his caresses, arched so that her breast fit more snugly into his palm. He thumbed the nipple, groaning when it hardened, then bent his head to suckle. He imagined her pussy swelling with a moisture he soon would taste with his tongue.

"You are so beautiful," he murmured as they moved toward the bed.

After laying her down on the mattress, he put his mouth again to her breast. He licked a hardened tip, circling with his tongue, flicking and teasing and unable to get enough. He kneaded the soft flesh while the reddened nipple seemed to throb in his mouth. Each pull of his lips called to his own lust like fire in his balls. His cock strained to bury itself inside her—any orifice so long as it was wet and tight—but he restrained himself, wanting to push her to her own pleasure before taking his own.

With her musky fragrance teasing his nostrils, he kissed his way down her silken stomach to nestle his head between her legs. At her soft mound he paused, pulling on the hairs with his lips. Her low laugh made him smile. Drunk now with her scent, he forced himself to open her with his tongue as slowly as possible. She trembled with a low moan as he slid between her glossy lips, tasting her honey, spreading it upward until her hairs trailed off the tip of his tongue. He went back to lap again. And again. Softly, insistently. With each swipe of his tongue, he delved a little deeper, licked at her clit with a bit more pressure. Her hips undulated with him in a fluid dance. Her hands tangled in his hair, her moans of pleasure like an aria. But this time as her breathing became more labored and her throaty urgings more insistent, he withheld her climax. Something inside him demanded that instead of orchestrating her orgasm, he share it, joined with her. So, at the crucial moment, he lifted his head.

Delphine jerked hard on his hair. "Cristoforo, please!"

"*Si*, I know," he said through gritted teeth.

Moving quickly, he fitted his cock to her wet slit, took a deep breath and sank inside her. *Dio.* He closed his eyes, overwhelmed. Although he'd entered her dozens of times, this time was different. Nothing in his whole life had ever felt so satisfyingly right. Not when he lost his virginity. Not the feeling of his father clapping a proud hand on his shoulder when he'd won the trophy in football. Not even the perfection of holding mallet and chisel in hand. No, joining with Delphine this way surpassed everything. His entire body vibrated with approval, like a sculpture whose last chip had at last been hewn. He wanted to believe this feeling of completeness had nothing to do with Delphine and her symbolic gesture and everything to do with the good wine, food and company they had just left, but when she shivered beneath him, her eyes fluttering closed and he finally completed that first stroke inside, he admitted the truth to himself. He loved her.

Earlier at the party when Carina's mamma had asked her innocent question, the idea of making a baby with Delphine had tugged at his heart. He could easily imagine her rocking their son to sleep, an unfamiliar American lullaby on her lips, or laughing as she tickled their daughter's chubby tummy. Since that moment, that idea refused to go away. In fact, it grew into a yearning so strong that he felt it in his gut like a hunger that only she could satisfy. He wanted a future with her. He wanted a family with her. Beneath the urbane, cultivated persona she showed the world was a woman who embraced art, thirsted for knowledge, strived to better herself. He had experienced her nurturing side firsthand. And the sex? Making love to her eclipsed any other pleasure on earth.

Resting his weight on his elbows, he pulled out almost completely, then slid back in, maddeningly slowly.

"Look at me, Delphine."

She complied, fixing her Aegean blue eyes on his. As he started another measured stroke in and out, he absorbed every nuance of feeling he saw there. Each rolling thrust of his hips was reflected on her face, doubling his pleasure, feeding him in a profound way he couldn't put into word or thought. His rhythm built, his thrusts came harder and still he held her gaze. When at last she reached her peak, her hips rose off the bed and she cried out. He lost control at the same moment, and as his cock erupted, he clenched his jaw to keep a spontaneous confession from spilling from his mouth, even though he'd never felt so utterly whole.

* * * * *

The next day Cristoforo got up early and went to his study. Delphine looked disappointed when he didn't linger for a sun-drenched morning in bed, but he had a phone call to make that he had avoided far too long as it was. *Dio*, his heart pounded as he finally scheduled his eye surgery.

When he hung up, his hands were still shaking. Although he felt as if a two-ton block of marble had been lifted from his shoulders, he was far from carefree. The experimental operation carried a high degree of risk, and chances were high he'd end up blind much sooner than if he just let the disease run its course.

Furthermore, the question of Delphine's feelings for him remained. Did she care about him beyond the parameters of her contract or was her devotion to him just part of her job? The fact that she'd shown him her hair seemed to suggest something. She had been so particular about it for as long as he'd known her—admittedly not long—but even so, her demeanor after her hair had been let down seemed so vulnerable that he couldn't help but think he'd achieved a degree of intimacy she hadn't been willing to allow before. It gave him hope.

* * * * *

When Cristoforo went into town on a mysterious errand, Delphine did some preliminary packing and tried to figure out how to tell him she was leaving. Both tasks were equally difficult. The kittens discovered that suitcases made excellent playgrounds, and handling the gifts Cristoforo had given her squeezed her heart, but she proceeded gamely anyway. Love was a liability in her profession, one against which she had no insurance.

Although she was proud of how far she'd come in life, she was under no illusions about what she was and how others viewed her.

Cristoforo paid her for sex.

In order for their relationship to change, she'd essentially have to ask to be his...his girlfriend, and even assuming she could debase herself enough to do that, if he then rejected her... Her eyes pricked with tears and her throat started to close up at just the thought. She knew if he rebuffed her in truth, it would be a hundred times worse, because that's what love did. It left you too vulnerable. Whatever control you had over your life not only disappeared, but fell into the hands of someone else.

So, later after a simple supper, she gulped down some wine and attacked the problem head-on. Damned if she'd act the weakling, so paralyzed with fear that she ended up prolonging the torture.

She had a plan. She just needed to execute it.

"Cristoforo," she said, "I have some bad news. I have to leave tomorrow."

"Leave? *Perchè?*" he said, his brows drawing together. "What do you mean?"

"I — my aunt is sick. I have to go back to the States to take care of her."

"What is wrong with her?" Then he sliced a hand through the air. "Wait. It is not important. We get a nurse for her. Problem fixed."

She slowly shook her head. "That's very kind of you, but she needs *me*, not a nurse. My flight leaves at one p.m. tomorrow out of Peretola."

As he stared at her wordlessly, she steeled herself for an explosion, but he just stood abruptly. With a deep breath, he took his wineglass and went to stand by the window, his back to her. Several moments passed before he spoke again. When he did, he sounded wearier than he had when she'd first arrived.

"When you come back?"

She stood up too and forced the words from her lips. "I don't know."

"Ah," he said, nodding. "I see."

Delphine waited, her stomach in knots as again he said nothing for a long while.

Finally, he straightened and cleared his throat.

"Then I need to find new mistress," he said curtly. "Maybe you have names to suggest."

* * * * *

Delphine managed to make it to her room before surrendering to tears. She hadn't felt so betrayed since her "stepfather" Elias had snubbed her at the movies. Her mother had seen him standing in line for popcorn with his real family and steered the fifteen-year-old Delphine away, but too late. Elias met Delphine's eyes briefly, then turned his head away as if he didn't know her. Her mother futilely attempted to rationalize his behavior, but a piece of Delphine's heart had withered that day.

From that moment on, Delphine could only see her mother as a martyr with no self-respect—a woman who condemned herself to a life of lies and delusion and sustained herself on the leftover attention of a man who didn't truly love her. Delphine vowed never to allow a man that kind of power over her.

And yet that's just what she'd done.

She thought she'd been so careful. She'd thought the key to guarding her heart was in equating sex with business and never ever considering love as an option, but Cristoforo's indifference to her departure hurt her deeply. Part of her had hoped he would fall down on his knees and beg her to stay, saying he couldn't live without her. But he hadn't. He'd merely asked for help in finding a replacement.

So the tears fell, each salty drop a testament to—

Delphine jumped as the door slammed open and Cristoforo burst into the room. He strode up to her and took her none too gently by the shoulders.

"You no have aunt!" he exclaimed.

"Yes I do," she protested weakly.

"*Stronzate!*" His fingers dug into her arms and his eyes blazed with anger.

Delphine's face burned, but she lifted her chin anyway. "I don't know what you're getting so worked up about. My contract clearly states I have the right to terminate our relationship with two days' notice. Besides," she said, pulling away angrily, "it doesn't really matter if I leave or not. You can just get a replacement."

She was gratified to see pain twist his features.

"Delphine, I am sorry I say that. My temper is strong and my brain was not working."

The remorse in his dark eyes took the edge off her anger and she nodded once.

"Listen to me, Delphine." His grip on her shoulders loosened. "What I say before is impossible. Even if I look all over whole planet, I never find someone like you."

As those words washed over her, he kissed her deeply, taking her face in his hands and pressing his warm lips to hers. His tongue slid into her mouth and she felt a longing so strong she had to grab on to him.

"I want you to stay," he said against her mouth. "I call the doctor today and I am to get surgery next month."

"Oh God. Surgery? On your eyes?"

"*Si*. The doctor say if I do not have it, I am blind in two years. If I do have it and there is success, I am probably okay."

"But what if it's not successful?"

"Then I am blind now and do not get two years."

Delphine's resolve weakened. How could she go and leave him to face surgery alone? If it didn't work, she knew it would be a hundred times worse than after he'd destroyed the Beethoven. And yet, if she didn't go now, she was afraid she never would.

He must have seen her refusal in her face, because he went on in a rush.

"Do not talk yet. I have one another thing to say. *Ti amo*," he said roughly. "You understand what '*ti amo*' means?"

Delphine gaped at him. "I— I don't believe you."

"You think I lie? No, Delphine. I say it with my body last night. I say it with my mouth today. I even say it with this."

He reached into his pocket and took out a small leather box.

Delphine gasped as he opened the box to reveal a dazzling platinum ring. The world stopped turning. She stared wordlessly at the sapphire nestled between two brilliant, square-cut diamonds.

"You see? I do not talk about the surgery so you stay here. I tell you that because it is not right to ask you to get married with me and you do not know what the doctor says."

She couldn't seem to breathe. This couldn't be happening. It didn't seem possible. She stood there speechless as he cupped her face in his rough hands.

"Talk to me, Delphine," he said. "What you feel for me? I see your fat red eyes. I know you cry. You cry for me? Because you leave me? You do not have to go." He kissed her again, tenderly this time, over and over—her lips, her cheeks, her forehead. "Please stay, *zuccherino*. Get married with me. Make babies with me."

Delphine couldn't think. She didn't want to think. Joy filled her. Every fiber of her being expanded with happiness until she felt she was going to burst with it.

"Oh my God. Yes," she sobbed, throwing her arms around his neck. "Yes, yes, I'll marry you."

Cristoforo took her head in his hands and kissed her hard, stabbing his tongue into her mouth. Desire rushed through her in a wave. It flared between her legs. It penetrated every molecule in her body until nothing else mattered except his lips, his hands, his stiffening cock.

She hooked a leg around his hip and rubbed herself against his erection, and, gasping, Cristoforo broke away. His eyes radiated such fierce desire that it was like looking at the sun. Pieces of clothing flew until, naked, they fell onto the bed where he parted her thighs and entered her with one strong thrust.

Delphine cried out as her body, wet and welcoming, yielded to the invasion. He loved her. They were going to build a life, a family, together. She felt as though she was acting out the fairy-tale ending of a movie, and yet nothing could be more real than Cristoforo's strong body above hers, his harsh exhalations, his hips pistoning as he drove into her over and over again.

"Say the words to me, Delphine," he gasped, sweat beading on his forehead. "It is just two words. Say them to me now."

At first, Delphine didn't understand what he was talking about, and Cristoforo's brow wrinkled when she didn't respond, but then it came to her. Of course. In Italian it was only two words.

Looking deeply into his espresso eyes, she took his face in her hands. "*Ti amo*, Cristoforo," she said, her heart brimming with love. "*Ti amo, ti amo, ti amo.*"

With a gruff noise of satisfaction, Cristoforo kissed her. As his cock plunged in and out, harder, faster, she strained against him. Their bodies were slick with sweat now, their breathing loud and labored. The pleasure and emotions built inside her until her entire body trembled on the brink, and when she went over, she took him with her. Together they shuddered in ecstasy, their love strengthening with each throb of pleasure. More tears leaked from her eyes as he spent himself inside her, grunting his release.

After he'd caught his breath, he bent his head and kissed her neck.

"Next week, eh?" he said, dropping his weight to his elbows. "Next week we get married."

"So soon?" Still aglow from her orgasm, Delphine brushed the hair off his damp forehead.

"*Si*, because we cannot make babies until we are married in church," he said firmly. "And I cannot wait to see little Delphines running around the house."

"Only *bambinas*?" she asked, unable to wipe the smile off her face. "No *bambinos*?"

"Ah, we make many of both," he said with a gloating smile of his own. Then, with a sly look, he gave a little half thrust. "You know we have to do this very much to make babies."

Laughing, Delphine cried more happy tears. "I have absolutely no problem with that."

*　*　*　*　*

From the personal journal of Delphine Valtieri
27 June

My handwriting is messy because we're in the air on our way to Paris. I can't believe I haven't made an entry since before the wedding. Actually, I can believe it. Cristoforo has been doing his best to get me pregnant, and his best is pretty impressive!

I'd never planned to have a family, probably because I was afraid to hope that such a thing was possible for me, but now that Cristoforo's surgery is over and the disease seems to have halted, he talks a lot about the future. I'm sure that he'll dedicate himself to his family with as much fervor as he does his art.

In just a little while we'll be landing at Orly. Tonight we have to appear at the German embassy for the unveiling of the new Beethoven statue that he managed to complete in record time, but then after that our time is our own. Cristoforo has promised a big surprise for me. Knowing him, it involves sex or chocolate or both. Lucky me.

About the Author

෨

Kate Willoughby got hooked on romance in the late seventies when she read Sweet Savage Love by Rosemary Rogers. Inspired, she and her best friend wrote a contemporary love story involving a multi-millionaire playboy and the restaurant hostess determined to cure his drinking problem. Unfortunately (or fortunately, depending on how you look at it), that manuscript has been lost forever.

Fast forward to college, where she took a creative writing course. Kate still wanted to write love stories, but everyone else in class was composing Important Literature and Thought-Provoking Poetry. A few devastating critiques later, she gave up, discouraged and embarrassed. Eventually her muse got over the trauma and pestered her to try her hand at writing again. Although she has other e-books published, A Man of Vision is her first Ellora's Cave story.

Kate resides in Los Angeles with her husband of fifteen years and their two sons. When the testosterone in the house builds up to unbearable levels, she escapes by reading, cooking, and scrapbooking with friends.

Kate welcomes comments from readers. You can find her website and email address on her author bio page at www.ellorascave.com.

Tell Us What You Think
We appreciate hearing reader opinions about our books. You can email us at Comments@EllorasCave.com.

Why an electronic book?

We live in the Information Age—an exciting time in the history of human civilization, in which technology rules supreme and continues to progress in leaps and bounds every minute of every day. For a multitude of reasons, more and more avid literary fans are opting to purchase e-books instead of paper books. The question from those not yet initiated into the world of electronic reading is simply: *Why?*

1. *Price.* An electronic title at Ellora's Cave Publishing and Cerridwen Press runs anywhere from 40% to 75% less than the cover price of the exact same title in paperback format. Why? Basic mathematics and cost. It is less expensive to publish an e-book (no paper and printing, no warehousing and shipping) than it is to publish a paperback, so the savings are passed along to the consumer.

2. *Space.* Running out of room in your house for your books? That is one worry you will never have with electronic books. For a low one-time cost, you can purchase a handheld device specifically designed for e-reading. Many e-readers have large, convenient screens for viewing. Better yet, hundreds of titles can be stored within your new library—on a single microchip. There are a variety of e-readers from different manufacturers. You can also read e-books on your PC or laptop computer. (Please note that Ellora's Cave does not endorse any specific brands.

You can check our websites at www.ellorascave.com or www.cerridwenpress.com for information we make available to new consumers.)

3. *Mobility.* Because your new e-library consists of only a microchip within a small, easily transportable e-reader, your entire cache of books can be taken with you wherever you go.

4. *Personal Viewing Preferences.* Are the words you are currently reading too small? Too large? Too... ANNOYING? Paperback books cannot be modified according to personal preferences, but e-books can.

5. *Instant Gratification.* Is it the middle of the night and all the bookstores near you are closed? Are you tired of waiting days, sometimes weeks, for bookstores to ship the novels you bought? Ellora's Cave Publishing sells instantaneous downloads twenty-four hours a day, seven days a week, every day of the year. Our webstore is never closed. Our e-book delivery system is 100% automated, meaning your order is filled as soon as you pay for it.

Those are a few of the top reasons why electronic books are replacing paperbacks for many avid readers.

As always, Ellora's Cave and Cerridwen Press welcome your questions and comments. We invite you to email us at Comments@ellorascave.com or write to us directly at Ellora's Cave Publishing Inc., 1056 Home Avenue, Akron, OH 44310-3502.

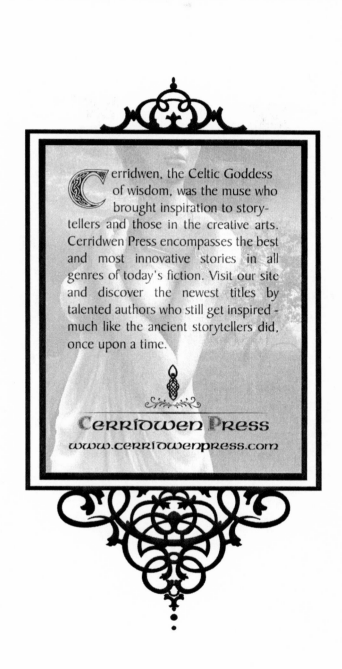

Cerridwen, the Celtic Goddess of wisdom, was the muse who brought inspiration to storytellers and those in the creative arts. Cerridwen Press encompasses the best and most innovative stories in all genres of today's fiction. Visit our site and discover the newest titles by talented authors who still get inspired - much like the ancient storytellers did, once upon a time.

CERRIDWEN PRESS
www.cerridwenpress.com

Discover for yourself why readers can't get enough
of the multiple award-winning publisher

Ellora's Cave.

Whether you prefer e-books or paperbacks,

be sure to visit EC on the web at
www.ellorascave.com

for an erotic reading experience that will leave you
breathless.